Ronald Revisited

Ronald Revisited

The World of Ronald McDonald

Bowling Green University Popular Press
Bowling Green, Ohio 43403

Copyright ©1983 by Bowling Green University Popular Press

ISBN: 0-87972-247-9
      0-87972-248-7

Contents

In The Beginning Was

Stop as you Pass

and try a glass of our delicious soda water. Nothing looks so tempting or justifies the anticipation of a cold, sparkling, palate tickling and thirst killing drink as a glass of our soda water with pure fruit juice flavorings or ice cream.

Lakeside Pharmacy

Opposite: Advertisement from the 1908 "Coeur D'Alene Journal." Throughout the 1890's and early 1900's, Coeur D'Alene, Idaho served as a resort area for Spokane's mining **nouveau riche.** Within the Eldritch landscape of a vacation's psycho-space—relaxation, pleasure, escape, unique experience—the Lakeside Pharmacy's curb service attained a level of plausibility not offered by Main Street, U.S.A. Today, unreality remains an integral part of the McDonalds scene. However, it is no longer encountered at the counter, but rather on the television, the end of day vacation. **Below:** The Track Drive-In, Los Angeles. A sense of technological efficiency pervaded drive-in thinking from the late 1930's onward. In 1949, owner-inventor K.C. Purdy opened the Track and replaced car hops with metal bins. This innovation supposedly speeded up service 20-25% while saving 25% in labor costs. "Business Week" claimed the Track "brought the drive-in closer to the ultimate in mechanization."

Opposite: Carl's Drive-In, Los Angeles. Architect: Henry Werner. The September 1946 "Architectural Record" presented an extensive study on the drive-in restaurant. Henry Werner's lead article emphasized the functionalism of this "new" architectural form with its extensive use of glass and neon. The circular design, which provided maximum parking and best use of space was advocated.

The Drive-In...

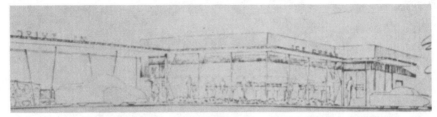

Drive-In, Richmond, California. Architects: Rhoda and Moist Hardison. Although described by "Architectural Record" as a "departure" from the "circular prototype," the square building with a canopied runway was another popular design of the post-war years.

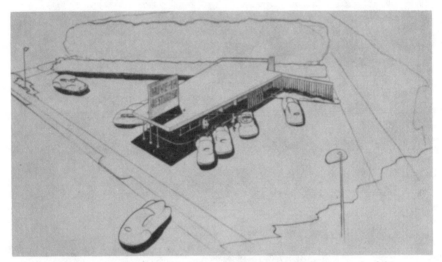

Donart Drive-In, Long Beach, Cal. Architect: Thornton Abell. This is an example of the post-war era designs which the "Architectural Forum" found to be "sharp distinctive forms which are themselves eyecatching."

Drive-In, Van Nuys, California. Architect: Louis Shoall Miller. This is an example of the post-war era designs which the "Architectural Forum" found to be "sharp distinctive forms which are themselves eyecatching."

Introduction

by Marshall Fishwick

> *The voice I heard this passing night was heard*
> *In ancient days by emperor and clown...*

John Keats Ode to a Nightingale

*I*nto our pop-spaceship we go, to revisit *The World of Ronald McDonald.*[1] Already the earlier visit seems long gone. When we made it, in 1978 A.D., a born-again Baptist insisted on being called Jimmy the President of the United States. Inflation and fast food had become part of the "American way of life"; trouble was brewing in Iran. Most people assumed that any President who wanted to be called "Jimmy" would find a clown like "Ronnie" a national asset. And so—as far as we can tell—he did.

But alas, the American people did not find Jimmy a national asset, and discarded him in 1980 A.D. Into the void stepped another Ronald (let's call him Ronald II) whose politics paralleled those of McDonald's owner-founder Ray Kroc. Though times got tougher and tougher, and scholars argued about when the recession would become a depression, both Ronalds stayed the course. Ronald I's appeal didn't contract—it expanded. When the economy slows, fast food sales quicken. In times of Big Trouble a man's best friend is a Big Mac.

When McDonald's 1982 *Annual Report* appeared, there were billions and billions of reasons to be happy—counting hamburgers and dollars earned. In the year of the highest number of corporate bankruptcies in American history, company profits were soaring, 7,259 restaurants in 31 countries were flourishing, and McDonald's had become the largest food-service in Japan. Ronald II was also happy. The economy was improving along with his national rating; despite record unemployment, most politicians were assuming he would run and win again in 1984.

Speaking of billions and billions, we should make note of a second pop-spaceship adventure that appeared since 1978. Carl Sagan has given us *Cosmos* as book, television program and trinketry—all have achieved unprecedented popularity. If Ronald is our Number One Clown, Sagan is our "Number One Celebrity Scientist." Some critics note there are many similarities.[2]

Let no one ridicule the clown, wherever he be in space or time. No one knows exactly where or when clowns originated. We were "clowning around" long before becoming *homo sapiens*—monkeys make marvelous clowns—and there is still a little clown in each of us. Ritual clowning is older than recorded history, shrouded in mystery, stretching back into primitive societies—perhaps into prehistoric caves. Wall paintings in tombs at Beni Hasan in the Nile Valley show that clowns, acrobats and magicians were entertaining rich and poor as early as 2500 B.C. Long before the Christian Era, itinerant clowns roamed—much like the mountebanks that blanketed Medieval Europe, or the medicine show men, frontier America. There were jugglers in Xanadu, acrobats in Crete, Greek and Roman buffoons were legendary, "bread and circuses" primary. Slapstick and buffoonery were central to the Roman *fabulae togatae*, which eventually took the place of Greek comedies.[3]

What is a fair or parade without a clown? Derived from the Latin word *feria* (festival), the first fairs brought worshipers and pilgrims to sacred places, like St. Bartholomew's in England. Clowns filled crucial roles in Shakespeare's plays and gained new color and prominence in the Italian *commedia dell' arte*, an improvised art form. Ronald McDonald is a descendant of the *zanni*, Arlecchino and Pierrot, or comic servants of the commedia, such as the sly and witty Harlequin and the awkward Pedrolino, whose costume of baggy trousers, loose-fitting blouse, and wide brimmed or peaked hat is still worn by many clowns. Over the centuries the role of "clown" emerged, first as a stock supporting figure, then as a leading character in his own right. Ronald has become the living symbol of McDonald's.

Elizabethan clowns, called merry-andrews, were displaced in the 18th century when Harlequin and companions appeared in pantomimes with harlequinade and transformation scenes. Joseph ("Joey") Grimaldi displaced Harlequin as a clown and set the white-face tradition. "Joey" influenced the circus clown, who first appeared at Philip Astley's riding school (afterward Astley's amphitheatre), as a comic and a talking clown.

In the 1860s a low-comedy buffoon appeared under the name of Auguste, who had a big nose, baggy clothes, large shoes and untidy manners. He worked with a whiteface clown, and always spoiled the latter's trick by appearing at the wrong time to mess things up. In Germany and Austria a stock figure, Hanswurst, appeared in the 16th century and was popular through the 19th. Other buffoons included the grimacing, musical, singing, rubber and vanishing clowns. With the three French Fratellini brothers, the Auguste-clown act became an art: Francois was the whiteface Pierrot and Paul and Albert were the buffoons. The circus had seemed up into the Television Era the natural habitat of American clowns, the best known example being Emmett Kelly.[4] Long and illustrious is the heritage of today's top clown, Ronald McDonald.

One of today's leading theologians, Henri Nouwen, has called our attention to the deep significance of clowns. We respond to them, he points out, not with admiration but sympathy, not with amazement but with understanding, not with tension but with a smile:

Clowns remind us with a tear and a smile that we share the same human weaknesses. Thus it is not surprising that pastoral psychologists have found in the clown a powerful image to help us understand the role of the minister in contemporary society.[5]

Ronald has taken the more modest (and meaty) task of helping us understand hamburgers. To be more accurate, we should say *Ronalds*—for now there are scores of them, the majority being on the road for fairs, fund-raising, parades and restaurant openings, the favored few being in front of cameras making magazine ads and television commercials. Even though one can get a pre-packaged "Ronald McDonald Biography" from McDonald's headquarters, there is no indication of why and when Ronald was born. Groupthink was involved, and one is referred to Cooper and Golin, "a major Chicago public relations firm."

Before Ronald there was Speedee. In early years he was featured exclusively through print: a pert puckish little fellow with a wink in his eye and these words: "I'm Speedee—Look for Me at McDonald's Speedee Drive-ins. Tender, Juicy All-Beef Hamburgers, Only 15¢." (By 1983, that sounded like another era, another economy.) In 1962 the Company conducted research which revealed McDonald's customers more readily identified McDonald's with the "golden arches" than with Speedee. The results of the survey may have been affected by the widespread local-market use of McDonald's first advertising jingle, "Look for the golden Arches," which had been introduced two years earlier. Nevertheless, Speedee was retired, and the golden arches replaced him as the Company's new advertising symbol.

But kids like flesh-and-blood characters: why not a clown? The resulting Ronald made his debut (along with the largest drum in the world) at Macy's annual Thanksgiving Day Parade in New York, November 25, 1963. As we have all come to know, Ronald lives in McDonaldland, but is at home anywhere. Intelligent and sensitive, he's always clown-like. He loves hamburgers, jokes and children. He can do almost anything, and defies the law of gravity. Antics of other McDonaldland characters complement Ronald, but never upstage him. Ronald McDonald is a super-star: and the company's official spokesman to children. He has acquired not only a voice but a world of his own, the world's best-publicized clown.

Ronald came on network in 1964, and other fantasy-characters were gradually added over the years. Most of them have been "toned down" since their original appearance. "Evil Grimace," for example, has become simply "Grimace," a lovable purple blob. The Hamburglar started as a frightening and mischievous fellow—but has become a mere bungler. Most scripts have been written by Needham, Harper and Steers, McDonald's national advertising agency. Storylines are based on products, and vary according to advertisement policy and needs. Ronald, dubbed "official spokesman" since 1967, has filled that role admirably. More important, he has become a *living entity*, a *ding an sich*, for millions of people ... a perpetual and immortal clown. His creators have proclaimed him "more famous than Lassie or the Easter Bunny." One may argue this, without denying that he is part of our media-landscape: the genial host of McDonaldland, with all that implies. And what do his creators think about Ronald's prospects? "He has a very bright future with the McDonald's Corporation."[6]

Is McDonaldland modeled (consciously or unconsciously) on Disneyland? Is Ronald a sort of Sorceror's Apprentice, who can turn the flow of hamburgers on, but cannot stop them? Does he even *want* to stop them? Will he drive all other competitors, all other foods, out of the land? That, at least, is the Orwellian question which some scholars insist on raising.

Since King Moody has been chief TV commercial "Ronald" since 1970, it is his face that most of us know and identify with the name; now he trains other Ronalds.[7]

What, exactly, does Ronald do? In the words of the "official biography":

Ronald does everything kids would like to do—skating, boating, flying around in the air, magic, riding on camels and best of all, going to McDonald's to eat hamburgers, his favorite food. Ronald spends all his time going from one McDonald's restaurant to another to see his friends, the children. If his friends are sick he visits them at the hospital. Ronald's favorite thing to do is to make children happy, to make everyone laugh.

Ronald has made not only children, but adults who own McDonald's stock or work under the Golden Arches happy, too. Ronald chronicles a commercial bonanza, powered by a mighty munching army consuming billions of hamburgers not only in America but around the world. But there is much more to it than that, says Professor Conrad Phillip Kottak, an anthropologist at the University of Michigan:

McDonald's has become nothing short of a secular religion, the shelter between the Golden Arches, a sacred place. One finds here spirituality without theological doctrine.

When we enter, Kottak notes, our surroundings tell us we are in a sequestered place, apart from the messiness of the outside world. We know what we are going to say, what will be said to us, what we will eat, how it will taste, how much it will cost. Ronald, what have you done to us?

Such a question is easier to ask than to answer. Language is a powerful complex tool, taking (like Proteus) multiple forms, shapes, meanings. Words, like things, change fast. Enter the Era of Fast Foods.

That McDonald's was able not only to reflect but also to help shape the innate desires and needs of a generation is widely acknowledged. Ronald's motto Q.S.C. (Quality, Service and Cleanliness) was a kind of Q.E.D. to the propositions of our time. To have expanded from one restaurant in 1955 to thousands here and abroad validates the "modern commercial miracle." What is harder to get at is the intangible meaning—the mythic and ironic overtones—of this "miracle." What is the meaning of Ronald's world? Why is it (in David Orr's phrase) "a powerful spore of popular culture on the

American landscape.""?

The impact of fast foods, not only on our stomachs but on our psyches, has only begun to be realized and reported A pioneer effort was made by *Time* magazine,whose July 4, 1977 issue featured as cover and commentary "Eating on the Run." The open road has become fast-food alley. It is not our endless plains and purple mountains that the young poeticize now. They reflect a new landscape and poetry:

> Shakey's Pizza, Tastee Freez
> A&W, Hardee's.

> Howard Johnson, Red Barn, Blimpie,
> House of Pizza, Big Boy, Wimpy.

> Wendy's, Friendly's, Taco Titos,
> Sandy's, Arby's, Los Burritos.

The giant under the Golden Arches is McDonald's, who not long after the magazine appeared sold his 23 billionth hamburger. "Fast food is now truly ubiquitous in American life," Paul Gray concludes. "Even those who want no part of it cannot avoid hearing its advertising, seeing its installations, or smelling its aromas wherever crowds gather to relax or be amused."

Historians knew that fast foods have been around for centuries. The Romans had one-dish instant service shops all over Rome, and their empire; winning generals have been working on fast-food formulae for centuries. The sandwich, key invention for fast foods, was the work of an English earl, not an American cook. But if (as Jean Brillat-Savarin claimed in 1826), "The destiny of nations depends on the manner in which they nourish themselves," the United States may well be the first nation whose destiny manifestly depends on hamburgers. *Time* was so impressed with this truism that it featured McDonald's on the cover (Sep. 17, 1973 issue) and wrote on "The Hamburger Empire." The article confirmed what other publications would test and document: in the world of fast foods, McDonald's was plainly Number One. But neither statistics, polls or ratings can measure the scope and impact of Ronald. He is, after all, our *friend*. He makes us laugh. He tells us that we deserve a break today—so we take it.

Only the narrow-minded would adjudge McDonald's success as merely economic or geographical. The corporation has affected, even altered, our lifestyle. It has applied a manufacturing style of thinking to a people-intensive service situation. If machinery is to be viewed as a piece of equipment with the capability of producing a predictably standardized, customer-satisfying output while minimizing the operating discretion of its attendant, that is what a McDonald's retail outlet is. Through painstaking attention to total design and facilties planning, everything is built integrally into the machine itself, into the technology of the system.

Such claims tend to raise two different reactions from humanists. One is to note that after all these years, our human intelligence seems to have solved the problem of cheap, clean food, produced quickly. The other is to see, in the face of those programmed attendants, the fulfillment of George Orwell's *1984*. McDonald's offers the hamburger without qualities for the man without qualities ... the supreme triumph of all that is insane in American life.

So—in the humanistic tradition—let's turn to etymology and to history for some clues.

No one knows who ate the first hamburger—or where or when that event occurred. Various current dictionaries have settled for this sort of standard definition: "a sandwich consisting of a patty of meat in a split round bun." They go on to trace sandwich to the Earl (of Sandwich) and hamburger to the city (Hamburg, Germany). The largest seaport in continental Europe, Hamburg has been for centuries a crossroad of cultures and cuisines.

Sailing throughout the Hanseatic league, ships from Hamburg must have discovered a Russian delicacy called "tartar steak." It was ground raw meat—one can still get it in parts of the world. Back in Hamburg, they probably preferred to cook it: behold the *hamburger!*

Nonsense, various cuisine-chauvinists claim. It was conceived in France (naturallement), Italy, Austria, England (where else would there be an Earl of Sandwich?). In New Haven, Connecticut, there used to be a place which claimed to be "The Birthplace of the Hamburger." New Haven has to argue that out with other "birthplaces," such as St. Louis, where they were "serving 'em hot" at the 1904 World's Fair. Perhaps we should conclude the matter by paraphrasing Gertrude Stein: "A hamburger is a hamburger is a hamburger."

From the anthropological viewpoint, the hamburger has somehow solved basic time-space problems. Given our landscape, livestock and lifestyle, *this* is what everybody can afford to eat, often. Hamburgers are cheap, abundant, tasty, nutritious, convenient. But we aren't just dealing with something to stuff into our mouths—but about a thousand memories of a thousand meals, picnics, ball games, vacations. Eating a hamburger can be, and often is, ritualistic. Eating them with others is a form of communication; we consume not only a burger but a cipher. No wonder the pop artists are fascinated with hamburgers. They are close to the center of contemporary popular culture. Over the years I have asked students to make comparisons between hamburgers and automobiles, explaining the communality. They come out with results like this:

Hamburger's Home	Car's Label	Common Denominator
Mom and Pop (independent)	Pinto, Corvair	Risky; often the wrong choice
Fast Food chain	Nova, Toyota	Cheap, uniform, sturdy

Coffee Shop	Mercury, Impala	Safe, undistinguished, overpriced
Sit-down restaurant	Oldsmobile	Big, dull, dependable
"Specialty" hamburger restaurant	Datsun Z210	Trendy, splashy, ostentatious
"Haute Cuisine" Establishments	Rolls Royce, Mercedes	Quietly elegant, filet mignon quality

Not content to stay with the Nova's and Toyota's, McDonald's has tried constantly to upgrade service, decor, image; this brought forth in 1968 a multi-million dollar training facility (where all licensees and managers must study) called Hamburger University, in Elk Grove Village, Illinois.[8] At first centering on technical expertise, the university now offers what it calls a "college-type format, including management sciences." This leads to a Bachelor of Hamburgerology, with a minor in French fries.

While other academics may take all this as a joke, McDonald's doesn't. They have sought and got official accreditation, and studies show that many students arise at 6:30 a.m. and put in 14 hour days—a record that not even the Marines would be ashamed of. After graduation: out in the field!

In the field, licensees and managers are incessantly hounded by roving inspectors (called "field supervisors") to make sure that the restaurant floor is mopped at proper intervals and the parking lot tidied up hourly. If a manager tries to sell his customers hamburgers that have been off the grill more than ten minutes or coffee more than 30 minutes old, Big Brother in Oak Brook will find out. Headquarters executives calculate exactly how much food each restaurant can be expected to throw away each day, and are ready to chastise a chronically deviant manager who has no good explanation.

Grillmen, "window girls" (order takers) and other hired hands conform to strict rules. Men must keep their hair cropped to military length, and their shoes (black only) highly polished. Women must wear dark low shoes, hair nets and only very light makeup. Viewing the results, Harvard Business School Professor Theodore Levitt describes McDonald's as "a machine that produces, with the help of totally unskilled machine tenders, a highly polished product. . . . The only choice available to the attendant is to operate it exactly as the designers intended."

This, I suggest, is why the burger ("ham" got lost in colloquial speech) has become a major phenomenon of our time; why burger joints spring up on highways, city boulevards and small-town streets like mushrooms (which they often architecturally resemble). For every dollar spent on food eaten away from home, an estimated 40¢ goes to fast-food emporiums. The total sales each year is in the billions. That's a lot of beef.

With that much at stake, there is naturally a lot of competition. Look around you, at the dazzling permutations on the basic hamburger, bearing odd, hyped-up names which take some time to master, much less understand. But a snack that hits the spot on one day is likely to do so every day, thanks to tight control of quality and portion size by the large chains. Familiarity with fast food does not, apparently, breed contempt.

To those who find formal restaurants intimidating and expensive, the in-and-out eateries are godsends. No snooty headwaiters, no discomfort over which fork to use; the teen-agers who always seem to be taking orders at the counter are just like the ones next door, or on magazine covers, billboards and TV. Eli Whitney, take note: by 1978, American kids munching tasty burgers had become interchangeable parts. No wonder Ronald was happy with his world.

Before Ronald came Ray—Ray Albert Kroc, born of Slavic parents in 1902 on Chicago's West Side. If Hamburger is the real hero of our true-to-life drama, then Ray is at his right hand, stop watch clicking to keep the burgers bustling. Kroc appears many times in the chapters ahead; only his essential story need be recorded here. Though there is no indication of a close friendship, Kroc served with Walt Disney as a Red Cross ambulance driver in World War I. Having tried several other jobs, Kroc settled down in 1923 as a paper cup salesman for Lily-Tulip. In 1941 he got franchise rights for friend Earl Prince's new multi-mixer, and started Prince Castle Sales Division. This was eight years before Richard and Maurice McDonald opened up a hamburger stand in San Bernardino, California, and twelve years before the McDonalds ordered eight multi-mixers, enticing Kroc himself to go out and see what was behind this super-order.

By concentrating on burgers and fries, served in disposable wrappers, and by reducing the ordering process to a simple code, the brothers had developed an assembly line operation that could deliver food quickly and cheaply. Specialization, efficiency, uniformity and volume had long been sacred for American industry. But as Kroc the veteran salesman sat beneath the golden arches in the California sun, watching the endless flow of customers, he realized what was missing. Somebody had to put the show on the road!

In the new corporate poplore, Kroc is to hamburgers what Ford is to Model T's; these are the "historic three days" (Christian resurrection overtones?) during which Kroc "discovered" McDonald's. Then the miracle which the P.R. staff (disciples?) never tire of retelling took place:

1955 - Kroc's first McDonald's opens in Des Plaines, Ill.
1956 - With a total net worth of $90,000, Kroc borrows $1.5 million.
1961 - $2.9 million buys all rights to the McDonald's concept.
1962 - Total system wide sales: $76.3 million.
1963 - Major menu innovation: double burger and double cheeseburger.
1964 - Number of units more than double that of 1960—now 570.
1965 - McDonald's goes public and continues to make huge profits.
1966 - McDonald's becomes a national name; Ronald goes on national network.
1967 - The end of the 15¢ hamburger era and the beginning of Ronald's role

as "official" spokesman of McDonald's on national television.

1968 - Big Mac and Hot Apple Pie added; 1,000th store in America's heartland, Des Plaines, Ill.

1969 - International Division formed: the "billion served" sign changed to "five billion"; women crew-persons for first time.

1970 - "You Deserve a Break Today" new slogan, and McDonaldland new setting for TV commercials.

1971 - Hamburglar, Grimace, Mayor McCheese, Captain Crook and the Professor join Ronald; McDonald's open in Japan, Germany and Australia.

1972 - McDonald's becomes a billion dollar corporation, 2,000th store opened in Des Plaines, and Ray Kroc receives Horatio Alger Award.

1973 - Egg McMuffin is introduced; 2,500th store opens in Lockport, New York, and McDonald's makes *Time* cover.

1974 - First Ronald McDonald House opens in Philadelphia, company sells 15 billionth hamburger.

1975 - McDonald's celebrates its 20th birthday by graduating 10,000th student from Hamburger University, building first drive-in, and launching a new ad campaign ("We Do It All For You.")

1976 - As sales surpass the $3 billion mark and the 4,000th store is opened, crews get new uniforms and a new ad campaign ("You, You're the one.")

1977 - McDonald's offers complete breakfast, organizes All American High School Basketball Team, and buys land for a "New World Headquarters" in Oak Brook, Illinois. Ray Kroc's 75th birthday.

1978 - As the 5,000th restaurant opens in Japan, and the 15,000th graduate from Hamburger U. gets his diploma, the 25th billionth hamburger is served.

So matters stood on our 1978 study-visit to *The World of Ronald McDonald*. Obviously the mass-produced mechanized hamburger had given Kroc a fortune and Ronald a world: bright, happy, clean, bedecked with Ronald McDonald goodies and glasses. Promotional campaigns give children a free hamburger and soft drink on their birthdays. Napkin and straw dispeners are placed in the customer area, to allow youngsters to "do things" for themselves. Mothers, who make most meal decisions, endorse their children's preference. The food is economical, fast, quality-controlled and appealing. Wherever in the world you enter you can count on what you would get—even what you will be told (in various languages) as you leave, "Have a good day!"

But things have been a bit rocky—for the company and the nation— since our 1978 visit. Inflation soared and profits shrank. Ronald suddenly had competition, some of it Darwinian. Rivals popped up everywhere, under such banners as Wendy's, Arby's and Burger King. The Battle of the Burgers got underway, with newcomers struggling tooth-and-bun to get a larger share of the $20 billion fast food market.

Quick to respond to the threat, McDonald's coined a slogan for rough days: "Seize Restaurant Superiority." Paul Schrage, executive vice president of the markets, thought S.R.S. would have immediate impact, and predicted "a shakeout of weaker, less aggressive fast food companies" in the days ahead.[9] He also urged all friends of Ronald to shout forth the new National Anthem:

> Nobody can do it like McDonald's can.
> Nobody, nobody else in this whole land!
> You're the reason we do it —
> Nobody can do it like McDonald's can.

In addition to sending out the clown, McDonald's stepped up its advertising in newspapers, magazines and billboards. The company, defending its position as Number One, saturated the radio, running the gamut from traditional to country-western to disco, featuring well known stars like Tammy Wynette, Gloria Gaynor, Rose Royce, Paul Anka and Seals and Crofts. All this brought the annual promotion budget for 1982 to over $362 million. That's a lot of bucks to sell a lot of beef. Effective bucks, too: the annual total system-wide sales exceeded $7 billion.

Realizing that the stakes were simply gastronomical, warring factions plotted their strategy. They wooed and bribed each other's executive officers, sent out recipe reconnnaissance teams, recruited informants to sneak and leak secret documents, and set aside "combat funds" to plan commando raids. "Worm rumors" in opponents' hamburgers were released—close to the "dirty tricks" category. Suits and countersuits resulted. Worms squirmed. By 1982, the Battle of the Burgers was sizzling— and the end is not in sight.[10]

The armaments were slogans, promotions, commercials, new products and free premiums: balloons, whistles, "Star Wars" glasses, puzzles, prizes and comic books. For example, Burger King officials estimate that every two weeks, the company has given away 6 million such premiums to kids as "a reward for coming to Burger King."

At its seven-story corporate headquarters in Miami, the Burger King Corp. kicked off its Operation Grand Slam with a direct challenge to the World of Ronald McDonald. Wendy's and Arby's were no less resolute, if not so well armored. The common resolution was to match trick for trick, clown for clown, dollar for dollar. The question of the war was a billion-dollar question: "Who's got the best darn burger in the whole wide world?"

For one man, at least—Ray Kroc—there is only one answer. Like Ronald, he wants to be a father-figure to millions of hungry kids. Customers are "my people" and the Company "my baby":

> "This is my baby. It's not that we're super, but nobody else in the field has this kind of fatherhood. Willard Marriott and old Howard Johnson did, once. But now, *I'm* the Hamburger Man."

A sentimentalist? Hardly. "This is rat eat rat, dog eat dog," Kroc says of competition on the strip. "I'll kill 'em before they kill me. Anyone who wants the consumer's eating-out dollar is our competitor. We don't belong to the associations. They ask me to speak. I don't speak. If they want financial things, all they have to do is buy one share of McDonald's stock and come to our shareholders' meeting. They can go to the financial analyst meetings. We appear there. But we're not going to spill our guts to competitors to give them ideas."

Times may be hard, but Ray Kroc is frank to admit he lives "the good life" on his California ranch, having earned every penny he spends. He spelled this out to a reporter from *Insititutions*:

"I have 22 twin bed rooms, each with private bath and I have seminars out there. I don't know whether you've seen the Big Mac bus? Well, I bought one for an experiment here in Chicago. I bought a 40-foot Greyhound bus and had it customized. It cost $150,000, carries 17. It's absolutely beautiful inside. It's like a yacht on wheels. I have a shower and a bathroom, a galley and a bar. Television, telephone. And a make-up table if the gal wants to make-up or something. I have the logo on the side and the back of the bus. And I have a 72-foot boat."

The man who is captain of that boat—and of his soul—is an electronic age Horatio Alger, proud to be at the top of the ladder. But he is far too clever to let his company, or the thousands of places in which Ronald peddles his burgers, remain static. Kroc has been quick to see the new concern with minorities, ethnic groups, women's movements, nostalgia, regionalism. Ronald is selling a standardized, mass-produced product, but he is selling magic too. That is his secret weapon.

"When you're in this business," says Ronald's master, Ray Kroc, "you're in show business. Every day is a new show. It's like a Broadway musical. If they hum your tune, you're a success."

Ronald has them humming; not only in America, but all over the world. The idea of Ronald is contagious. There are dozens of American hamburgers, The Everywhere Community is becoming international—not just as global communication, but as identical products and processes. National boundaries, and separate words, merge:

TWOALLBEEFPATTIESSPECIALSAUCELETTUCE
CHEESEPICKLESONIONSONASESAMESEEDBUN

But in the words that follow, by authors with varied backgrounds, disciplines and opinions, we hope both to split and analyze them, and the fast food phenomenon in general. The one thing on which authors and critics are in agreement is the statement by Chris Schoenleb, marketing vice president of Burger King: "It's not a question of *whether* we're going to eat billions of burgers, but *where* we're going to eat them." That's why the giants are into a verbal war of pattie propaganda. McDonald's relies on its crack division: send in the clowns!

By now we understand that buying a hamburger is really a ritual. But the contenders want you for more than an occasional ritual. They want you for breakfast, and are willing to bake fresh biscuits every morning to get you there. They want you for dinner, for snacks; for birthdays, holidays, weekends. They want you when Mom doesn't want to cook or when Dad doesn't want to eat Mom's cooking, or when Dad himself threatens to cook. They want you to become—in market lexicon—a heavy user, the hamburger eater who stops in at least once a week.

Schoenleb figures "If every customer made one additional visit per month, that would get us an additional $100,000 per store annually."

They want you so badly they'll spend millions for your business, bribe your kids with toys and do anything possible to make you believe their hamburger is really different—tastier, bigger, faster, and more fun to eat than anyone else's.

The early rumblings of war began when a top McDonald's executive, Don Smith, defected to become president of Burger King. It didn't take long to see what he had in mind—to out-Ronald Ronald.

"Before Don's arrival, I think we were resigned to our No. 2 position. Don doesn't accept that philosophy. He believes it's possible to be No. 1," said Jerry Ruenheck, Burger King's vice president in charge of operations. Plainly, Don wasn't just clowning around. He had become a living example of one of Ronald's cartoon friends: the Hamburgler.

We shall hear more about him, and other topics, in the pages ahead: wizards, drive-ins, landscape, interior design, ethnography, linguistics, calorie-counting, psychology, philosopy, fast-food happiness, architecture and people's habits. Opponents will square off: Berger vs. Burger, Mao vs. Mac, Onion vs. Pickle. All this may lead you to think that we are only clowning around. Not so. Fast food is not merely a business, but clue and key to our culture. We think that, like many another clown, Ronald deserves our serious attention.[11] When you have finished, we hope you will agree. Now, let's get on with our visit.

Notes

[1] The original visit began in a special issue of the *Journal of American Culture*, 1:2, summer 1978, and was reissued as a book—Marshall Fishwick, editor, *The World of Ronald McDonald* (Bowling Green, OH.: Popular Press, 1978).

[2] Carl Sagan, *Cosmos* (New York: Random House, 1980). The dangers of this billions-and-billions man are pointed out by Walker Percy, in *Lost in the Cosmos* (New York: Farrar, Straus and Giroux, 1983). He is amused by Sagan's "innocent scientism, the likes of which I haven't encountered since the standard bull session of high school and college—up to but not beyond the sophomore year." (p. 201) But there is too little malice and too much ignorance to offend—which is the way many of us feel about Ronald peddling his burgers to the cavernous stomachs of the world.

[3] There is a fascinating body of literature on fools and clowns, which may be said to date in "modern" times from Carl Flogel's *Geschichte der Hofnarren* (Leipzig, 1789), and include such major studies as John Doran, *The History of Court Fools* (London, 1858), M. Wilson Disher, *Clowns and Pantomimes* (London, 1923), Allardyce Nichol, *Masks, Mimes and Miracles* (New York, 1931), Mircea Eliade, *Images and Symbols* (New York, 1961), Tristan Remy, Clownnummern (Cologne, 1964), William Willeford, *The Fool and His Scepter* (Chicago, 1969), Harvey Cox, *Feast of Fools* (New York, 1970), and Henry Nouwen, *Clowning in Rome* (New York:

1979). See also footnote 11 below.

[4]See Marian Murray, *Circus: From Rome to Ringling* (Westport, CT: Greenwood Press, 1973).

[5]Henry Nouwen, *op. cit.*, p. 34.

[6]Letter to Marshall Fishwick from Cindy Williams, Administrative Coordinator, McDonald's Corporation, July 19, 1977. Subsequent letters in 1982 and 1983 repeated the prediction.

[7]McDonald's, which treats social science surveys almost as reverentially as it does French fries, sponsors annual "Awareness Studies," which verify the 96% recognition factor for Ronald. This makes him a close second to Santa Claus, and an easy victor over any American commercial rival.

[8]For more details see *Time* Magazine, Sept. 17, 1973.

[9]See *Advertising Age*, April 23, 1979, p. 94.

[10]For details, see Carl Hiassen's syndicated piece for the Knight-Ridder newspapers, Oct. 10, 1982, entitled "The Battle of Burgers is Sizzling."

[11]For those who want a deeper background in the clown than we have provided in this short "Introduction" we add a clown bibliography to supplement footnote 3:

Bernadin, N.M. *La Comedie Italienne en France et les Theatres de la Foire et du Boulevard, 1570-1791*, Paris, 1902.

Canel, A. *Recherches Historiques sur les Fous des Fous Rois de France*, Paris, 1873.

Chambers, Sir E.K. *The Mediaeval Stage*, 2 vols. Clarendon Press, 1903.

Clement, Mme., nee Hemery. *Historire des Fetes Civiles et Religieuses des usages anciens et moderns du department du Nord*. Paris,1834.

Duchartre, P.L. *The Italian Comedy*, Authorized translation from the French by R.T. Weaver. London, 1929.

Erythraeus, Janus Nicius. *Pinacotheca Imaginum Illustrium Doctrinae vel ingenii laude Virom.* Guelgerbyti, 1729.

Forbes, A.P. "Lives of St. Ninian and St. Kentigern," in *Historians of Scotland*, vol. v. Edinburgh, 1874.

Frazer, Sir James. *The Golden Bough*, 3rd ed. London, 1911-15.

Hunt, Douglas and Kari. *Pantomime: The Silent Theater*, New York: Atheneum,1964.

Kelly, Emmett. *Clown*. New York: Prentice-Hall, 1954.

McVicar, J. Wesley. *Clown Act Omnibus*. New York: Crown, 1960.

Picot, E. *Pierre Gringoire et les comediens italiens*. Paris, 1878.

Poggio Bracciolini. *The Facetiae or Jocose Tales of Poggio*, now first translated into English with the Latin Text, 2 vols. Paris, 1879.

Rudwin, M.J. *The Origins of the German Carnival Comedy*. Berlin, 1920.

Swain, Barbara. *Fools and Folly During the Middle Ages and the Renaissance*. New York: Columbia Univ. Press, 1932.

Wesselski, A. *Narren, Gaukler and Volkslieblige*. 5 vols. Berlin, 1910-20.

Don't forget to update by getting Ronald's free *McDonald's Fun Times*—but you'll have to buy a burger to get the paper!

Interior of McDonald's, Airport Road, Toledo, Ohio. Photo, courtesy Glenn J. Browne

"Rose Window," in McDonald's, Ann Arbor, Michigan. Photo, courtesy E.L. Huddleston

Hamburger Stand Industrialization and the Fast-Food Phenomenon

by Bruce A. Lohof

In 1936 Charlie Chaplin unveiled one of the most famous of his satirical commentaries on life in the twentieth century. *Modern Times,* he called it—the film and the century—and his protagonist was a factory worker who stood at his station on the assembly line tightening a perpetual sequence of bolts, each with a single turn of a single wrench. Monotonously he thereby became an accessory to the replication of some standardized product or other. The motion picture was not named "best of the year" (an honor that went instead to a completely forgettable M.G.M. biography of *The Great Ziegfeld).* Its setting did have a certain recognizable madness, however, which doubtless explains why Chaplin's imagery has since become a cultural symbol.

Not that the helpless pawn of standardized industrial forces was a Chaplinesque invention. Historians among the audience of *Modern Times* knew its protagonist well. Long before him the handloom weavers of England had bowed before the power looms of the eighteenth century even as their fellows in a myriad of other callings had sooner or later fallen beneath some similar juggernaut. The conditions that Chaplin attacked with pathos and satire had in all seriousness and with great violence been confronted a hundred years earlier by the Luddites. Indeed so compelling and ubiquitous had been the narrative that Chaplin's themes were major leitmotifs in the history of the industrial revolution: the subordination of the skilled artisan to the sophisticated mechanism, and the replacement of the unique item by the standardized product.

The times have changed now and, outside the Third World at least, civilization has moved through secondary and tertiary revolutions into what is often characterized as a post-industrial condition. And yet the dichotomies of artisan versus mechanism and unique versus standard— couplets so central to the revolution of the nineteenth century—still exist here and there in post-industrial settings. Indeed one such place is suggested by *Modern Times* itself: as aficionados will recall, Chaplin had his masochistic protagonist actually suggest that the purposes of the factory might be further served by a feeding machine that would oblige the laborers to eat without loss through down time. The suggestion was thought too complicated by management, but the most cursory glance at the American landscape of the 1970s and 1980s suggests that it need not have been. Franchised eateries stand cheek by jowl along every post-industrial city's neon strip. A handful of nationally recognized trade names—each itself a near icon—with thousands of individual eateries snuggled beneath them gives evidence of both the mechanical feasibility and the manifold profitability of feeding machines. The industrial revolution in short has come to fast food, and it is well to examine its advent. In doing so we may recapture in our own time the processes by which industrialization occurs. Moreover we may learn something about the impact that industrialization and its imperatives have had on American culture, a culture that quite literally takes much of its sustenance in the form of the machine-made hamburger.

The pre-industrial history of the fast-food phenomenon in the United States disappears somewhere into the *diner* (an Americanism of nineteenth-century vintage). Originally a railroad car especially equipped for the preparation and serving of food, the diner came to be a derailed shell or an erstwhile trolley following its calling in a single location. Or perhaps a more recognizable form of pre-industrialization in fast food is the *greasy spoon* (a colloquialism with roots apparently as deep as the 1920s), that franchised or company-owned edifice of the post-war period, that Royal Castle or White Castle or White Tower or Toddle House that in many cases continues to punctuate the American cityscape. Take for instance any one of the many Royal Castle restaurants that between 1938 and 1975 were constructed and operated by the Miami-based firm Royal Castle System, Incorporated. Even in the worst of years Royal Castle made more than twenty millions of dollars in sales.[1] In terms both financial and symbolic then the local Royal Castle was a fitting archetype of pre-industrialism in fast food.

The sample might conform to any of the four types that the Royal Castle System constructed during its thirty-seven years in fast food: "D," the earliest of the four, was a rectangle thirty-five by forty feet, a forward corner recessed into a front entrance. Type "DD" followed, essentially a "D" structure augmented by a smaller module whose interior was fitted for table service. The "J" came next, a slightly smaller building—twenty-eight by forty feet—whose exterior featured the same illuminated facade that dominated gasoline service station architecture during the period. And finally came the "K" type, a square of thirty-five feet with an exaggerated hip roof. Only the "K" departed from tradition by obscuring its kitchen behind a partition, a service passage joining preparation and serving areas. The other types were vintage greasy spoon: delineating their interiors was the service counter; flanking the counter a row of stools and a galley-style kitchen.

Structures of such modest artistic pretensions have of course generally

Royal Castle Restaurant, "D,"
Courtesy George Chillag

The Royal Castle, "DD,"
Courtesy George Chillag

Royal Castle, "J"
Courtesy George Chillag

Royal Castle, "K"
Courtesy George Chillag

lain beneath the purview of scholarly scrutiny. A few architectural historians have stooped to comment however, some with disgust, others with glee, and all on the apparent divorce of image from function. The critic Reyner Banham for instance was clearly disturbed by such matters when he explained how one might construct a "hamburger bar" by purchasing "a plain standard building shell from Butler Buildings Corporation or a similar mass-producer and add[ing] symbolic garnish [or signs] to the front, top, and other places that show."[2] In contrast, the architect Robert Venturi and his associates have applauded this genre of structure. Explaining how in many elitist "megastructures" the "systems of space, structure, and program [or function] are submerged and distorted by an overall symbolic form," in buildings such as a Royal Castle restaurant—the Venturi people call them "decorated sheds"—"systems of space and structure are directly at the service of program, and ornament is applied independently of them."[3]

One can then either denigrate with Banham the garnished shell and its inconsistencies of work and form, or celebrate with Venturi the decorated shed and its liberation of image from function. Either way it is worth noting that a Royal Castle restaurant, like a gasoline service station, is a good example of what John Kouwenhoven and others have called the "vernacular tradition." Each of the tradition's characteristics—"economy, simplicity, and flexibility"—is on clear display.[4] Each of the Royal Castle types was designed for economical maintenance, with the floors, concrete and glass walls, and either aluminum or the ubiquitous porcelain enamel fixtures. With the exception of the "K" and its excessive roof line, each is free of meaningless ornamentation. And each is an invention in the broadest sense of the term: an architectural contrivance that can be replicated over and over again without modification in design, and can be located wherever a fast-food eatery seems desirable. Indeed like their vernacular counterpart the service station, certain Royal Castle types— particularly the "D" and the "DD"—are so flexible that they are properly understood as a series of modules or basic structural elements that can be horizontally stacked to produce a variety of restaurant types with a small repertoire of module designs.

In the days before the industrial revolution enveloped the fast-food business the door to a busy Royal Castle restaurant was an entrance to an animated collage. Here a derelict dozed in his coffee. Here a nurse fresh from a night's sleep breakfasted on bacon and eggs while a cabbie weary from a night on the streets relaxed over a hamburger. Here a nondescript couple consumed any of the fifty-odd items that appeared on the Royal Castle menu. The establishment in short was a jostle of apparently disparate activities, each in pursuit of its separate agenda.

Lending unity and coherence to this jostle however was the presence of the protagonist, the artist-in-residence: the *fry cook* (yet another colloquialism, this apparently of unknown origin). As the protagonist he served as the common denominator among these uncommon agendas because he—and usually with single-handed dexterity—had taken each

The Royal Castle Galley.
Courtesy George Chillag.

order and had prepared and served its contents. More important he was an artisan in the most classical sense of the term: he had undergone an apprenticeship, he was able to exercise special skills and manipulate special equipment, he pursued an applied art. His education had been of the most basic sort—on-the-job—so experience rather than some more formal order of training accounted for his expertise. His work bench so to speak was the galley kitchen stretching from grill to ice maker, with coffee urns and soup warmers, toasters and waffle irons, griddles and sinks all strategically interspersed.

Scattered across the galley was an array of tools with names as arcane and functions as specialized as those of the tanner or the chandler. And finally his product—mean fare to be sure—played soup and sandwich to the chef's souffle as surely as the anonymous gargoyle played to Michelangelo's *Pieta*, as surely as in more general terms the product of any artisan plays to the more sophisticated but nevertheless similar product of the artist. Was the handloom weaver the protagonist of textile production before the introduction of the power loom? Or the cooper the protagonist of barrel-making before the advent of the mass-produced steel drum? So as certainly the fry cook was the artisan-in-residence in this archetype of pre-industrial fast food, the greasy spoon.

In 1975 however after nearly four decades in the fast-food business, the Royal Castle restaurants and their artisans left the marketplace. Clearly they had become the victims of technological obsolescence, for down the road was new competition, a new variety of structures that housed a new central character and offered a new and standardized product. Industrialization had come to fast food.

The Burger King Corporation, a subsidiary of the Pillsbury Company was in 1980 operating or franchising 2,700 fast-food stores world-wide. Its sales were exceeding 1.8 billion dollars annually, making it one of the largest fast-food firms in America.* And each of its restaurants is the home of the industrialized hamburger.

Like its pre-industrial predecessor the Royal Castle System, the Burger King Corporation has constructed a variety of restaurant types during its decades of existence. In the 1950s the company relied upon the "Walk-up," a simple rectangle whose interior housed equipment for the preparation of food but lacked a seating area, rest-room facilities, and other amenities usually associated with American restaurant design. The "Handlebar" store followed. So named because of its dominant roofline decoration, the "Handlebar" was a rectangular structure, forty-five by fifty feet. In adherence to the flexibility of the vernacular tradition—and reminiscent of the Royal Castle's "D"-"DD" coupling—the "Handlebar" was merely a "Walk-Up" augmented by a seating area.

In recent years however Burger King stores have invariably conformed to either the "Red Roof" or "Natural Finish" types. Rectangular buildings

*Only McDonalds Restaurants and the U.S. Army are larger

Burger King, "Walk-Up"
Courtesy Burger King Corporation

Burger King, "Handlebar,"
Courtesy Burger King Corporation

Burger King, "Red Roof"
Courtesy Burger King Corporation

Burger King Restaurants, "National Finish"
Courtesy Burger King Corporation

of between forty-five by fifty feet and fifty by fifty-five feet depending upon the anticipated sales and desired seating capacity, these recent types are distinguishable from their predecessors as well as from each other by their distinctive decors. Gone is the earlier handlebar logo; in its place is either a red mansard roofline or an ecology motif: cedar shakes, brickwork walls and warm color schemes.

Too much can be made of these decors, of course, for the lessons of Banham and Venturi should always be borne in mind. Recalling the one's garnished shell and the other's decorated shed it quickly becomes clear that the Burger King Corporation has simply retired older for newer images. Moving one's attention from decoration to structure it becomes evident that the divorce of image from function which alternately appalled Banham and thrilled Venturi still prevails. Architecturally food preparation and seating areas lie side-by-side within rectangular boxes and the vernacular tradition is intact. Hence the eye is caught by that familiar economy of maintenance and simplicity of design. Noticed also is the flexibility and replicability of the structures. And finally, in the Burger King store as elsewhere within the tradition one finds the vernacular reliance upon a horizontal stacking of modules. Hiding behind a different logo then and clothed in a different wardrobe of motifs is the same vernacular tradition.

Inside the store however all is different. As our attention turns from architecture to cookery we cannot help but notice the conspicuous absence of the greasy spoon's protagonist and artisan-in-residence, the fry cook. Nor can we ignore his shining, stainless steel successor, a feeding machine that would have warmed Charlie Chaplin's satirical heart. Here between the fry cook and the feeding machine is the first of the industrial revolution's dichotomies: the artisan versus the mechanism. Not far behind is the revolution's second dichotomy: the unique versus the standard. For our new protagonist is the Burger King broiler and it is producing Burger King's burgers by the thousand. Industrialization has come to fast food.

Like other machinery in the world of industrialization the Burger King Corporation's hamburger machine—or *line-up*, as it is referred to in the trade—rationalizes the construction of its product. Accordingly the process is first separated into its discreet tasks. Each task is then assigned to its proper station, mechanical or manual, a post that has been carefully designed for a precise purpose. And finally each of these stations is assigned its appropriate place along the assembly line. In the world of Burger King the line-up begins with a broiling mechanism. Moving along endless-grate conveyors, buns of bread and patties of ground meat travel at precise speeds through intense temperatures. When properly cooked these patties and buns leave the grates and descend small chutes, the one to be sandwiched within the other. These sandwiches are then moved to the next station, a preparation table where a variety of accessories and condiments is applied as prescribed by the customer.* Here the sandwich is completed, packaged and forwarded to the point of sale.

The Burger King line-up is of course no more sophisticated than its

*Hence the advertiser's jingle: "...special orders don't upset us,/all we ask is that you let us/have it your way."

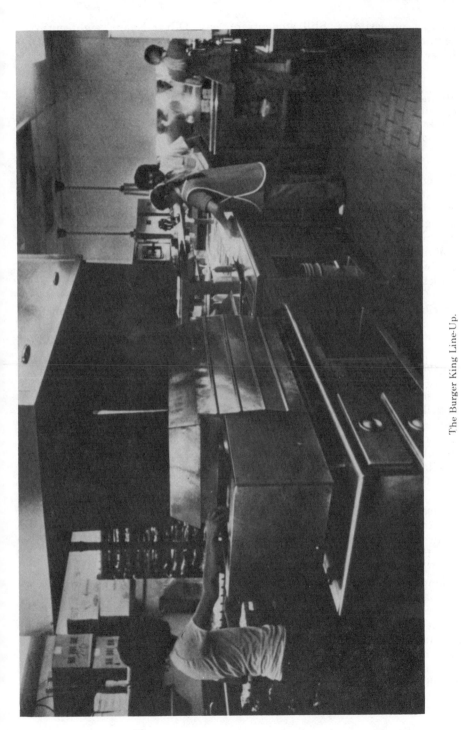

The Burger King Line-Up.
Courtesy George Chillag.

product necessitates. Still students of, say, Oliver Evans' eighteenth-century plant at Redclay Creek or Henry Ford's twentieth-century works at River Rouge will nevertheless recognize the line-up's mechanical essence. As the historian Siegfried Giedion has explained:

Mechanizing production means dissecting work into its component operations...[and] in manufacturing complex products such as the automobile [or as we see relatively simple products such as the hamburger sandwich], this division goes together with reassembly.[5]

When contrasted with the pre-industrial nature of the Royal Castle System's greasy spoon, the Burger King line-up conjures an overtly industrial milieu. The basic elements of the factory have obviously been introduced to the fast-food phenomenon. Moreover, this introduction has brought with it two other inevitable changes. One, the advent of the feeding machine has introduced the possibility—some consumers would say the dulling certainty—of a standardized, recognized product. As one commentator has written: "Burger King...wants the food it serves in New York to be as identical as humanly possible to that served in New Mexico or New Orleans." But conformity of this magnitude is of course not *humanly* possible; only machinery can provide so standardized a product. Concomitantly the rise of the machine has meant the fall of the artisan. Standing in the place of the fry cook, his lengthy education, his careful skills, and his arcane galley, is the glistening metal line-up and its inexperienced attendants. The Burger King Corporation claims that a single hamburger machine represents an investment in excess of seventy thousand dollars. It also claims that the average restaurant employee is an unskilled teenager who will work for the prevailing minimum wage and last perhaps four months on the job. What other data could more graphically illustrate the replacement of the experienced artisan with the sophisticated machine and its callow caretakers. In fast food as elsewhere the truth of Giedion's title cannot be escaped: mechanization takes command!

But what can they mean, all of these busy Burger King stores, all of these derelict Royal Castle restaurants, and all of the thousands upon thousands of other fast-food eateries that under competing logos punctuate the American landscape? Neither architecture of artistic merit nor engines of awesome sophistication can be found here. What lessons then are there, that this apparent trivia should be contemplated?

First we can look to the architecture of fast food to find another ready example of the vernacular tradition in building. And though as aesthetes we may be put off by the vulgarity of the tradition we cannot as students of the culture ignore its ubiquity. Vernacular architecture is all around us. If it is not as we have earlier seen a gasoline service station for the refueling of our automobiles, it is a Burger King for the refueling of our stomachs or a tract house for the renewal of our bodies. Inspirational as we might find the architecture of a Wright, a Sullivan, or a Stone, it is the vernacular tradition in which we live our lives. And the economy, simplicity and flexibility is readily evident in the houses of fast food.

Second, we can look inside the fast-food phenomenon to find an ongoing example of what it has meant to make an industrial revolution. And for students of industrialization who live as we do in cultures long since industrialized such examples are as useful as they are rare. In comparing the greasy spoon with the industrial hamburger one finds those imperatives of mechanization that students from before Adam Smith to after Giedion have explained to us: one, the standardized, uniform product; and two—if we may return all the way back to the seat of Charlie Chaplin's malaise—the subordination of the skilled artisan to the sophisticated mechanism.

These are the lessons, technological and cultural, of the industrialized hamburger.

You Are What You Speak:
Menu Language Where America Feeds

by Sam G. Riley

When I was a child, I spoke as a child; I ordered as a child; I ate as a child. Now that I have reached my middle years, a sulky inner voice occasionally reminds me it is time to put away childish things insofar as my dining habits are concerned.

Let me enter a fast-food franchise, however, and I find myself placed in jeopardy. To get anything to eat there, I may be forced to employ cute, child-like language that no thinking adult would otherwise use.

To eat so simple a thing as a hamburger, it would be necessary to also swallow one's pride by first asking the teenager behind the counter for a Big Mac or a Whopper or a Big Boy or something else that sounds equally repugnant.

While ordinary, old fashioned restaurants still call a filet mignon a filet mignon, and while nicer seafood houses for the most part still refer to boiled shrimp as boiled shrimp, the fast-food industry has seen fit to trick out its menus with cutsie-poo product names. America has accepted this practice readily enough, uttering these names aloud at a myriad counters across the land, probably in the manner of a man who sees many billboards out of the corner of his eye as he drives along in his automobile, but doesn't let many of them register in his conscious mind. We see but do not *see*; we speak but do not always hear ourselves speaking.

The spectacle of an adult person giving in to the use of such puerile language might be compared to Doris Day at her present age pulling back her hair in a ponytail and playing the ingenue role in a Tammy movie. Good intentions do not always produce pleasant results.

To be fair, one must admit that this linguistic problem varies greatly within the fast-food world. The pizza chains are relatively blameless. They have refained from naming their respective pizzas the "Sicilian Orb," the "Big Wheel," or whatever. Possibly this is because of the nature of the product; we are still free to order our pizza with a choice of toppings: pepperoni, ground beef, olives black or green, onions and for the very brave, jalapeno peppers or anchovies. Standarization attracts dumb trade names; variety drives them away.

I am also reasonably at ease whenever I find it convenient to visit a quickie steak house. To be sure, many of their dishes have childish names, usually in a Western motif. The Golden Corral, for instance, offers the Pardner, a chopped sirloin; the Sixgun, a broiled tenderloin, sliced thin; the Baron, a club steak; the Herdsman, a sirloin; and worst of all, the Belt Buster, a larger sirloin. My God! Imagine yourself actually standing there at the counter saying, "Gimme a Belt Buster with fries." With due apologies to Robert Burns, I submit:

> O wad some power the right way to steer us
> To hear oursels as others hear us.

One does not have to be a raving elitist to bridle at asking aloud for a Belt Buster.

Similarly, the Western Sizzlin chain would have us ask for a Trailblazer (Boston strip), a Dude (New York strip), a Maverick (sirloin) or a Gunsmoke (a larger sirloin).

But, and here is their saving grace, the quick-steak chains offer us a happy alternative. They have *numbered* each dish, allowing the squeamish diner to simply say, "Let me have a No. 7, well done," and in so doing, retain his adult human dignity.

The Bonanza chain should here be given appropriate recognition, and it has almost entirely avoided the unseemly practice of creating pet names for slabs of meat. The only item on their menu that even smacks of cuteness is the Bonanzaburger, and out of sheer gratitude one can readily forgive them that one lapse.

Chicken chains, too, are largely free of this product-name pestilence. Dreaming up cute names for chicken parts is apparently a challenge to which marketing experts have not yet fully risen. Instead, we are left to ponder another dilemma: original recipe or extra-crispy?

A foreboding of chicken cuteness to come, however, may be found in, of all places, a seafood chain. Long John Silvers offers a battered and fried item called Chicken Planks, and even cuter, Chicken Peg Legs—quite in keeping with their private theme, but out of sync with adult dignity when spoken aloud. In the same vein, Western Sizzlin sells Chicken Nuggets, and McDonalds has Chicken McNugget.

The menu language of Arby's, a roast beef chain, is also relatively inoffensive. Aside from the unfortunate use of 'N, as in Beef 'N Cheddar or Ham 'N Cheese, the only item on their menu I find impossible to utter is the Arby's Super Meal (a roast beef sandwich, french fries, and a large Pepsi).

More troublesome is the Dairy Queen, with its Mr. Misty ice drinks, (in cherry, lemon-lime, grape, orange, or raspberry) and its dessert called, incredibly, the Double Fudge Nutty. Worst of all, linguistically speaking, is their Big Foot, a foot-long hot dog. Picture yourself standing there with other people listening to you, ordering in a clear, steady voice a Big Foot, a Mr. Misty and a Double Fudgy Nutty. The adult mind boggles.

Then there are America's burger chains, where one orders the burgers of the machine age, safely interred in styrofoam. One might pause and reflect that the popular clown/itchmen Ronald McDonald and the Burger King truly are symbolic of the retail end of this industry. The language they would have us use when we order their products causes us to *participate* in their clownishness. If I could don Grimaldian garb and put on whiteface like Ronald, I might feel more kindly disposed to intoning, "Gimme a Big Mac, a large fries and a chocolate shake" when I stop at McDonalds for a quick lunch.

I for one refuse to say the words Big Mac, Whopper, Yumbo, Whaler, or Heaven help us, Big Deal Meal. If I want a Big Mac, I resort to pointing vaguely at the plastic menu display on the wall and mumbling, "Give me one of those double hamburgers."

"You mean the Big Mac?" asks the pimple-faced lad behind the counter.

"That's the one," I reply, smug in the satisfaction of having beat the system by turning their cute names back on them, forcing *them* to give up a small chunk of *their* dignity.

What we are observing here is one end of an American social trait called the "phenomenon of the adultized child and the infantile adult." Researchers looking into the effects of television on American audiences have concluded that children who watch programs intended for adult and audiences in a sense "grow up" earlier than did pre-TV era children whose childhoods came and went before the mid-1950s. On the other hand, the researchers found, many adults watch programs that are produced for children—Sesame Street, The Electric Company, Mr. Rogers' Neighborhood, Saturday morning cartoons, etc. In the process, the researchers said, children have become more adult-like, adults more child-like.

Without doubt today's child is adultized more quickly than once was the case. On the adult side, the evidence it not quite so clear, but consider with fear and trembling that the newspaper—or at least the periodical printed on newsprint—that enjoys the largest circulation in America is the *National Enquirer.* Cynics might say that its editorial mix is aimed not at the mentality of a child, but at that of the yet unborn. But I digress.

See an otherwise rational adult belly up to a fast-food counter and place his or her order in the language of the day, and you could be nearly convinced that the phenomenon of the infantile adult might have become reality.

Taking top honors for aggressively cute, cloyingly childish menu language are two of the chains that offer some of the best eating in franchise land—Shoney's and Steak and Ale. Much of Shoney's early success was attributable to a large hamburger called the Big Boy. A later entry on their menu was another sandwich called the Brawny Lad. I have never had either and have had to settle for the Quarter Pond of Ground Round, which I am able to say aloud without blushing. "Gimme a Big Boy and a Brawny Lad?" Unthinkable!

Cutest of the cute is Steak and Ale, which in every respect save menu language is one of the nation's best franchise restaurants. Seated comfortably there in ersatz English country-in splendor, one is asked to use some really preposterous terminology. To get a filet steak, the customer must ask for the Duke's Filet. For a marinated chicken breast, the hungry patron must force himself to say, "Let me have the Poacher's Platter, please." For a combination of the two, one must ask for the Prince and Pauper. Should one want a baked potato with any of the above, sure and it's an Irish Gem he must be orderin'. Dragon Burgers are on the menu here as well as a beef kabob dish called, believe it or not, the Sir Lance-A-Lot.

May Walt Disney have mercy on our souls.

FAST FOOD FLASH

by Jon Carroll

McDonald's is smarter than Jimmy Carter, smarter than John Kenneth Galbraith, maybe even smarter than you.[1] Just when conventional wisdom had predicted that Big Mac had run out of markets and gone stale on gimmicks, just when convoys of experts had determined that the fast food market had become cluttered with imitators and was about to pluralize itself out of hegemony, McDonald's has strengthened its strangle hold on the industry.

Kentucky Fried Chicken's profits were plucked badly last year. Burger King, ditto. But in 1976, McDonald's corporate profit jumped 25%. This means a sales base of $2.7 billion in this country, or 19.6% of fast food sales. Which is what you call your special sauce.

As it happens, fast foods account for an astounding 28 percent of the equally amazing $50 billion we spend on eating out every year. McDonald's stands above the rest of the fast food market just as the Yankees used to stand above the American League.

How came this miracle to be? By what right has McDonald's been granted a license to control the nutritional habits of the world? Are they linked in with the Force, the controlling power of the universe? No, they have become one with the Smarts, the universal principle which guides all accountants. They are careful: Big Mac tested Egg McMuffin for four years before putting it into general circulation, and now breakfast accounts for 10 percent of the company's sales, or $350 million worth of muffins per annum. They are prudent: Franchisers are vouchsafed a single outlet at a time—rather than franchising rights for a whole city or state—which means that the people who own McDonald's franchises actually visit the stores. And they are bold: When the rest of the industry was still congratulating itself about the cost efficiency of take-out food, McDonald's was realizing that sit-down restaurants were the wave of the future.

Which is the point of the current words you see before you, nicely designed to fit around the pictures, just as the new McDonald's decoration are designed to fit nicely around your hamburger habit. McDonald's is smart (see above). McDonald's understands the importance of mass decor. When America was seeking homogeneity, back in the great era of television aesthetics (when how

36

good it was didn't matter; what mattered was how bad it wasn't), McDonald's understood that Americans wanted the comfort of regularity and uniformity, that they were willing to sacrifice quality in exchange for freedom from salmonella. But when Americans no longer wanted that, when they abandoned their nuclear holocaust postures and emerged from their psychological bomb shelters, McDonald's was ready for them. Let a hundred flowers bloom; let neighborhood power dominate the all-beef patties. We got your surfer motifs for your beachside outlets; we got your animated hamburger playgrounds for your heavily kidded franchises; we even got your Beverly Hills S/M glitter flash for Wilshire Boulevard. At precisely the right historical moment, McDonald's sensed the onslaught of diversity.

In point of historical fact, it was McDonald's move out of suburbia that necessitated that McDonald's go stylish. In the slurby boonies, there was no other architecture of consequence to contend with. The arches only had to play against traffic signals and a tree or two. But downtown, McDonald's sometimes found itself ripping down buildings to put up its outlets. Of itself, that was enough to provoke considerable anger on the part of the residents who thought more of what was coming down than the prospect of more Big Macs.

After taking a lot of heat (in Cambridge, Massachusetts, one of the city's two pre-Civil War Greek revival landmark buildings was blitzed to make way for a McDonald's, a mistake not likely to be repeated), Burger Central in Illinois issued its decree: Anything a franchisee wanted to do in the way of decor was okay. If he (or she) wanted glitter, all that needed to be done was a call to the designer working for McDonald's real estate and construction department. And if what was provided didn't quite meet the franchisee's fantasy, then the franchisee was free to hire an independent designer.

After all, it is not only a matter of fitting into a neighborhood, but perhaps into a shopping center which already has design restrictions (fake fishing village, ersatz Regency, quasi-Norman).

Since the franchisee pays for the design, it is limited only by the realities of the marketplace and his or her budget, which means the possibilities are endless but not infinite.

There cannot be, we are assured by a spokesperson for McDonald's, much in the way of a desperate mistake. The owners of the franchises understand—how could they not?—their business: It is "family" food, by which is meant no branches of the firm in high hang-out low-class areas.

And while the decor may be glitzy, it can never cross that, ah, certain line. Beverly Hills glitter may be okay. High pimp funk is not.

The spark leaps across the be-pattied mind: It is precisely the sort of design genius one might first associate with Disney, only it goes just a bit beyond. Sure, Disney has Tomorrowland, but it's still tame, it still isn't quite Star Wars enough (and the McDonald's glitter is). And all the rest of Disney is so utterly cute you could throw up. Well, the Big Mac people know the value of a stomach not upset.

Given this, it's safe to say there's no stopping them. Resistance is useless. McDonald's knows what you want before you want it. You may deserve a break today, but you're not going to get one.

God may or may not be dead, but Ronald McDonald surely is immortal. There will be burgers forever! Two patties, special sauce, shredded lettuce, pickles, onions, cheese—all on the sesame seed bun. And the green shamrock shake! Who could ask for anything more? Where's the Bromo?

Notes

[1]This article is reprinted by permission. It appeared in *New West* on September 12, 1977.

The Landscape of McDonald's

by Kenneth I. Helphand

The Clown and the Golden Arches are part of a mythic landscape, along with Howard Johnson's orange roofs and Mail Pouch barns. What is their role as an environmental artifact? A symbolic landmark? A cultural cipher in our landscape?

Seeking answers, I propose to examine McDonald's in the automotive landscape, then relate it to the "Everywhere Community," franchising, and placelessness. The themes of clustering, urbanization, and internationalization will inevitably arise, as we use McDonald's as example and indicator of general trends in the American landscape.[1]

The details of "the early days" of McDonald's are covered elsewhere in this book. Early, and until recently almost all, McDonald's were drive-in franchise restaurants. Their original locations were mostly confined to highway "strips," commercially oriented urban arterials. Grady Clay, in his book *Close-Up: How to Read the American City* presents a history of the American highway strip.[2]

The strip has become an environmental scapegoat, an archetypal symbol of the crass economic determinism of the American landscape. However, Clay notes:

The strip is trying to tell us something about ourselves: namely, that most Americans prefer convenience; are determined to simplify as much of the mechanical, service, and distribution side of life as possible; and are willing to patronize and subsidize any informal, geographic behavior setting that helps. The value systems of the strip derive from the open road rather than from the closed city.[3]

The strip and its landmarks of Golden Arches and Mobil signs are manifestation of similar cultural drives. However, the much maligned strip has had its defenders. In 1956, one year after the first McDonald's franchise, the human geographer, J. B. Jackson, wrote an article called "Other Directed Houses."[4] As always, he recognized the significance of mobility in American life, its association with new forms of leisure, and the development of a "popular," "other directed" architecture. This "other directed" architecture of the highway strip was aimed primarily at pleasing and attracting the passerby. He suggested a positive attitude towards the strip, its "garden of moving colored lights," and exhorted us to transform them "into avenues of a gaiety and brilliance, as beautiful as any in the world." His exhortations have largely gone unheeded, and the strip is seen by many as a necessary evil where the populace guiltily consumes its Big Macs.

With McDonald's remarkable financial growth went a corresponding growth in their corporate consciousness as a community institution. This consciousness extended into the landscape and the late sixties ushered in a new restaurant image. The "other directed" architecture of the drive-in, take-out, highway oriented golden arches was replaced by the sit-down mansard roof of community conscious design. This was a response to several developments. There was a need to remodel older restaurants,[5] a sensitivity to growing criticism of roadside franchises as garish strip enterprises, and the need for the development of a symbolic structure to appeal to the broadened base of McDonald's clientele. The roadside strip maintained its significance, but its character was changing. New centers were developing along it, new clusterings in shopping centers and even franchise malls. In suburban areas especially, these were nascent community environments, places of informal and formal congregation. (How many childrens' birthday parties are celebrated at McDonald's?) The roadside commercial restaurant of McDonald's with its golden arched roof was transformed into what was perceived as a more community responsible and responsive architectural and landscape design. McDonaldland was born and billions more sold.

McDonald's in less than a generation has become an American roadside landmark. Landmarks are point references and are characterized by a distinguishable form, visability and significance.[6] McDonald's meets these physical characteristics with its readily identifiable arches, architecture, and its tote board of billions sold. Franchise sites are chosen with maximum visibility in mind, and the significance of McDonald's as a landmark leads to the next area of discussion, as symbols of the everywhere and anywhere communities we inhabit.

McDonald's and the Everywhere Community

The fresh charm and virgin promise of America was that it was so different a place. But the fulfillment of modern America would be its power to level times and places, to erase differences between here and there, between now and then. And finally the uniqueness of America would prove to be its ability to erase uniqueness.

Elsewhere democracy had meant forms of personal, political, economic, and social equality. In the United States, in addition, there would be a novel environmental democracy. Here, as never before, the world would witness the "equalizing" of times and places.

The flavor of life had once come from winter's cold, summer's heat, the special taste and color of each season's diet. The American Democracy of Times and Places meant making one place and one thing more like another, by bringing them under the control of man.[7]

This environmental democracy has its contemporary realization in the age of the everywhere community, "invisible" communities of consumption and statistics, loose affiliations and communal identification based upon shared material consumption and participation in a common democratized cultural experience. Boorstin brilliantly traces the history of the Age of the Everywhere Community in *The Americans: The Democratic Experience*. The landscape, like a book, can be read. It communicates values, ideas, tastes, and is "history made visible."[8] It is the concretization of a culture and its values. The everywhere community begets an everywhere landscape and the images of the everywhere landscape are sometimes transformed into idealized landscape elements. The golden arches landmarks of McDonald's are sought out. They symbolize security and predictability to their clientele. Quality is less important than the replication of a previous experience. Holiday Inn, the world's largest hotel chain advertises, "the best surprise is no surprise," and one can feel secure that the McDonald's experience in Baltimore is the same as that in Eugene, Oregon.

In an industrialized culture of interchangeable parts, mass production, and standardization, we have interchangeable items of consumption. Correspondingly the landscape takes on the appearance of these same industrialized processes. It is mass produced, interchangeable and standardized. Importantly, these characteristics can be viewed ambivalently and of course generate places we love to hate. An indicator of the contrast in values is the reactions to a statement by Harvard Business School Professor Theodore Levitt:

A McDonald's retail outlet is a machine that produces a highly polished product. Through painstaking attention to total design and facilities planning, everything is built integrally into the machine itself, into the technology of the system. The only choice available to the attendant is to operate it exactly as the designers intended. McDonald's is a supreme example of the application of manufacturing and technological brilliance to problems that must ultimately be viewed as marketing problems."[9]

In *Autoamerica* by Chip Lord of Ant Farm, an architectural design collaborative, quoted Professor Levitt and went on to say:

So, again, the trend is for the machine to take on more of man's role. Just as the trend in the manufacture of cars is removing us from the experience of driving, so McDonald's removes us from the experience of producing, preparing—and tasting—food. McDonald's is not a restaurant; it is a store selling a predictable product in an eternally clean environment and guaranteeing the most minimal, polite human encounter. It has turned the attendant *and* the consumer into efficient machines.[10]

The McDonald's corporation also quote Levitt, with obvious pride.[11] McDonald's is a community landmark in the landscape of the Everywhere Community, joining shopping centers, highway interchanges, Hojos and Holiday Inns.

The Everywhere Community has aspects of being anywhere. As Boorstin has noted, the destruction of the uniqueness of places is not new to the American experience. Yi-Fu Tuan says place is a center of meaning constructed by experience.[12] When the experience is replicable, when it is the same as the one that one had yesterday a thousand miles away, what then is the meaning of both the place and its related experience? A price is paid for environmental and experiential democracy. In the continual transformation of the landscape, what happens to the meaning, significance and the unique qualities of each place, is a question continually confronted by all those involved in planning and designing our environment. There exists now in America and internationally an accelerated tendency towards environmental homogenization, as places lose their uniqueness and special, idiosyncratic character in the face of an increasingly mobile, more powerful and communicative culture.

The contemporary landscape is a dialect of the uniqueness of each place and the cultural forces which destroy that uniqueness. It is a tension between the particularity of a Franklin Boulevard in Eugene, Oregon (highway strip) and the forces which generate its design. These include uniform national road standards, motels, gas stations, and franchises of standard design.

American economic know how has developed an economic strategy which facilitates the development and extension of the Everywhere Community. This is franchising. International Franchise Association defines franchising as "a continuing relationship in which the franchisor provides a licensed privilege to do business, plus assistance in organizing, training, merchandizing, and management in return for a consideration from the franchisee."[13] Importantly, the "franchisee is his own boss, but he looks to the parent company, the franchisor, for every form of assistance imaginable, from cash loans or credit to designing, building, staffing, promotion and publicizing the business."[14] Charles Vaughn, former director of the Boston College Center for the Study of Franchise Distribution, said, "McDonald's can probably be considered one of the prototypes for the industrial revolution in marketing."[15]

The implications for the landscape parallel this process, with a local business looking to a regional or national parent company for the design of the franchise. In the case of McDonald's and other large corporations, this will include aid in site selection, architectural and landscape design and construction, and even periodic changes in design styling. Therefore, McDonald's in the eastern U.S.A. is substantially the same in the south, north and west. This homogeneity is encouraged. The place as well as the product should be predictable. Recently, however, the McDonald's Corporation is introducing greater local variation in restaurant design, but on the whole it is a packaging change while the contents remain constant.

The trade journal, *Modern Franchising*, has monthly features on "Franchise City" which maps franchises in American cities.[16] If we look at the landscape as a manifestation of an economic system much of our commercial landscape is a franchise landscape. The landscape has the characteristics of franchises; standardized, packaged, predictable, and answerable to the home office.

Franchising leads us to the final section of recent trends and McDonald's: the clustering, urbanization and internationalization of McDonald's.

Clustering

The latest stage in the development of the strip shows clusterings of establishments. The 1972 "Patio at Northland" in Columbus, Ohio was an early example of a franchise cluster or a franchise mall, as they are called. This intentional clustering will probably occur more in the future. University of Oregon students, in a Landscape Architecture design studio have made proposals for the design of franchise malls with interesting results. Employing current and potential possibilites, they have included the provision of more community amenities at such malls including outdoor eating areas, entertainment possibilities, playgrounds (which already exist at many franchise operations including McDonald's) and most importantly, a recognizable center, a locus of activity.

Located largely in suburban areas these clusters are a small part of the gradual "urbanization" of the American suburb.

The highway and suburbia have contributed to the growth of a landscape of a distinct character. This includes the development of new building types and activities. Of these the regional shopping center is the most dramatic, but it also includes entertainment districts, warehouse lockers and the planned unit development. The forms of this landscape are still little understood, but as of the last census a plurality of Americans identify themselves as suburban vs. urban or rural. That plurality lives in a landscape which is responding to the satisfaction of many of their needs and desires. Clustering is one suburban response to the need for identifiable community, public places in the landscape.

McDonald's has not participated in any franchise malls although they are increasingly integrated into the development of shopping centers. However, they are often the prime generator of unintentional clusters where a McDonald's is followed by a Taco Bell, Baskin Robins, a competing hamburger franchise, etc. These clusterings are beginning to give a sense of urbanity to suburban landscapes with higher densities of people, goods and services. Many new shopping centers manifest this as they become more like a "downtown," mixing shopping, work and entertainment functions.

The Urbanization of McDonald's: The Suburbanization of the City

The next trend is perhaps the opposite of the last. Our suburban and road environments have fostered a landscape of franchises, largely automobile oriented commercial establishments. These franchises are now expanding their market into a territory they previously excluded themselves from, the urban core. McDonald's has numerous urban franchises, which they call townhouse units, some with, most without, off street parking. Unlike the roadside golden arches and mansard roof, their exterior design tends to blend in with the urban milieu. However, they bring the identical product of the urban scene and the characteristic elements of a different kind of landscape. One characteristic of the urban landscape is its lack of predictability, its often apparent chaos, its anonymity, its diversity and incongruity. Within this urban milieu is interjected the standardized predictability of a national franchiser and the urban populace can join the rest of the country and "enjoy a break today."

McDonald's characteristics are symptomatic of broader trends. A "suburbanization" of downtowns was popularized by Victor Gruen, architect and author of *The Heart of our Cities*.[17] Gruen applied principles developed in suburban shopping center design to downtown areas and has been widely imitated. The paradigmatic plan included a pedestrian, car free core with invisible services and support facilities surrounded by parking lots and garages. At a gross scale hundreds of American cities have followed this formula.

McDonald's International

The modern franchise business has touched off economic revolution in traditional patterns of American marketing and the revolution is being taken up all over the world.[18]

In 1969 McDonald's International Division was formed. By 1977, 394 McDonald's were in operation in twenty countries outside the U.S. This included 66 in Tokyo alone and even three in Hamburg, Germany; the associated culinary mythology not being lost on McDonald's International.

McDonald's International operates substantially similar to McDonald's in the U.S. There are slight menu variations to conform largely to local beverage tastes: wine in France, beer in Germany, tea in England. Otherwise there is a great pride in the fact that the food is the same the world around. The 3000th McDonald's opened in London in 1974, the 4000th in Montreal in 1976. While the growth of the International division is only a small percentage of the corporate picture, it is a telling indicator. The Everywhere Community is becoming international. Importantly it is not just in global communication and shared culture information, but now beginning to share identical products and identical landscape elements.

McDonald's has gone from an individual roadside fast food operation to an international corporation. I have tried to be an observer and to only note trends in the landscapes as I see them. McDonald's beckons us to examine the contemporary landscape; the trip, the Everywhere Community, clusters, suburbanization, internationalization. McDonald's is a product of our culture and a harbinger of what our landscape may become.

Notes

[1]McDonald's Systems Inc., *McDonald's Twentieth Anniversary, April 1975*, p. 5.

[2]Clay, Grady, *Close-Up: How to Read the American City*, (New York: Praeger Publishers, 1973) p. 92-93.

[3]*Ibid.*, p. 108.

[4]Jackson, J.B., "Other Directed Houses" in *Landscapes; The Selected Writings of J.B. Jackson*, ed. E. Zube, (University of Massachusetts Press, 1970).

[5]*McDonald's Twentieth Anniversary*, p. 28.

[6]Lynch, Kevin, *The Image of the City* (Cambridge, Massachusetts: MIT Press, 1960).

[7]Appleyard, Donald, "Why Buildings Are Known," *Environment and Behavior*, Vol. 1:2, December 1969.

[8]Boorstin, Daniel, *The Americans: The Democratic Experience* (New York, Vintage Books, 1974), p. 307.

[9]Jackson, J.B., "Settlers Slow to Grasp Importance of Agriculture," *American Issues Forum: Courses by Newspaper, Eugene Register-Guard*, (Nov. 6, 1975).

[10]Ant Farm, *Autoamerica* (New York, E.P. Dutton & Co. Inc., 1976), p. 62.

[11]*Ibid.*, p. 62.

[12]*McDonald's Twentieth Anniversary*.

[13]Tuan, Yi-Fu, "Place: An Experiential Perspective," *Geographic Review* (Vol. 65: April 1975).

[14]Kursh, Harry, *The Franchise Boom*, Englewood Cliffs, New Jersey (Prentice Hall, 1968), p. 22.

[15]*Ibid.*, p. 22.

[16]"McDonald's Makes Franchising Sizzle," *Business Week* (June 15, 1968), p. 102.

[17]*Modern Franchising Magazine*, Des Plaines, Illinois.

[18]Kursh, p. ix.

The author would like to thank Dennis Detzel of McDonald's for his assistance in preparing this article.

McDonald's Interior Decor

by Gene Huddleston

The quick service restaurant has succeeded the drug store and drive-in as a unique middle-class youth oriented gathering place which has a larger social significance than might first appear. The poet Karl Shapiro has put in images some chief characteristics of the drug store of the 1940's, and the film *American Graffiti* has made a meaningful comment on the drive-in of the 1950's. Now anthropologists are having a hand at the quick service restaurant, noting the varied rituals manifested in this quasi temple.

Inevitably students of popular culture have been attracted to this significant phenomenon of American life, and inevitably the largest of these food chains has come under special scrutiny. My investigation of the interior design of McDonald's—more particularly paintings, murals, photographs, plaques, tapestries and collages—has involved photographing as many interiors as possible and determining the significance of the data gathered, as well as answering questions raised by Marshall Fishwick in his article "Mushroom Magik" in the special issue of the *Journal of Popular Culture* in 1973 devoted to architecture. In it he observed (p. 116), "the same history and evolution that makes Cape Kennedy and the Apollo rocket possible also explains the appearance of McDonald's . . ." The logic is that if we understand McDonald's architecture, we will also understand the "mindset" that produced the architecture. But at present, says Fishwick, we know very little about the field. Among the crucial questions that need to be answered are these (p. 116): How do contractors arrive at design conclusions . . . How do developers, contractors, and realtors collaborate in design matters? How many decisions are local, how many are made in far-distant design factories? Because of McDonald's systematic approach to construction and operation as well as the cooperation evidenced by managers and other officials, it is possible to approach these questions directly.

To get at the sources of the design decisions related to art in McDonald's requires examination of the three general sources of the art in an order moving from the simplest forms to the most elaborate and from the least costly to the most costly. The first general source is local and ranges from some locally hired artist—trained or primitive—or relative of the store manager or franchise holder to community participation—genuine people's art. By far the most common source is "factory" art. Through either mechanical, electronic or manually controlled operation, an interior design firm produces either special orders or items from a catalogue to the restaurant owner or manager requesting the service. Company owned stores feature "factory art" more so than locally owned operations, but many franchise holders use it also. For convenience's sake, the third source is called professional art. Because there is no limit to what a local franchise holder can spend on decorating his store, he might resort to a major architectural firm or interior decorator, who would proceed to place art in the store that is not mass produced or cheaply reproduced like factory art (at least it gives this appearance), nor does it have the crude folksy, and often eccentric touch of local art. It may be sophisticated and "arty" or it may cater to children through Disney-like make-believe. But its main characteristic is its relatively high cost and hence high status.

A sense of the particular is evidenced in local art. And McDonald's main office encourages this decentralization and destandardization as much as possible, being sensitive to charges of a mindless uniformity often leveled against the chain and knowing, too, that making the folks feel "at home" is important, since most of a store's business comes from within a 3 mile radius of the store. Mr. Ted Hunt's ideas for remodeling provide a specific example of the movement from factory art to local art. Mr. Hunt, manager of a franchise store soon to be redecorated, plans to work with his wife, an art teacher, in removing the present paintings, which are factory produced acrylic on panels, with a Spanish mission motif, and replacing them with photographs laminated onto panels 2' x 4' on which were formerly painted cathedral bells, which were removed from their places on the walls next to the mission panels by Mr. Hunt when he took over management of the store. The subject of these paintings will be famous alumni of Michigan State University, only a block away from the restaurant. These photographs will be changed every 6 months to provide a center of interest for the student clientele.

Whether this plan comes off remains to be seen, but such homemade and pragmatic solutions to the design doldrums induced by factory art are not uncommon to McDonald's. A manager (or owner) in Richmond, Indiana, taking advantage of a railroad's offer to give away old cabooses, converted one to an annex. A much more uncommon approach to user-oriented design is community art. This exciting approach to advertising and merchandising is illustrated by a McDonald's in Chicago whose owner, taking advantage of a bare wall on a building next door, invited parents and kids in the community to fill in a mural 50 by 60 feet or so. Everyone was enthusiastic about participation and pleased with results. And it did wonders for business.

When factory art is on an insipid or hackneyed theme—say hunting and fishing—it is merely tiresome, but when it attempts to disguise itself as local art, it is humorous because the fakery is so evident. One of the major suppliers of factory art to McDonald's has been J. Bookbinder Industries, Inc. of Compton, California. This firm used to design movie sets. Everyone knows that during the great days of Hollywood a company seldom went on location if it could build a set instead. So the "mindset" of J. Bookbinder Industries probably has been so oriented toward fakery that the fake has become real. And by their reasoning the real becomes dull.

The often absurd fakery of factory art can be illustrated with the decor in a franchise McDonald's store in East Lansing, Michigan. The theme of this store is scenic Michigan. When the store was constructed, the local franchise holder's management team gathered some two dozen black and white 8 x 10's from the Michigan Tourist Council of pleasing vistas in Michigan and sent them to California for conversion by Bookbinder to acrylics on panel, about 4' x 6' in size. An unknown and anonymous artist, who probably had never seen firsthand Michigan's Pictured Rocks on the shoreline of Lake Superior, reproduced the scene with no sense of its sublimity. Of course, the photographer initially shooting the scene might have had no artistic insights, either, of the kind associated with the noted Ansel Adams' depictions of Pacific coast near Carmel, California. Aside from the flatness of this conversion, there is another puzzling, almost humorous, landscape panorama in the same restaurant. Here the anonymous artist had painted in originally a human figure looking out over a natural prospect from a high rock ledge. Apparently this figure, a man's, was in the photograph the painter was copying from. But for some reason, he decided to obliterate this figure, by erasing or painting over or using a similar technique. But a trace of the image is still there, giving a ghostly quality to the scene if one observes it carefully (since these paintings are often mounted directly above booths, one is not supposed to stare too long at them).

One might note that conversions like these are less "fake" than others which modern technology is developing, often to the point where (as in a recent news item on computerized sculpture) the faked reproduction looks more "real" than the creation of the artist. One can conceive a McDonald's manager or franchise holder (or his architect or interior decorator) reading this announcement that recently appeared in *Interiors* and making use of it:

"The 3M Company offers Architectural Paints, an unusual computerized process that constructs mural-size four color graphic images with paints rather than with photo dye. The technique is based on computer scanning of a conventional color transparency by a photo-electric sensing system and transmission of the color information to micro-paint spray guns. The cloth, paper or other carrier material travels under the guns on a rotating drum. Any size can be specified. . . ."

Prices of these "paintings" are competitive with conventional photos. Trumbull's "Signing of the Declaration of Independence," reproduced by this method, would brighten any restaurant and fool all but connoisseurs of fine art.

In the trade journal *Restaurant Business*, a similar service, offered by Etchcraft Company, takes illustrations of commemorative events in early American history and converts them to line sketches on plaques. One could go on and on describing decorative wall ideas from firms advertising in the magnificently opulent journals on commercial art and graphics. Because of the diversity of these interior design firms and the range of art they offer to clients, it is very difficult to define when wall paintings and other decor cease being "factory" art and start becoming "professional art." Good art in America is expensive, as anyone who frequents galleries or antique dealers knows. Hence, in the field of commercial art, one gets what he pays for. Owners and managers of McDonald's are usually not seeking to impress the wealthy. It doesn't matter if it's *kitsch* as long as it pleases the manager (and his wife, I'm told) and the customers. One cannot picture someone about to open a McDonald's taking advantage of the kind of factory art featured by Hubert Paley Studios of 100 Fifth Avenue, Manhattan, in a recent ad; shown is a reproduction of a painting called "The Runners" which is described as acrylic on shaped canvas with relief figure, 72" x 36". The ad notes that such art is their forte: "Original one-of-a-kind works of distinction and aesthetic appeal direct from artist at prices 30% to 50% below comparable works in galleries."

But since no limit is placed on what can be spent on interior decor in McDonald's one occasionally comes across restaurants at which thematic settings are carried out on a lavish scale of color and design which are usually aimed at attracting children. Or a genuine effort is sometimes made at beauty, on a high level, usually when a McDonald's steps out of its typical middle-class neighborhood setting and invades territory where one normally wouldn't expect a McDonald's. This type usually is urban and doesn't have a parking lot. Not being on the usual neon strips, it must compete with boutiques and other businesses surrounding it on their terms.

Thematic settings do not alone make the art "professional." As I have pointed out, even those McDonald's employing factory art often attempt a thematic interior. A McDonald's in Saginaw, Michigan, naturally exploits the one-time lumber-capital-of-the-world theme, and the manager got Bookbinder to convert some old photos of the great white pine forest days, and he resourcefully added a touch of local art by hanging on the walls near the pictures objects of timber cutting, such as a cross-cut saw, a pike pole, wagon wheels, double-bitted axes, etc. The use of a theme becomes "professional" when the total design of the restaurant eating area is based on the theme. Either a competent architect or sophisticated design firm, or both, has been at work. The theme might be trains, with seats and tables shaped like a locomotive and tender, with expensive looking prints of ancient locomotives and appropriate advertising posters out of the 19th century on the walls. The theme might be airplanes, with a huge bi-plane in the middle of the floor, with kids eating in the cockpit, off the wings, or off the elevator or the tail assembly. The theme might even be the quarter deck of a sailing vessel with compass, helm, etc. Space ship interiors are right now in the construction stage. Maybe the restaurant is in the Italian section of town. Hire a designer to give it that ethnic look. Maybe the restaurant is in a town (Kokomo, Indiana) associated with the early days of the auto industry—give it an antique car motif. Maybe the restaurant has a Ronald McDonald playground outside; then use an animated cartoon-type interior with bright colors and Ronald and his cohorts (supplied by Set Makers in California) literally plastered in bas-relief on the walls. It's Disneyworld or Knott's Berry Farm or Busch Gardens, where parents and children are transported to a quasi African veldt for an afternoon of escape. Or it feeds upon nostalgia for the days when grandpa sang "In the Good Old Summertime" with the local barber shop quartette. Wherever McDonald's has invaded urban areas or busy commercial centers, one might find an interior which is completely unexpected for a quick-service restaurant. Here the franchise holder has given an architect *carte blanche* in interiors, subject of course, to certain seating materials and space limitations set forth by McDonald's. Notable among these are the English Inn in Chicago with its sparkling chandeliers and pictures of knights and coats of arms and the one at ritzy Water Tower Place on North Michigan Avenue featuring lots of wood paneling and subdued lighting. *Architectural Record* (January 1976) reports how the "typically chaotic" McDonald's look was made over in a new San Francisco installation in Embarcadero Center by architects EPR Associates through "careful detailing and a tight range of finish materials." Suspended ceilings consisting of large cubes and rectangles in varying depths and sizes are the most noteworthy features of this contemporary styling, which, according to the magazine, is "gracious, inviting—even elegant." At 966 3rd Avenue, New York, reports *Interior Design* (May 1975), a major architect, taking on the project "as something of a challenge," created a theme "based on simple references to nature—a photographic view of a winter landscape, or hanging plants under simulated skylights. While the skylights are fake, the plants are very real, so real that the problem with them is not maintenance but theft. The need for their replacement is steady. Project director for the firm handling the installation was Gordon Micuris, stage and set designer.[2]

One conclusion to this study is unequivocal. Variety in interior decor does exist in McDonald's; and thematic unity within in individual stores also exists. McDonald's corporate policy does encourage diversity within bounds of space, seating, and material requirements. But the policy makers are finding, I imagine, that it is very hard to overcome an image once created. *Architectural Record,* for example, takes the view that the architects of the new San Francisco Embarcadero McDonald's "made over the typically chaotic and much-criticized McDonald's look by careful detailing and a tight range of finish materials." And *Interior Design's* feature on the New York Third Avenue installation is headed "McDonald's: A Variation of the Formula."[3]

The other findings to this study tentatively suggest directions for future investigation. Technology in the service of art is an important component of "factory" art. Specifically, the role of computerization in art creation raises philosophical questions that go beyond evaluating the function of "factory" art in quick service restaurants. Many great artists have made multiple copies of what turned out to be their greatest works, and usually their motive was to increase the monetary gain for their "product." Copying to an artist is a mechanical operation; so what is different between manual copying and machine copying in terms of value? Students of popular culture might well explore *Advertising Age* and other trade publications for clues as to the significance of graphics being automated. The very opulence of the magazines advertising design services of the types I have been examining invites attention, for this opulence indicates their enormous influence and prestige. If the "medium is the message," these magazines have something to say.

For the old questions of the relative values of cultivated vs. vernacular art, elite art vs. kitsch, the answers gleaned from McDonald's decor must be most tentative because they involve taste as generated by social and economic status. But one can generalize about the most obvious values in local, factory and professional art observed in McDonald's. Factory art, which undoubtedly predominates at both company owned and franchise outlets, varies in quality, but overall its images and symbols are insipid, uninspired, and superficial. Art from so-called "professional sources," depending on the level of taste of the decorator selecting it and the budget for the project, might seem the closest of any McDonald's art to cultivated art. But container and contained do not match. A hamburg stand is a hamburg stand whether its design is a prefab lunch counter or an imitation of the Taj Mahal. Such conscious striving after "class" often results in mere gaudiness. A specific example is the Ann Arbor, Michigan, McDonald's set in a business area adjacent to the U. of M. campus, with its outstanding feature a large stained glass circular window, reminiscent of the rose windows of medieval cathedrals. And rare old photos on the wall, set in pleasing patterns, of nineteenth-century Ann Arbor landmarks introduce a gentle theme of nostalgia. The place is attractive, even a haven in storm of activity in a sense, but there is also a sense of the place being overdone, like a poor relative trying hard to make an impression, when it is compared with a bar-restaurant down the street, known as the Pretzel Bell, or P-Bell, which grew up with the University and which features genuine Tiffany lamps and tier upon tier of photographs of varsity athletic teams. It used to be the place everyone went to chug-alug beer when he turned twenty-one; it's probably still a campus "institution."

A more complex example of over-done art on the "professional" level is the McDonald's in Greencastle, Indiana, which won the state prize for the chain in 1976 and a national award as well. De Pauw University is the chief "industry" in this town of 8,000, so the decor is aimed at the college trade. The color scheme is varying shades of green and gold, the school colors. Overhead Tiffany lamps are inscribed with "De Pauw" in discreet lettering. A large, photographic portrait of Washington De Pauw, the founder, and three mural sized photos of university buildings were furnished by the University Public Information Office. Dominating the main restaurant section is the De Pauw seal, about 6 foot in diameter, and highlighted by a small spot light.

This was the motif as originally conceived and executed by designers, Sharp Associates of Indianapolis. But soon the decor was criticized for being "too much De Pauw." In this criticism was recognition by users of the facility that the design was overdone. The people using the restaurant, and, therefore, those most affected by its design, had spoken. Thus management had to modify the design to include authentic local sources of art. These are exhibits prepared by the art department of the four area high schools—one a three-dimensional shadow box type; another a montage; another a large color photo of the school done by students; the fourth a collection of color photos of athletic events.

No, even the professionally designed McDonald's can never represent cultivated art, that is, art whose enjoyment takes money, taste, and leisure. McDonald's is a middle and lower-middle class institution. It belongs to the people. Yes, even the English inn McDonald's in Chicago, according to its manager, gets its customers from shoppers with their kids, tourists with their kids, and young people without their parents. What I've called local art is thus best suited to integrate design with use. Interaction between the users of a building and its designers—such as delineated by psychologist Robert Sommer in his *Design Awareness* (1972)—will result in the kinds of local art variously known as native art, folk art, vernacular art, primitive art, people's art, and community art. Whether this art will proliferate more than it has depends perhaps upon the extent to which McDonald's management encourages local store operators to become truly responsive to needs and tastes of the people using their stores. they now have freedom in design decisions. The development at Greencastle, Indiana, bodes well for the future.[1]

Notes

[1] I could not have completed this paper without the generous help of: Professor Russel Nye of Michigan State University; Mr. Denis Detzel of McDonald's Corporate Social Policy Office; Ms. Marge Hall, assistant to Mr. John Hagen, holder of the McDonald's franchise in East Lansing-Okemos; and Mr. Ted Hunt, manager of an East Lansing McDonald's.

[2] Classifying McDonald's art by subject presents more obstacles than classification by source. But out of the plethora of themes observed one gets the impression that nature and nature nostalgia predominate, perhaps because most McDonald's are suburban in location. Whatever the topic, it is usually tied to the specific locality of the restaurant. If not natural scenery, some local industry, institution, or attraction inspires the art. In selection, the art seems directed more at ruggedness and masculinity than toward tea-room gentility, perhaps because of the dominance of the nature theme and the heavy construction of the interior furniture specified by the corporation. For a time McDonald's in centers of dense urban population did not seem to be tied to place as a motif for art, but that is changing. The *New York Times* (April 20, 1977) reports that McDonald's is catering to urban neighborhoods by using decor appropriate to the neighborhood—e.g., in New York the garment, flower, and fashion districts. A store on Fifth Avenue near the Empire State Building imitates Victorian Britain's famed Crystal Palace. But whatever the city, stores in less affluent areas are likely to utilize existing structures and be more utilitarian and generalized in decor.

[3] And in an article in *American Heritage* (April 1977) extolling the value to nostalgia buffs of diners—converted streetcars and the prefab variety—the author says of the "fast-food franchise chains," which replaced diners after they had grown too fancy, that they "gave those who were comforted by such things the illusion of having the same cheap food in the same room whether they were eating in Fresno or Bangor."

Rituals at McDonald's

by Conrad P. Kottak

The world is blessed each day, on the average, with the opening of a new McDonald's restaurant. They now number more than 4,000 and dot not only the United States but also such countries as Mexico, Japan, Australia, England, France, Germany, and Sweden. The expansion of this international web of franchises and company-owned outlets has been fast and efficient; a little more than twenty years ago McDonald's was limited to a single restaurant in San Bernardino, California. Now, the number of McDonald's outlets has far outstripped the total number of fastfood chains operative in the United States thirty years ago.

McDonald's sales reached $1.3 billion in 1972, propelling it past Kentucky Fried Chicken as the world's largest fast-food chain. It has kept this position ever since. Annual sales now exceed $3 billion. McDonald's is the nation's leading buyer of processed potatoes and fish. Three hundred thousand cattle die each year as McDonald's customers down another three billion burgers. A 1974 advertising budget of $60 million easily made the chain one of the country's top advertisers. Ronald McDonald, our best-known purveyor of hamburgers, French fries, and milkshakes, rivals Santa Claus and Mickey Mouse as our children's most familiar fantasy character.

How does an anthropologist, accustomed to explaining the life styles of diverse cultures, interpret these peculiar developments and attractions that influence the daily life of so many Americans? Have factors other than low cost, taste, fast service, and cleanliness—all of which are approximated by other chains—contributed to McDonald's success? Could it be that in consuming McDonald's products and propaganda, Americans are not just eating and watching television but are experiencing something comparable in some respects to a religious ritual? A brief consideration of the nature of ritual may answer the latter question.

Several key features distinguish ritual from other behavior, according to anthropologist Roy Rappaport. Foremost, are formal ritual events—stylized, repetitive, and stereotyped. They occur in special places, at regular times, and include liturgical orders—set sequences of words and actions laid down by someone other than the current performer.

Reprinted with permission from *Natural History* Magazine, January 1978. Copyright © The American Museum of Natural History, 1978.

Rituals also convey information about participants and their cultural traditions. Performed year after year, generation after generation, they translate enduring messages, values, and sentiments into observable action. Although some participants may be more strongly committed than others to the beliefs on which rituals are based, all people who take part in joint public acts signal their acceptance of an order that transcends their status as individuals.

In the view of some anthropologists, including Rappaport himself, such secular institutions as McDonald's are not comparable to rituals. They argue that rituals involve special emotions, nonutilitarian intentions, and supernatural entities that are not characteristic of Americans' participation in McDonald's. But other anthropologists define ritual more broadly. Writing about football in contemporary America, William Arens (see "The Great American Football Ritual," *Natural History*, October 1975) points out that behavior can simultaneously have sacred as well as secular aspects. Thus, on one level, football can be interpreted simply as a sport, while on another, it can be viewed as a public ritual.

While McDonald's is definitely a mundane, secular institution—just a place to eat—it also assumes some of the attributes of a sacred place. And in the context of comparative religion, why should this be surprising? The French sociologist Emile Durkheim long ago pointed out that some societies worship the ridiculous as well as the sublime. The distinction between the two does not depend on the intrinsic qualities of the sacred symbol. Durkheim found that Australian aborigines often worshiped such humble and nonimposing creatures as ducks, frogs, rabbits, and grubs—animals whose inherent qualities hardly could have been the origin of the religious sentiment they inspired. If frogs and grubs can be elevated to a sacred level, why not McDonald's?

I frequently eat lunch—and occasionally, breakfast and dinner—at McDonald's. More than a year ago, I began to notice (and have subsequently observed more carefully) certain ritual behavior at these fast-food restaurants. Although for natives, McDonald's seems to be just a place to eat, careful observation of what goes on in any outlet in this country reveals an astonishing degree of formality and behavioral uniformity on the part of both staff and customers. Particularly impressive is the relative invariance in act and utterance that has developed in the absence of a distinct theological doctrine. Rather, the ritual aspect of McDonald's rests on twentieth-century technology—particularly automobiles, television, work locales, and the one-hour lunch.

The changes in technology and work organization that have contributed to the chain's growth in the United States are now taking place in other countries. Only in a country such as France, which has an established and culturally enshrined cuisine that hamburgers and fish filets cannot hope to displace, is McDonald's expansion likely to be retarded. Why has McDonald's been so much more successful than other businesses, than the United States Army, and even than many religious institutions in producing behavioral invariance?

Remarkably, even Americans traveling abroad in countries noted for their distinctive food usually visit the local McDonald's outlet. This odd behavior is probably caused by the same factors that urge us to make yet another trip to a

McDonald's here. Wherever a McDonald's may be located, it is a home away from home. At any outlet, Americans know how to behave, what to expect, what they will eat, and what they will pay. If one has been unfortunate enough to have partaken of the often indigestible pap dished out by any turnpike restaurant monopoly, the sight of a pair of McDonald's golden arches may justify a detour off the highway, even if the penalty is an extra toll.

In Paris, where the French have not been expecially renowned for making tourists feel at home, McDonald's offers sanctuary. It is, after all, an American institution, where only Americans, who are programmed by years of prior experience to salivate at the sight of the glorious hamburger, can feel completely at home. Americans in Paris can temporarily reverse roles with their hosts; if they cannot act like the French, neither can the French be expected to act in a culturally appropriate manner at McDonald's. Away from home, McDonald's, like a familiar church, offers not just hamburgers but comfort, security, and reassurance.

An American's devotion to McDonald's rests in part on uniformities associated with almost all McDonald's: setting, architecture, food, ambience, acts, and utterances. The golden arches, for example, serve as a familiar and almost universal landmark, absent only in those areas where zoning laws prohibit garish signs. At a McDonald's near the University of Michigan campus in Ann Arbor, a small, decorous sign—golden arches encircled in wrought iron—identifies the establishment. Despite the absence of the towering arches, this McDonald's, where I have conducted much of my fieldwork, does not suffer as a ritual setting. The restaurant, a contemporary brick structure that has been nominated for a prize in architectural design, is best known for its stained-glass windows, which incorporate golden arches as their focal point. On bright days, sunlight floods in on waiting customers through a skylight that recalls the clerestory of a Gothic cathedral. In the case of this McDonald's, the effect is to equate traditional religious symbols and golden arches. And in the view of the natives I have interviewed, the message is clear.

When Americans go to a McDonald's restaurant, they perform an ordinary, secular, biological act—they eat, usually lunch. Yet, immediately upon entering, we can tell from our surroundings that we are in a sequestered place, somehow apart from the messiness of the world outside. Except for such anomalies as the Ann Arbor campus outlet, the town house McDonald's in New York city, and the special theme McDonald's of such cities as San Francisco, Saint Paul, and Dallas, the restaurants rely on their arches, dull brown brick, plate-glass sides, and mansard roofs to create a setting as familiar as home. In some of the larger outlets, murals depicting "McDonaldland" fantasy characters, sports, outdoor plastic seats and tables. In this familiar setting, we do not have to consider the experience. We know what we will see, say, eat, and pay.

Behind the counter, McDonald's employees are differentiated into such categories as male staff, female staff, and managers. While costumes vary slightly from outlet to outlet and region to region, such apparel as McDonald's hats, ties, and shirts, along with dark pants and shining black shoes, are standard.

The food is also standard, again with only minor regional variations. (Some restaurants are selected to test such new menu items at "McChicken" or different milkshake flavors.) Most menus, however, from the rolling hills of Georgia to the snowy plains of Minnesota, offer the same items. The prices are also the same and the menu is usually located in the same place in every restaurant.

Utterances across each spotless counter are standardized. Not only are customers limited in what they can choose but also in what they can say. Each item on the menu has its appropriate McDonald's designation: "quarter pounder with cheese" or filet-O-fish" or "large fries." The customer who asks, "What's a Big Mac?" is as out of place as a southern Baptist at a Roman Catholic Mass.

At the McDonald's that I frequent, the phrases uttered by the salespeople are just as standard as those of the customers. If I ask for a quarter pounder, the ritual response is "Will that be with cheese, sir?" If I do not order French fries, the agent automatically incants, "Will there be any fries today, sir?" And when I pick up my order, the agent conventionally says, "Have a nice day, sir," followed by, "Come in again."

Nonverbal behavior of McDonald's agents is also programmed. Prior to opening the spigot of the drink machine, they fill paper cups with ice exactly to the bottom of the golden arches that decorate them. As customers request food, agents look back to see if the desired item is available. If not, they reply, "That'll be a few minutes, sir (or ma'am)," after which the order of the next customer is taken.

McDonald's lore of appropriate verbal and nonverbal behavior is even taught at a "seminary," Hamburger University, located in Elk Grove Village, Illinois, near Chicago's O'Hare airport. Managers who attend choose either a two-week basic "operator's course" or an eleven-day "advanced operator's course." With a 360-page *Operations Manual* as their bible, students learn about food, equipment, and management techniques—delving into such esoteric subjects as buns, shortening, and carbonization. Filled with the spirit of McDonald's, graduates take home such degrees as bachelor or master of hamburgerology to display in their outlets. Their job is to spread the word—the secret success formula they have learned—among assistant managers and crew in their restaurants.

The total McDonald's ambience invites comparison with sacred places. The chain stresses clean living and reaffirms those traditional American values that transcend McDonald's itself. Max Boas and Steve Chain, biographers of McDonald's board chairman, Ray Kroc, report that after the hundredth McDonald's opened in 1959, Kroc leased a plane to survey likely sites for the chain's expansion. McDonald's would invade the suburbs by locating its outlets near traffic intersections, shopping centers, and churches. Steeples figured prominently in Kroc's plan. He believed that suburban church-goers would be preprogrammed consumers of the McDonald's formula—quality, service, and cleanliness.

McDonald's restaurants, nestled beneath their transcendent arches and the American flag, would enclose immaculate restrooms and floors, counters and stainless steel kitchens. Agents would sparkle, radiating health and warmth. Although to a lesser extent than a decade ago, management scrutinizes employees' hair length, height, nails, teeth, and complexions. Long hair, bad breath, stained teeth, and pimples are anathema. Food containers also defy pollution; they are used only once. (In New York City, the fast-food chain Chock Full O' Nuts foreshadowed this theme long ago and took it one step further by assuring customers that their food was never touched by human hands.)

Like participation in rituals, there are times when eating at McDonald's is not appropriate. A meal at McDonald's is usually confined to ordinary, everyday life. Although the restaurants are open virtually every day of the year, most Americans do not go there on Thanksgiving, Easter, Passover, or other religious and quasi-religious days. Our culture reserves holidays for family and friends. Although Americans neglect McDonald's on holidays, the chain reminds us through television that it still endures, that it will welcome us back once our holiday is over.

The television presence of McDonald's is particularly obvious on holidays, whether it be through the McDonald's All-American Marching Band (two clean-cut high school students from each state) in a nationally televised Thanksgiving Day parade or through sponsorship of sports and family entertainment programs.

Although such chains as Burger King, Burger Chef, and Arby's compete with McDonald's for the fast-food business, none rivals McDonald's success. The explanation reflects not just quality, service, cleanliness, and value but, more importantly, McDonald's advertising, which skillfully appeals to different audiences. Saturday morning television, for example, includes a steady dose of cartoons and other children's shows sponsored by McDonald's. The commercials feature several McDonaldland fantasy characters, headed by the clown Ronald McDonald, and often stress the enduring aspects of McDonald's. In one, Ronald has a time machine that enables him to introduce hamburgers to the remote past and the distant future. Anyone who noticed the shot of the Woody Allen film *Sleeper*, which takes place 200 years hence, will be aware that the message of McDonald's as eternal has gotten across. Other children's commercials gently portray the conflict between good (Ronald) and evil (Hamburglar). McDonaldland's bloblike Grimace is hooked on milkshakes, and Hamburglar's addiction to simple burgers regularly culminates in his confinement to a "patty wagon," as Ronald and Big Mac restore and preserve the social order.

Pictures of McDonaldland appear on cookie boxes and, from time to time, on durable plastic cups that are given away with the purchase of a large soft drink. According to Boas and Chain, a McDonaldland amusement park, comparable in scale to Disneyland, is planned for Las Vegas. Even more obvious are children's chances to meet Ronald McDonald and other McDonaldland characters in the flesh. Actors portraying Ronald scatter their visits, usually on Saturdays, among McDonald's outlets throughout the country. A Ronald can even be rented for a birthday party or for Halloween trick or treating.

McDonald's adult advertising has a different, but equally effective, theme. In 1976, a fresh-faced, sincere young woman invited the viewer to try breakfast—a new meal at McDonald's—in a familiar setting. In still other commercials, healthy, clean-living Americans gambol on ski slopes or in mountain pastures. The single theme running throughout all the adult commercials is personalism. McDonald's, the commercials tell us, is not just a fast-food restaurant. It is a warm, friendly place where you will be graciously welcomed. Here, you will feel at home with your family, and your children will not get into trouble. The word *you* is emphasized—"You deserve a break today"; "You, you're the one"; "We do it all for you." McDonald's commercials say that you are not simply a face in a crowd. At McDonald's, you can find respite from a hectic and impersonal society—the break you deserve.

Early in 1977, after a brief flirtation with commercials that harped on the financial and gustatory benefits of eating at McDonald's, the chain introduced one of its most curious incentives—the "Big Mac attack." Like other extraordinary and irresistible food cravings, which people in many cultures attribute to demons or other spirits, a Big Mac attack could stike anyone at any time. In one commercial, passengers on a jet forced the pilot to land at the nearest McDonald's. In others, a Big Mac attack had the power to give life to an inanimate object, such as a suit of armor, or restore a mummy to life.

McDonald's advertising typically de-emphasizes the fact that the chain is, after all, a profit-making organization. By stressing its program of community projects, some commercials present McDonald's as a charitable organization. During the Bicentennial year, commercials reported that McDonald's was giving 1,776 trees to every state in the union. Brochures at outlets echo the television message that, through McDonald's, one can sponsor a carnival to aid victims of muscular dystrophy. In 1976 and 1977 McDonald's managers in Ann Arbor persuaded police officers armed with metal detectors to station themselves at restaurants during Halloween to check candy and fruit for hidden pins and razor blades. Free coffee was offered to parents. In 1976, McDonald's sponsored a radio series documenting the contributions Blacks have made to American history.

McDonald's also sponsored such family television entertainment as the film *The Sound of Music*, complete with a prefatory, sermonlike address by Ray Kroc. Commercials during the film showed Ronald McDonald picking up after litterbugs and continued with the theme, "We do it all for you." Other commercials told us that McDonald's supports and works to maintain the values of American family life—and went so far as to suggest a means of strengthening what most Americans conceive to be the weakest link in the nuclear family, that of father-child. "Take a father to lunch," kids were told.

Participation in McDonald's rituals involves temporary subordination of individual differences in a social and cultural collectivity. By eating at McDonald's, not only do we communicate that we are hungry, enjoy hamburgers, and have inexpensive tastes but also that we are willing to adhere to a value system and a series of behaviors dictated by an exterior entity. In a land of tremendous ethnic, social, economic, and religious diversity, we proclaim that we share something with millions of other Americans.

Sociologists, cultural anthropologists, and others have shown that social ties based on kinship, marriage, and community are growing weaker in the contemporary United States. Fewer and fewer people participate in traditional organized religions. By joining sects, cults, and therapy sessions, Americans seek many of the securities that formal religion gave to our ancestors. The increasing cultural, rather than just economic, significance of McDonald's, football, and similar institutions is intimately linked to these changes.

As industrial society shunts people around, church allegiance declines as a unifying moral force. Other institutions are also taking over the functions of formal religions. At the same time, traditionally organized religions—Protestantism, Catholicism, and Judaism—are reorganizing themselves along business lines. With such changes, the gap between the symbolic meaning of traditional religions and the realities of modern life widens. Because of this, some sociologists have argued that the study of modern religion must merge with the study of mass culture and mass communication.

In this context, McDonald's has become one of many new and powerful elements of American culture that provide common expectations, experience, and behavior—overriding region, class, formal religious affiliation, political sentiments, gender, age, ethnic group, sexual preference, and urban, suburban, or rural residence. By incorporating—wittingly or unwittingly—many of the ritual and symbolic aspects of religion, McDonald's has carved its own important niche in a changing society in which automobiles are ubiquitous and where television sets outnumber toilets.

The Ethnography of Big Mac

by David Gerald Orr

Ethnography as an interdisciplinary field in which all of the phenomena and documents produced by cultural groups and regionally distinct societies are examined has enjoyed rich success in its recent application to the problems posed by American formal expression. Ethnographers are now relentlessly pursuing widely different aspects of American material culture. Currently, at the University of Pennsylvania's American Studies Department (Department of American Civilization), various kinds of ethnographies are taught and subjects as far ranging as the development of the Mormon religious sect and the early eighteenth century society of Boston are discussed. All of these are now carefully considering the evidence left by objects and buildings. Ethnography has made a second, even more significant impact on another area of study, the community. The University of Delaware's excellent Odessa Program[1] annually considers the community surrounding the eighteenth century Delaware town now known as Odessa and the evolution of its impact on its neighboring towns and non-nucleated agrarian sites. The community is considered from every conceivable academic approach. The maritime community is studied, for example, with respect to its surviving practitioners, its nautical artifacts, its documents and records, as well as its cultural geography, sociological definition, and historic continuum.[2] The study of Odessa, as well as those areas suggested by the Pennsylvania examples focus on two basic humanistic questions: What constitutes social and cultural change? and secondly, What factors influence the development of human institutions? By responding to these issues, Ethnographers make statements which are not only crucial in the interpretative process of history but also produce, sometimes entirely involuntarily, large bodies of both verbal and non-verbal data. The sequence now has become painfully familiar to ethnographers; the focus is chosen, the harvest of material begins, the quantification of data proceeds, and the results are most often unpredictable. The great service of the process is the simple collection of material itself. The cataloging of artifacts and structures contributes to our growing desire to completely assess our national cultural heritage; to *Know* what we have, where we have it, before writing a thesis or contributing notes to professional societies. The short two year study of Odessa, for example, surveyed the architectural presence of the community and discovered that most of the fine building took place in a decade reflected by other examples of physical growth and prosperity. The *meaning* of that period of "good living" was dramatically defined by the structures themselves. Additionally, the study of the watermen rescued a priceless chunk of the "world we have lost" from total oblivion. Interviews were conducted which led to more significant analyses of not only the material heritage but indeed the entire ambience of marsh and wharf. This self-effacing act of painstaking data banking is a step too often ignored in most of the humanities. Ethnographic research by its mandatory process of data retrieval of all sorts of primary records makes a superb statement about our society. Most importantly the new stimulation provided by the meshing of ancillary disciplines sharpens the critical sense of both faculty and students.

Material culture study emerges from this web of data as an important discipline and one which acts as a nexus for much of what ethnographies reveal. Direct sensory confrontation of objects provides and amplifies an equally direct kind of knowledge about cultures. Even in the popular context, material cultural analysis can comprise a "community of experienced particulars".[3] This becomes crucial when one considers the material evidence of systems like McDonald's since so much of their physical formal intrusion is ephemeral. The associative value of building visual systems of experienced phenomena (Hamburger container to bag to table to building to urban/suburban setting) educates, illustrates, and explains our own age.

The past few years have been exciting ones for the student of our own material culture legacy. Exciting progress has been made in the fields of architectural history, art history, technological history, and historical and industrial archeology. Tightly defined parameters once present in these fields have been shattered and all of them are interlocking in a common effort to discover a more holistic view of culture.[4] More often than not, physical forms represent the best data available for study. Taut material culturally focussed ethnographies are now contemplated for even subjects like World War One Trench Warfare.[5] Battle ethnographies of this type give a clear vision, if still a vision, of relatively unattractive areas of analysis. The undistorted picture of World War One presented by the real objects in correct relationship and matrix is unforgettable, and should be required for all who seek to understand the generation which followed 1918. The American commercial post-World War II phenomenon known as Fast Food Vending lends itself magnificently to such a perspective. The materials which follows in this essay will attempt to provide a format in which the nuances of McDonald's Corporation, as an industry leader in Fast Food sales, can be interpreted in the light of our own culture. Instead of dismissing the vast amounts of ephemeral material culture produced annually by McDonald's as insignificant and valueless; why not examine it, consider it soberly as a reflection of our own goals and aspirations, and at least, look at it. Some of the essays in this collection accomplish this. The study of material culture is not limited to just the most progressive and elitist aspects; it is the study of *all* material culture.

The Fast Food Industry began in America as an important correlative to express railroad travel with its insistence on rigidly kept schedules and passenger transfers.[6] Yet, it was the automobile with its accompanying weatherproof road network, which firmly established the industry, chiefly in the

decade following the end of World War Two. The incredible spectrum of individual types which characterized the appearance of the roadside stops, gas
filling stations, and restaurants, of the late 20's, 30's, and 40's, quickly gave
way in the fifties to the inexorable march of what some scholars have humor-
lessly denoted as "Commercial Heraldic Industrial" forms. The old individual
visages and façades, aimed primarily at the kinetic vehicular traffic, were
imaginative, oftimes zany, and occasionally marvelous. But they were all more
or less autonomous. The *One-Spot Flea Killer*, for example, once perched
majestically above old Route One near Laurel, Maryland, was a fresh visual
oasis for the tired inter-urban commuter who traveled the busy thoroughfare in
the late forties and fifties; silently enduring the monotonous banality of the
strip architecture which lined the roadside.[7] The *One-Spot Flea Killer*,
structured as a small two story building sandwiched between two Terrier
silhouettes, was a real delight. Slowly the years of neglect took their toll; the
ears of the dog vanished, the sides of the little building crumbled until finally,
in the late sixties, it went down. It was instantly missed by the regulars of old
Route One but it never was recorded by HABS, HAER, or the National
Register.[8] I believe its demise argues strongly for the more sensitive surveying
of threatened structures, including those of a recent and more popular vintage.
At any rate a new genre of roadside and highway building was fast approach-
ing; spawned by the high speed auto and the cement octopuses of the Interstate system. This new typology was flashed on television daily as it evolved
from variety to sameness, from humor and a sense of wonder, to a rigid
heirarchy of fixed form; the commercial icons of Burger King, Stuckey's, Esso,
and McDonald's.

The meteoric ascendancy of McDonald's to its present position as
undisputed fast food industry leader is a saga best related elsewhere.[9] Some of
the highlights, however, should be reviewed. First, Ray Kroc's success seems
to be heavily dependent on his late 1950's (and todays?) consumers' desire for
cleanliness, fast service, and a reliably regular degree of product quality. This
was originally telegraphed into Q.S.C. (Quality, Service, and Cleanliness) by
the McDonald's management.[10] The twenty year growth of the firm is a
modern commercial miracle. The first restaurant in the chain opened in the
Chicago suburb of Des Plaines, Illinois, on April 15, 1955.[11] By 1975, there
were approximately 3,400 hamburger restaurants at home, with 300 abroad.[12]
A new McDonald's a day is the current pace of openings in the United States.[13]
One reason for their early success was the marked manner in which the first
McDonald's restaurants differed from their contemporary cousins. They were
never equipped with jukeboxes, usually tolerated no loitering or "hanging
out", and employed no carhops, experienced no tipping, and usually endured
no long lines of impatient diners.[14] McDonald's licensees had to respect general
corporate policies and standards, which were rigidly and uniformly enforced,
and bought their food and other supplies from local markets when possible.
McDonald's Corporation records claim that the late fifties customer had only
to wait an average of fifty seconds to receive his hamburger, shake, and order
of French Fries.[15] By 1965, McDonald's had established a network of regional

offices to maintain its high operational efficiency. A modern management trainee program and facility opened in Illinois at Elk Grove Village in 1968.[16] Here, at "Hamburger University" new licensees, managers, and assistants learn their trade. The original "candy-stripe" restaurant stand gave way to the "patio" style format endemic today, physically reflecting a significant marketing change from carryaway to sitdown meals. Today, barely 145 of these prototypical buildings survive.[17] McDonald's has now captured student unions at large Universities (Ohio State and Cincinnati), museums (Franklin Institute in Philadelphia), ski resorts (Boyne Mountain in Michigan), zoos (Toronto), and recently even a Children's Hospital (CHOP in Philadelphia, opened in April 1977). The thriving financial situation of McDonald's is an important testator to the brilliance of their manufactory/technological mesh in its application to marketing.[18] Today McDonald's is a powerful spore of popular culture on the American landscape and cityscape as they move out from their traditional suburban citadels and away from their traditional highway/automobile ambience towards new areas ripe for conversion. Toward the inner city, toward public and civic institutions and cafeterias, they now aim their advertising focus, as they continue their relentless effort to discover and captivate rich markets.

There should not be any valid objection in using McDonald's fast food marketing system as a focus in which to frame the problems common to our contemporary experience. As we previously learned from Plymouth and Jamestown, White Towers and Las Vegas, so we can now profit from an in depth examination of a major American Corporation. Unlike other fields of study, McDonald's presents us with a tightly defined harvest of historical evidence. The problem is not finding the material; the problem is the careful sorting out of data and the redistribution of evidence. The Material Culture historian must now come to grips with the teleology of the McDonald's engineer and architect. McDonald's artifacts do not just "train the eye" and "educate the observer", as the old chestnuts state; they dazzle and bludgeon. Nevertheless, it would seem that an ethnographic approach zeroing in on McDonald's can be formulated and would prove useful. A "Big Mac Ethnography" postulated under the following headings suggests one direction such an examination could take. Other areas of research should also be explored; this outline is certainly not the precise route for this ethnography. Hopefully, it also underscores the need for research commitment to our recent past and its material culture.

I. Identification and Definition

There exists at the present time a clear need for some sort of agreed on taxonomic schema. How crucial this is depends upon the theories which rest on these definitions. Existing patterns of definition which rest on rigid meanings for such words as "vernacular", "traditional", and "folk" need to be clarified and debated. McDonald's, for example, exists for the twentieth century "Everyman" and this relationship desperately needs to be restructured. Certainly the difference between the products of the "Workmanship of risk" and the "workmanship of certainty" is a valid and distinct one. Perhaps this basic difference in the fabrication of artifacts will help separate McDonald's visual world from other vernacular systems.[19] Even traditional trichotomies (such as Nye's) may have to be abandoned in pursuit of this goal.

II. "Reading" McDonald's "Architecture": Meaning in Building.

Theodore Levitt[20] has stated that we tend to think about service in humanistic terms and about manufacturing in technocratic terms. Discretion becomes the enemy of order, strict quality controls and regularity. McDonald's, by its appeals to the non-ordered image of family living and dining sometimes confuses these themes. Therefore, considerable care goes into the design of McDonald's façade screens and its interior decor. Local visual demands, based on historic trends and ethnographic patterns, are met wherever possible. Thus a colonial motif is selected for a restaurant in an eighteenth century setting while maritime forms are selected as trim for the McDonald's located in ports and river ambiences. Sometimes, McDonald's will scale down its heraldic thrust in order to yield to more basic and traditional ideas. The CHOP McDonald's mentioned earlier in this essay seems stripped of most of its large scale advertising; mainly because it is located on an interior court. Therefore it concedes this material to the previously established decor of the hospital's marvelous skylit interior courtyard. McDonald's restaurants are carefully conceived entities which tightly control physical and visual movement. Symmetry governs the relationship of parking lot to structure. Flower patterns are done in order to accent "naturally" the established McDonald's colors. Exterior color trim and molding replicate and answer the same statements used on the inside. A McDonald's restaurant, like the Flavian Amphitheater (Colosseum) in Rome controls customer (crowd) flow. Egress and ingress are important in the successful operation of a McDonald's restaurant. Like a gravity feed water supply system, it seems that nothing stops inside a McDonald's; that all things, as Heraclitus has said, flow. Actually, it just seems that all things flow; in truth they stop and even tarry. But there is no design for idleness. The basic tenet is flow. It is behind the initial success of McDonald's; since it assures that customers are served rapidly and efficiently. The design seems more in the means than in the end. Again, I emphasize *seems*, as the visual world of McDonald's is one of illusion and fantasy. The "iconic transfer" of the golden arch, though immediate and powerful, is executed in a cleverly engineered space replete with other less intelligible forms.

III. The Significance of Antecedental Force

The historic relationship of McDonald's to its immediate predecessors is very important in any consideration of the evolution of the Fast Food Industry in the United States. Following World War One, one can trace the progress of the first roadside stands to the first real franchises established before World War Two. The change from White Castle (White Tower) to McDonald's is a very instructive one. Again, one sees the individual formal enthusiasm of the early drive-ins, many of them couched in the shape of the products they sold. The end result is the Commercial heraldic icon-structure. A sequence, carefully conceived and delineated, illustrating the basic components of change would be an important part of our ethnography.

Another important part of this study would be the complete analysis of the major changes in McDonald's architecture and forms. The engineers and firms responsible would be examined in the light of the marketing and financial problems they were made to address. This information would then correlate beautifully with the historic material gained by examining the birth of the industry as a whole.

IV. Documentary Archiving and Cataloging

This section touches at the very heart of any ethnographic enterprize. As mentioned earlier in this essay, the accumulative process associated with any well-organized ethnography is, in many cases, its finest methodological and substantative achievement. My own seminal endeavours in this field are really not enough.[21] A central data repository is mandatory for such field research. Building plans, types and photographs must be accurately indexed. Oral interviews, videotapes (and motion pictures) and field notebook reports are all to be archived in one place. Corporate records and notes are of course, confidential, and must be withdrawn from public scrutiny. Yet, some cooperation should produce materials which will shed light on the operations of McDonald's, without creating major difficulties. Commercials, for example, can easily be converted to sound motion picture film and made available for study. The cultural importance of such a source material has only recently been felt. Marshall Fishwick's work in this area should lead the way to the eventual establishment of a TV Commercial archive.

V. Oral History

Both oral interviews and written answers to questionnaires can contribute important data to our ethnography. Specific themes can be suggested for our field interviews but more often than not, even when dealing with contemporary problems, the "shotgun" method of conducting interviews is the best.[22]

VI. Iconic/Symbolic Role-Playing

This concern is at the heart of many of the essays in this collection. Yet, the precise position which McDonald's occupies tends to meld many of our concepts concerning icons and the functions they provide. The building itself *is* the icon; not just the golden arch or a smaller scale advertising calligraphy. McDonald's serves as a veritable asylum for icons. But what message is transferrable? What service is being provided and what values are being served? The traditional sensitivity of major architectural endeavours in reflecting their age is nevertheless present. Just as Mount Airy in Virginia and Reading Terminal in Philadelphia cast important light on eighteenth century domestic society and the late nineteenth century urban transportation net respectively; so McDonald's comments honestly on American values present in the seventies.

Unemotionally and with an almost neuter perspective, McDonald's defines the quest for order, structure, and an easily understood social hierarchy, present in our times. The Generalization, based on artifact and building, is sometimes ill conceived and off-target. Perhaps a sharply drawn ethnography of McDonald's will contribute to the value of such a formal interpretation.

VII. Foodways

Dietray engineers should be used as important consultants in order to properly assess the impact of Fast Food on a flaccid America. It is possible that this idea concerning the dietary effects of constant Fast Food patronage may have to be revised under the influence of such an intense examination. In reference to the "Junkfood Junky" syndrome commonly held to be presented by McDonald's menu, the Children's Hospital, Philadelphia, McDonald's added soup, two salads, and a MacSundae to their offerings.[23]

VIII. McDonald's in the Community

Many McDonald's restaurants are establishing themselves as bonafide community centers. A McDonald's located in Essington, Pa., has a large community bulletin board and supports local civic activities. Nationally, McDonald's strongly supports such local initiatives which sponsor local charities, athletic teams, etc. These are often incorporated into the advertising campaign with large posters used to broadcast the efforts utilized. For example, the traditional Temple University/University of Delaware football game becomes the clever nexus of a McDonald's advertising campaign. One week before the clash is held, *Beat Temple* buttons are handed out in Delaware McDonald's while *Beat Delaware* buttons are handed out in Philadelphia area restaurants. The result: hundreds of buttons appear in a packed football stadium, all appropriately emblazoned with McDonald's logos.

IX. Packaging Technology

McDonald's regularly changes the patterns and even the texture of containers; most of the time in a very, almost unrecognizable, subtle manner. The old advertising gimmick of giveaway items has been perfected by McDonald's and utilized to a degree far beyond that of their rivals. Toys, buttons, tickets to zoos and athletic events, mugs, and even drinking glasses[24] have been distributed by McDonald's. Packaging technology is a field long neglected by the student of American private enterpise but should be quickly mastered by any McDonald's ethnographer. Last Year (1976), for example, Keystone Foods Corporation, which owns Equity Meat (McDonald's meat supplier) produced more than a billion burgers for McDonald's.[25] Keystone plans on making a strong incursion into the cattle-rearing industry so that the meat packaging process will be rigidly controlled from "calf to customer".[26] McDonald's research in food packaging is easily the most advanced of any other food server. Problems, such as discovering a biodegradable package for its food products, keep the McDonald's engineers occupied.

X. The World of Ronald McDonald

Much of the ephemeral material received daily by McDonald's patrons contain illusions and fantasies which refer to a world peopled by hamburger-headed characters, a Fillet o'Fish lake full of strange beings, and other cartoon individuals. The Disneyesque theme park, created in the late sixties, is being constantly expanded and improved. This is a brilliant merchandising tool since the child's market brings in the concept of McDonald's as a "Family" restaurant.[27] The colorful decals on McDonald's giveaway drinking glasses appeals to the world of the young child, and leads directly to the adult market. *McDonaldland* toy sets were marketed during the 1976 Christmas season; complete with a full complement of realistically sculpted dolls of all the McDonald's characters. This sort of enterprise has an elevating and legitimizing influence on McDonald's food products since the fantasy world characters exist as toys on their own merit. Much can be said concerning this recent movement of McDonald's into the toy market. What role does Ronald McDonald play and why does he appear asexually? What is the relationship of this visual hamburger Eden to the marketing of fast food? The Grimace, originally conceived as a strange purplish monster who loves hamburgers, has changed his image somewhat on the glasses given away in 1977 from the image emblazoned on similar glasses handed out a year before. The Hamburglar, conceived originally as lean and threatening, is now depicted with obese features, a kind of fat face, and a rather harmless visage. This fantasy world is, in all respects, an important feature of our ethnography.

XI. Demography: Regional and Ethnic Eating Patterns

Who eats at McDonald's and who doesn't? Oral interviews and local statistics will provide answers to these questions. Where does ethnic inbalance take place and what causes it? Who works at McDonald's and in what capacity? Finally, Who runs McDonald's? Regional studies will give us much valuable information concerning the larger, more national, effect of McDonald's on our life style. Answers to these vital questions will tell us much about ourselves.

The above headings represent what I feel should be considered as the major focii by any ethnography. Some other areas such as Management and Internal Infrastructure, Regionalization of Marketing Techniques, and Internal Decor Typology, could also be considered as appropriate to our study. All of these strands must be melded together; especially the material culture data. No aesthetic question of "good" or "bad" must confuse our judgment or blur our purpose. Perhaps the great success of McDonald's has only fulfilled many an architect's wish:

"We should insist upon ample freedom for experiment within a largescale framework of regulated order."[28]

Notes

[1]This program, jointly sponsored by the Henry Francis DuPont Winterthur Museum and the History Department of the University of Delaware has been recently expanded to include a Folkloristic material culture approach and a State architectural surveyor. See also *Winterim Project Summary: Documenting, Preserving, and Interpreting an Historic Village, Odessa, Delaware, 1750-1800.* January, 1972, 1973. Typescript printed by History Department, University of Delaware and the Henry Francis DuPont Winterthur Museum, 262 pp.

[2]For two good examples see John Demos, *A Little Community,* Oxford University Press: New York, 1970 and Rowland Parker, *The Common Stream,* Holt, Rinehart, and Winston: New York, 1975. For a good Local History bibliography, see Patrick H. Butler III, *Material Culture as a Resource in Local History: a Bibliography* (Chicago: Newberry Library, 1977). Mimeographed copy on file. Oral history has produced great success with rural subjects (Foxfire project, Rabun Gap, Georgia) but why not a City Foxfire which, among other things, could study Fast Food? See Deborah Insel, "Foxfire in the City" *English Journal,* 164 (Sept. 1975): pp. 36-38.

[3]For the "community of objects" see Bernard Herman and David Orr, "Pear Valley *et al*: An Excursion into the Analysis of Southern Vernacular Architecture" *Southern Folklore Quarterly,* V. 39, no. 4, December, 1975, pp. 307-327.

[4]For Industrial Archeology: M. Abrash and D. Orr, "Industrial Archeology: Teaching a New Historical Field" *History Teacher* V. IX, No. 1, 1975; Robert Vogel, "Industrial Archeology—A Continuous Past" *Historic Preservation,* v. 19, no. 2, April/June, 1967.

One recent study can serve as a prototype for what is possible. See John J. Mannion, *Irish Settlement in Eastern Canada, A Study of Cultural Transfer and Adaptation,* University of Toronto Press: Toronto, 1974.

[5]See John Keegan, *The Face of Battle,* Viking: New York, 1976, especially pp. 204-280, a fine study of the Battle of the Somme. See also Martin Middlebrook, *The First Day on the Somme,* Norton: New York, 1972.

[6]For Roman Fast Food: See the standard works on Pompeii. Ancient Pompeii had many streetside bars where one-dish hot foods were quickly ladled out to impatient Romans.

[7]See especially Paul Hirshorn and Steven Izenhour, "Learning from Hamburgers; the Architecture of White Towers" *Architecture Plus* June, 1973, pp. 46-55; Robert Venturi, Denise Scott Brown, and Stephen Izenhour, *Learning From Las Vegas,* MIT Press: Cambridge, 1972; Peter Blake, *God's Own Junkyard: The Planned Deterioration of America's Landscape,* Holt, Rinehart, and Winston: New York, 1964. For the gas station see Bruce A. Lohof, "The Service Station in America: The Evolution of a Vernacular Form" *Industrial Archeology* Vol. XI, no. 2, Spring, 1974, pp. 1-13.

[8]HABS: Historic American Building Survey; HAER: Historic American Engineering Record. Both under the U.S. Dept. of the Interior. Sometimes HAER records a few Commercially important buildings.

[9]Max Boas and Steve Chain, *Big Mac,* Dutton: New York, 1976. With plenty of bombast and surprisingly little attention to the material culture, this polemic represents the only major study to date. The Annual Reports issued by McDonald's Corporation are mandatory.

[10]Biographical sketch, *Ray A. Kroc,* Cooper and Golin, Public Relations/Marketing, March, 1975, p. 1. A "V" has recently been affixed for "value".

[11]McDonald's Corporation Fact Sheet, March, 1975, Chicago, Illinois, p. 1.

[12]*Ibid.*

[13]David Anable, "Computerization of Hamburgers" *The Christian Science Monitor,* Weds., July 6, 1977, p. 2.

[14]A McDonald's located in the Richmond/Bridesburg area of Philadelphia has a somewhat different philosophy. They have been encouraging more extended stays by providing daily movies at 4:00 p.m. (of old Three Stooges and Little Rascal films).

[15]*McDonald's 1955-1975—Serving a Second Generation,* Cooper and Golin: Chicago, Illinois, n.d., p. 2.

[16]Boas and Chain, *op. cit.*, p. 76.

[17]At the end of 1974, only 166 were "candy-stripers". See *McDonald's Restaurant Locations and Designs*, Cooper and Golin, March, 1975, p. 1. The figure mentioned in the text is my personal count.

[18]Theodore Levitt, *The Marketing Mode,* New York: 1969.

[19]For the Workmanship of Certainty and Risk see David Pye, *The Nature and Art of Workmanship,* Van Nostrand Reinhold Company; New York, 1971, especially pp. 7-10.

[20]McDonald's distributed abstract of article appearing in the *Harvard Business Review,* September-October, 1972, "Production Line Approach to Service".

[21]This refers to the three year old efforts of myself and Mr. Daniel Kitchen of Philadelphia to assemble a large collection of McDonald's related and officially issued artifacts. Uniforms, buttons, paper handouts, toys, mugs, glasses, posters, and packaging have been collected. This project has been assisted by the cooperation of the local McDonald's District office.

[22]See Kenneth S. Goldstein, *A Guide for Field Workers in Folklore,* Folklore Associates: Hatboro, 1964.

[23]Advertisement in the *Daily Pennsylvanian,* April 11, 1977, p. 6.

[24]A summer, 1977 crisis was generated by fears that the glass decals printed on giveaway McDonald's glasses contained harmful chemicals. Apparently they did not. See articles in *Philadelphia Inquirer,* Sunday, July 10, 1977, p. 2-A and *The Morning News* (Wilmington, Delaware), Monday, July 11, 1977, p. 29.

[25]See Anable, *op. cit.*   [26]*Ibid.*

[27]Calvin Trillin, *American Fried—Adventures of a Happy Eater,* Penguin: New York and Baltimore, 1974, p. 206.

[28]C. Tunnard and B. Pushkarev, *Man-Made America: Chaos or Control?* Yale: 1963, p. 330.

New York's Biggest Mac

Mother, God bless her, is Big Mac's biggest threat. Whether she's Jewish, Italian, Chinese or whatever, she's the gal the Golden Arches are out to beat.

It's tough competing with her in the kitchen—tougher even than competing with Burger King, Burger Chef, Pizza Hut, Kentucky Fried Chicken or any of those other easy-to-eateries that are sprouting across the land. You never know what delicacy mom will come up with next. It could be moo shoo pork, fettucini Alfredo or a TV dinner. Other competitors, at least, just keep coming up with variations on a theme.

So says John H. Kornblith. And he should know. A vigorously competitive man, Kornblith is chairman and president of Twenty First Century Restaurants of America, Inc., one of the largest chains of McDonald's restaurants in the United States and the biggest Big Mac dealer in the Big Apple.

Maybe he's partially kidding when he lists the family chef as his chief business rival, but almost everything about the Kornblith-McDonald's chow line is designed to get mom and her family out of the kitchen and away to Ronald McDonaldland.

What's a big corporate giant like McDonald's doing competing with a nice little lady like mom?

Certainly McDonald's Corporation, maestro of the fine art of fast food, is big. Annual sales are in the $2.5 billion range. But the bigness of the burger Goliath really is something more akin to a confederacy of "Little Macs."

Kornblith is the biggest "Mac" in his town—a big town, granted—but he's only one of many licensees who are united in efforts to get young families with children out of the house for a fast meal in clean surroundings.

McDonald's began as a small operation run by a handful of people. So did Kornblith. Most of McDonald's licensees today are small operators (one or two stores).

Kornblith is both typical of the average operator—and atypical. He's one of thousands of licensees who have found that the McDonald's food line provides them with a common name-brand product, a tried-and-proven system of operation and a reasonable, but not total, amount of business freedom. He's atypical in the sense that he's the biggest operator in New York and serves on many of the operators' regional policymaking bodies.

Copyright 1976 by *American Way*, inflight magazine of American Airlines. Reprinted by permission.

Kornblith offered some food for thought about the chain's casual dining concepts during an interview in his Seventh Avenue office overlooking (and overhearing) Carnegie Hall.

Patting a super-sized wax replica of two all-beef patties on a sesame seed bun (purchased in a pop art gallery in San Francisco), he says the typical McDonald's menu, once limited to a fifteen-cent hamburger and ten-cent french fries, now has something to titillate the tastebuds of every member of the family. While not the kind of diet that carbohydrate- and calorie-conscious families should gobble up without restraint, the fast foods in McDonald's restaurants nevertheless are of a variety much vaster than they were when Ray Kroc, founder and chairman of McDonald's Corporation, talked Richard and Maurice McDonald into letting him franchise their California outlets nationwide twenty-one years ago.

The hamburger is still "king," Kornblith says, but it's been expanded to the Big Mac and the Quarter Pounder and surrounded by Fillet-o-Fish sandwiches, hot apple pies, McDonaldland cookies and a full breakfast menu.

In Kornblith's stores, the fifteen-cent hamburger is gone. It's now thirty-three cents. (The Big Mac is ninety-five cents.) French fries range from thirty-two to forty-eight cents, depending on the quantity, but dad can still feed mom and the two kids for a five-dollar bill and get some change back.

From a single restaurant in 1955, the McDonald's chain is now cooking up all-beef patties in all fifty states and twenty other countries. Kornblith joined the patty parade in 1958—three years after it began and five years before it sold its billionth hamburger. His seventeen outlets have contributed their fair share of the 17 billion hamburgers that have been sold since.

The McDonald's chain, whose growth has been called "the greatest in the history of the restaurant business and the pacesetter in the fast-food line," is basically a licensing operation. With more than one restaurant opening every day, only about 30 percent of them are owned by McDonald's Corporation, now headquartered in the Chicago suburb of Oak Brook. The other 70 percent are operated by independent businessmen like Kornblith—and also by a golf pro, a retired colonel, a Navy commander, a research chemist and a former fullback for the San Diego Chargers.

"In my case, I'm the principal owner of Twenty First Century Restaurants, which is a relatively large chain of McDonald's in New York City," Kornblith explains. "There are seventeen stores in the chain and another eleven in the planning."

As a McDonald's operator, Kornblith is in business for himself, but with a nationally famous name behind him. The initial capital investment required for an individual to join the burger bandwagon runs about $250,000 in New York City (less elsewhere) for fees, equipment, supplies and so on.

While Kornblith can run his own McDonald's show, so to speak, he cannot—not even with seventeen licenses and eighteen years in the business—run out and put up the Golden Arches anywhere he pleases. The Oak Brook parent provides "suitable sites" for its licensees, plus buildings, twenty-year leases and sometimes hard-surface parking lots. "Papa Mac," then, is always the proprietor, and the landlord collects his 3 percent fee on every sale.

The licensee gets the advantages of national advertising (and a voice in its content), signs, the benefit of volume contracts, specially printed containers and other supplies, formulas, consultation, a system of operation and a bachelor of hamburgerology degree. (The degree is awarded when an operator finishes his training at "Hamburger University," the corporate training school in Elk Grove Village, Illinois.)

McDonald's advertising content is created by a national agency in Chicago, but direction for the ads comes from individual operators as much as from McDonald's corporate marketing department, Kornblith insists. OPNAD is the name for the chain's Operators National Advertising fund, a voluntary cooperative through which a percentage of member restaurants' sales go for national advertising.

As an OPNAD member for five years and its chairman for three, Kornblith is generally satisfied with the content of the chain's commercial messages. Advertising aimed at McDonald's young customers continues to feature carrot-haired Ronald McDonald, as it has since 1966, and squeaky-voiced McDonaldland food characters. Adult advertising stresses quality, cleanliness and service—plus that familiar "You deserve a break today" tug to get mom and everyone else out of the kitchen.

Some stores do limited local promotions. They offer free french fries to kids who can rattle off the advertising slogan—the complicated, tongue-twisting one. (For those of you who want to stump the stores, it's "Two all-beef patties, special sauce, lettuce, cheese, pickles, onions on a sesame seed bun.")

"We're a system, but we're not a chain in the conventional sense," Kornblith adds. "We're a bit like New York itself. New York is really a big city of little communities rather than a giant conglomerate. McDonald's is a lot of individual entrepreneurs rather than a monolithic corporation."

Each operator is on his own. McDonald's does not lend money to its operators or guarantee their obligations. Each store is part of its own neighborhood. Each store even sets its own prices. Sometimes one McDonald's competes with another McDonald's. That happens when there are two stores in the same general market area, and the customer then has an option of going one way or another. Facilities usually make the difference

McDonald's Corporation tries to make its facilities' exteriors and landscaping harmonize with their natural surroundings. A McDonald's in Wisconsin, for example, features natural wood siding and shingles to blend in with the North Woods atmosphere. In the Southwest, white stucco exteriors and tile roofs capture the mood of the setting. And near Boyne Mountain, the Michigan schussboomer's resort, a McDonald's outlet resembles a ski chalet.

The new two-story Town House models are the urban answer to harmonizing hamburgers with skyscrapers.

What makes a man decide to go into the McDonald's business?

The same thing that makes mom quit the kitchen for a Big Mac. Children.

It's been said that the secret ingredient in the hamburger sauce must be "kidnip." If so, then the secret ingredient that entices golf pros and Navy commanders to open their own McDonald's is watching the "kidnip" in action.

"My affiliation with McDonald's came about as a very natural event," Kornblith recalls. "I was in Chicago at the time, nineteen fifty-eight. I had two of my three children with me. Cathy was eleven, and Gary was eight. We had just been to a doubleheader between the White Sox and the Yankees. It had extended into the late evening. We were in the car, and they were hungry. At that time, the McDonald's hamburger was just fifteen cents, and I think a great many people were afraid to eat a fifteen-cent hamburger, but we stopped at a store on the northwest side of Chicago, and I went in to get three hamburgers. I was very impressed with the fact that I was in and out within ninety seconds with what turned out to be food that was very tasty. I was impressed with the cleanliness, the quality, and the practicality of its taking care of young appetites. The next morning, I learned that McDonald's was headquartered in a Chicago suburb and that it would be relatively easy for me to meet Ray Kroc and other principals in the business."

Twelve months later, Kornblith opened his first McDonald's restaurant in East Brunswick, New Jersey. That store was the 185th in the chain. There are now more than 3,700.

At the moment, most of Kornblith's customers are young adults and young families with children, but the times they are a changin', and McDonald's is, too.

"Outlets are located in some very unique places," he says. "There are two McDonald's restaurants and three satellite snack bars in the Toronto Zoo. Ohio State University has a McDonald's in its Student Union building. The Franklin Institute in Philadelphia was the first museum to have a McDonald's. We're creative. Within the next few months, we'll be involved with an experiment in delivery. None of the McDonald's stores in New York City delivers at present, but two or three of us plan to experiment with the idea."

McDonald's frowns on the delivery concept because its standards call for food to reach the customer's palate while it's still reasonably warm. However, Twenty First Century operates a number of stores where 50 percent of the business is take-out, so the customer is sacrificing some heat by hopping it home himself.

"A cold Big Mac is not unknown," Kornblith admits. "But we have very high standards and a very high waste factor as a result. We throw away a lot of food."

Hungry Bowery bums are not likely to start congregating at the backdoors of every McDonald's in New York when word gets out. While there is some waste with a system that calls for trashing any hot item that sits in the bin for more than eight minutes, the procedures call for a "Joe Namath" on the hamburger assembly line. This "Big Mac quarterback" calls the food as customers enter the store, based on past experience and on a quick assessment of the people who are entering the store and eyeing the menu.

McDonald's Corporation, a publicly owned company since 1965, is not shy about revealing its profits. Its net earnings have grown without interruption each year, from $3.8 million in 1965 to $86.9 million in 1975.

Twenty First Century Restaurants, a privately held company, does about $20 million in annual sales. "We've made a profit every year—well, I won't swear to nineteen fifty-nine, when we opened two new stores—but we've been self-generating and we've never needed public money to keep going and growing," Kornblith says.

Meanwhile, his effort to get mother out of the kitchen is working. Since his seventeen McDonald's outlets began serving breakfast, he's begun to notice his Sunday morning patrons are predominantly young fathers with children in tow. Sunday mornings seem to be the time that mom has chosen to let the family fend for itself. Apparently, she's sleeping in, taking a well-deserved break from her exhausting competition with McDonald's.

The Man Who Sold the First McDonald's Hamburger

by Phillip Fitzell

Some many-billion-plus hamburgers ago the first McDonald's, an eight-sided glass-enclosed stand, was started by Richard and Maurice McDonald in San Bernardino, California. The counterman, who slid open the window at 6 p.m. on that day in December 1948 to sell the first McDonald's hamburger, was Arthur C. Bender—a man destined to become owner of the first franchise in the McDonald's chain, as it was developed under the direction of Ray Kroc.

Bender recalls that the McDonald brothers actually opened their stand, selling barbecue items, before World War II. At the time of the war, they leased the building out, but it eventually came back to them as the leasee defaulted. So they developed a center island concept, built almost like a glass fishbowl. From there, they began selling 15-cent hamburgers, 19-cent cheeseburgers, milk, coffee, buttermilk (soon afterward discontinued), orangeade, root beer, Coke, assorted pies, and potato chips. By popular demand, french fries and milk shakes were later added to the menu. Their hamburger stand became an immediate success.

Out of two front sliding windows, hamburgers and milk shakes were dispensed; and "around the corner" at another window, 10-cent french fries were available. Along one side of the building stood a popcorn vending machine.

People came from miles around to sample the products and even to make sketches or photograph this new phenomenon. Lines of customers added to the excitement.

In their first year of business, the McDonald brothers grossed nearly $100,000—unheard of for such a stand at that time. After four years of operations, they had pushed their volume to one-third of $1 million yearly—rung up on a single cash register!

Bender began working for the brothers for $1 an hour. He and the other "window people" were charged with keeping score on the number of french fries and milk shakes sold. At the time, they were experimenting with a multimixer for malted shakes, using ice milk and holding cabinets. Each shake had to be handdipped and a collar placed on every cup. Each collar, in turn, had to be washed after usage. As the volume of business increased, this method became impractical. The McDonald brothers went to a machine shop and had the mixer's spindles cut down, so that a 16-ounce cup could fit onto the unit without a collar.

Six months up to a year after opening, french fries were added to the menu. Since there was no space for the french fry kettles, the brothers had to add on to their building. They then installed a hot sink for rinsing the potatoes, cutters and peelers. The potatoes, Bender remembers, were never blanched, but fried right through.

Bender also recalls many job offers made to him during this time. He would be wiping the counter, and someone would walk up and offer him a management spot elsewhere. But he decided to stick with the successful McDonalds.

Meantime, they had decided to begin franchising their concept. The brothers negotiated their first contract with Neil Fox for a site on Indian School Road in Phoenix.

Fox paid them $900 for the franchise rights along with an option either to build his own stand or have it completed under contract. The McDonalds made dollar rebates on products sold to him. And they agreed to allow Fox to temporarily hire one of their employees to help get the store started. Under this system, Bender was dispatched to the Phoenix store to work for about a week. He notes: "One day, I'd be a counterman, a flunky; and the next day, I'd become a big shot know-it-all. Then I'd go back to being a counterman again." He helped the brothers open about six more franchised stores, all in California: Downey, Sacramento, North Hollywood, Azusa, Pomona, and Los Angeles. (Since then, some of these operations have failed, some have come into the McDonald's fold, while the Downey unit still continues under its original franchise.)

Enter Ray Kroc

The McDonald brothers, Bender indicates, eventually became disenchanted with franchising. They had about a dozen units underway, when Ray Kroc, a multimixer salesman in the Midwest, heard about his man on the West Coast selling mixers to the McDonalds "like they were going out of style." Kroc went out to investigate and became very interested in the McDonald's business. He bargained with them, agreeing not to touch their existing units and to pay them one-half of one percent of the gross on each store that he opened. In the negotiations, Kroc was limited in his take of the percentage of the royalty fee paid by the franchisee. Kroc got just 1.9 percent of each franchisee's yearly gross.

In this period, 1954-55, Kroc sold his first franchise in Fresno, Calif. to a San Bernardino resident for a $1,500 franchise fee plus 1.9 percent of the gross in exchange for exclusive rights to Fresno under a 10-year contract.

The Fresno franchisee wanted to hire Art Bender as manager of his store, but the franchisee was seized by a heart attack and died. Bender then verbally made an agreement with the widow to operate the store as manager with an option to buy it at a later date. Nothing was put onto paper.

Before Bender went to work in Fresno, however, he was temporarily hired by Kroc to help him open a pilot store in Des Plaines, Ill. in April 1955.

In July of that year, Bender went back to the Fresno store on Blackstone Avenue. He hired local people, who came in asking for work. His people became involved in all phases of the start-up, including construction of the building. Before opening, he conducted training sessions; and on opening night, even the purveyors, who supplied him with products and equipment, came over to help launch the unit.

For the employees, things had improved somewhat: They were now earning $1.05 an hour. But the hours, worked by everyone in two shifts, were rough, from 10:30 a.m. to 11 p.m. (with a Friday and Saturday closing at 1 a.m.).

It wasn't all smooth sailing. McDonald's even then faced community opposition. The Fresno store was called "that no good Los Angeles outfit." But Bender quickly recognized that the trick in turning public sentiment came with getting involved in community affairs.

For Bender, it meant working a 14-hour-a-day shift. After some time, he became impatient: He still didn't own the operation, although he ran everything. Kroc had offered him a job as operations man; so Bender decided to give notice to his employers and work instead for Kroc.

Bender's employers knew that if he left, the store would fail; so they agreed to sell him the business for $35,000. His big problem: Where to get the money?

With just $1,500 cash saved, Bender began to beg and borrow. His employers agreed to carry some paper for him. But he needed $14,000 to handle the business. The banks loaned him $6,000; his mother cashed in her war bonds. Finally, he completed the deal by raising $10,000.

(As the contract came up for renewal in 1965, Bender was able to secure another 10-year contract under the same terms, allowing him to bring that store in line with other stores in the McDonald's chain, which all now operate under 20-year contracts. It should be noted that the franchise fee has climbed to $10,000 plus three percent of a franchisee's gross and an additional rental fee. Early in business, Kroc learned from his partner Harry Sonneborn that more profits could be realized by first leasing land and developing a site, then releasing this property either to a franchisee or a company store. The rental fee started at about five percent and now is up to 8½ percent.)

Three years later in 1960, Bender again with borrowed money, leased some property to start his second store in Fresno. It took $15,000 in cash plus another $50,000 borrowed for equipment and signs. But that store met with strong competition, when a Bob's Big Boy coffee shop moved in nearby. Bender's sales there fell off by 20 percent, but later picked up again to become a high-volume store.

His growth in the franchise business was slow but solid. In 1965, he opened a third store and succeeded. In 1969, a fourth store was started, in 1971 a fifth, and in 1972 a sixth, all within his Fresno franchise. For 1974, Bender projects his volume at $4.5 million. His units now average anywhere from $65,000 to $70,000 per month.

For the most part, Art Bender's role in the McDonald's story has been played in the background. Similarly, his 28-year-old son, Ken, who now runs the six Bender stores (FRC Enterprises, Inc.) as vice-president, has also been a background figure. When his father was busy helping the McDonald brothers open their Azusa franchise, Ken was an eight-year-old, playing elf at a Christmas time promotion for the store. He also was on hand for the opening of the Blackstone Avenue store in Fresno, painting the floors, hammering, sweeping, etc. Through junior and high school, Ken worked as a grill man. In 1968, he helped his father set up a training program for store employees. Two years later, he went into training at the stores, working up to office manager, then general manager, and eventually to a full takeover in 1972.

Art Bender has continued working on a semiretired basis; but recently he underwent open-heart surgery, forcing him to devote all his energies to recovery.

It could be said that much of McDonald's strength come from its people—well-trained and dedicated. According to Art Bender, fast food operators keep grasping for new items as an answer to added volume. But the original concept of fast food, as successfully practiced by the McDonald brothers, is a limited menu. More items just slow down the operation. Nothing will create business more, Bender believes, than a good operation: "All the advertising, all the gimmicks, all the new menu items just won't do. It's the day-to-day attention to the operation that does it. Well-trained employees, who have an interest and pride in their work, keep the business on a one-to-one basis, between customer and employee."

Bender notes that Kroc was farsighted. Early enough, he recognized that "the business couldn't fly by the seat of its pants." It took a love for the business. Kroc hired the best talent he could get. He made sure that his people got all the information necessary for an optimum operation—information on pricing, on use of refrigerated cars, on what icings were required and the costs. He gave his people the right tools to work with, Bender recalls. Kroc told them about the potato market. He set standards for quality—for the meat: how it was ground, the size of the pattie, the handling, refrigeration, delivery, how it was packaged and the type of packaging. This applied to all items. He set up a research and development lab to test old products and seek ways to get optimum use out of them.

Bender continues: "It wasn't luck and there weren't any shortcuts for Ray Kroc. He just had a good concept and he stuck with it. He was a perfectionist. For many years, he went without a profit; and when he did make money, he reinvested it back into his people and facilities. In short, he didn't leave a crumb unturned in the McDonald's business."

Bender adds that credit for McDonald's success must go to Kroc. . . "He has a good mind and is a tremendous judge of people—recognizing quickly their potential or intelligence. And his genius comes in getting them trained to his way of thinking.

"I, too, learned from Kroc to stick to quality precepts. A purveyor would come in and offer me his product at 22 cents a dozen, while I was paying 36 cents per dozen. But I'd refuse, since it wasn't my quality. And I would throw away all our stale products."

Millionaires in the McDonald's story have been made both through ownership of its stock and through acquisition of exclusivity on real estate. But (as Art Bender can well attest to) for many owner-operators without the financial backing and real estate investment, making a million wasn't as easy. They would have to pay out an initial investment, then pour back their earnings into the business—reinvesting say $150,000 for remodeling, or paying large sums for replacement of volume equipment. Lately, Bender observes, equipment depreciates much quicker, lasting only five instead of 10 years.

The success of McDonald's transfers right down to its employees. One of Bender's window people was Jerry Smith, who had been working in a service station when that "no good LA outfit" moved in next store. Smith went over as a counterman and raised himself up to supervisor of operations for all the Bender stores.

Smith has watched McDonald's change from the inside, that is, from behind the counter. He's seen second and even a third generation of customers. He's observed the store's image change: "10 years ago, if a manager wore his McDonald's jacket on the streets, he'd almost be laughed upon. Today, managers can wear their uniform anywhere in town with respect."

In the early years, employees were separated from the customer by glass. Their "contact" was through two small sliding windows, Today, it's on a one-to-one basis, as employees stand in front of 10 "glassless windows."

Smith remembers that a store's crew comprised some 15 people. Everybody was in a fishbowl. But it was easier to get the crew charged up. Since the crew worked both shifts, everybody was known. The operation was less complicated and the store managers didn't need much business sense. Teamwork made it all work—a good feeling, even an inspiration, which the employees felt in serving their customers fast and efficiently.

Today, there are 50 people working a store. Since they work different shifts, they often are strangers. Smith adds that society, too, has changed to where young people feel they don't have to work. It's become the store managers's job to instill pride and dedication into employees. It's become much more complicated, he concludes.

Years ago, employees stuck with the business. In fact, in the six Bender stores, all but one of the present managers have come up through the ranks.

Larry DeVries, manager of the Blackstone Avenue unit, began as a 16-year-old trainee. He observes that just six years ago, the store was "a hamburger joint, but now it's become a good restaurant.Management has better tools to work with. The store has become more crew-oriented. In fact," DeVries says, "we try to know all the people in the crew. We even have rap sessions at my house or theirs, just to talk things out."

The change for McDonald's is a metamorphosis from a sterile-looking fishbowl building to an architecturally attractive restaurant with indoor seating and elaborate decor. According to Art Bender, the concept is still changing. He sees the limited menu disappearing at McDonald's. The change is toward a total restaurant concept—not a white tablecloth setting, but more of a sophisticated coffee shop atmosphere. There will be many of the items now on the menu plus additions; but the emphasis will continue to center on value, quality, and service.

Bender also predicts waitress table service for the future McDonald's. But the operation will maintain its fast turnover and low-price structure.

Look for more variations offered with the hamburger. And chicken and roast beef haven't been ruled out. The company for years has fiddled around with these items. But its success is based on putting out a product that's competitive in price but superior in quality to the competition's product. If chicken is adopted, first standards have to be developed. Portion control must be maintained. Putting chicken into 3,000 units isn't something that can be done overnight.

The Psychology of Fast Food Happiness

by Gregory Hall

McDonald's eateries are as common as chewing gum under cafe counters, and more genuinely American. A few facts are in order. As of 1973 McDonald's hatched on the average one fledgling fast food diner each day. In the restaurant business this amounts to a population explosion. It's still happening. Even more staggering is the number of cows that have been ground up for the billion McDonald's burgers sold roughly every four months. Resurrected, these herbivores would ring around an area larger than Greater London. But even this number is far exceeded by the number of American school children who adore Ronald McDonald second only to Santa Claus. Clearly, McDonald's is more than just another hamburger joint. It is a hamburger joint the wins the hearts of men. It is itself the product of peculiarly American preoccupations. Its product is fast food happiness.

In 1968, Guy Roderick, successful establishment lawyer, was charmed by McDonald's. He quit a Chicago law practice and joined the growing number of doctors, executives and lawyers who each year take up residence under the golden arches. As of 1973 Roderick owned four of hamburgerdom's mightiest and worked seven days behind the counter. Trading 20 years of legal science for fast food vending might seem like a step down, but Roderick insists the change brought him "a million dollars in happiness." What rare fascination does McDonald's hold for establishment professionals? Perhaps those disillusioned with the stress and responsibility of professional life opt for the less demanding, less creative and almost certainly profitable escape McDonald's offers. In return for an initial layout, the licensee gets to attend Hamburger University, and use the McDonald's real estate, name and formula, which earn the operator handsome profits. For many this is a prescription for happiness.

Why do so many hungry Americans prefer McDonald's meals? Because McDonald's is a form of therapy. Like many modern technologies tailored to the consumer market, McDonald's wants to entertain. But the entertainment is subtle, almost imperceptible. "When you are in this business," says Ray Kroc, "you are in show business. Everyday is a new show. It's like a Broadway musical—if people come out humming the tune, then the show was a success." Kroc, one time barroom piano player and war cohort of Walt Disney, knows how to entertain. His fast food circus stars a clown and a bevy of energetic uniformed kids who welcome the hungry into a carefully designed atmosphere.

"We offer people more than just fast food. It's an experience," says John Giles, national director for public relations. "It's an experience of fun, folks and food. We've sold 18 billion hamburgers, but we sell them one at a time." The McDonald's indoctrination begins with elaborate television commercials that illustrate the joyous restaurant atmosphere. Under the arches, we may feel the commercial-related *esprit de corps*. We may be entertained and fascinated by a group of unskilled adolescents who have been miraculously mobilized into an efficient, cheerful, coordinated unit. We may feel the invisible but ubiquitous Ronald McDonald poke and make us vulnerable to happiness.

In form the circus strategy was designed to capture families by first capturing the kids. But it aims equally at luring the passive child consumer from its shallow haunt in the adult ego. In the language of transactional analysis, our child ego state becomes dominant. It is the child who is able to feel the elemental joys of circus and food.

A certain psychological fulfillment is basic to McDonald's success. That is the real feat engineered by Ray Kroc and subordinates—the transformation of an American institution, the greasy-spoon hamburger joint, into a respectable, superclean, standardized, computerized food production machine that also makes people happy. The capture of America's tummies goes hand-in-hand with giving America a mealtime lift. It is technology used to create the aura of happiness—as contrast to the growing experience of constraints and frustrations imposed upon daily life by the engine of technical change in a world of discontinuity. In the words of a Fort Lauderdale, Florida 13 year old: "It's a fun place. It's like a circus. I feel happy here."

Escape from stresses of modern life is a national preoccupation aided, in large measure, by the automobile. It is interesting that the auto also plays a big role in precipitating many of the stresses from which it is used to provide escape, such as increased tempo, traffic, injury or death, financial responsibility, noise and pollution. The uterine confines of the car allow us to make instantaneous decisions to get away, to express and experience "freedom." As ideal transmitters of impulse, autos have become second skins, extensions of the human personality. In the same way, McDonald's is a projection, a response to a collective human desire for a certain kind of experience. The McDonald's ethic is closely allied to the values encouraged by the auto. This should be no surprise since the drive-in hamburger joint evolved as a symbiotic adjunct to the car. But McDonald's goes beyond reinforcing the speed-escape ethic. It is an experience qualitatively different and more varied than the auto.

Still, our fascination for McDonald's is like our fascination for the auto. Both are the lure of the slick efficient machine, as well as anticipation of the fantastic built on images of escape. In philosophical terms these cross currents are congruent with Nietzscheian categories, the Dionysian and Apollonian visions. The American experience has at one level been an interplay of these forces, an exploration of stresses set up between the exercise of individual freedom and compromises to a culture of control, between the perfectly ordered, crystalline dream and the ecstasy of spontaneous, uncontrolled, creatively sensuous experience. McDonald's builds these unconscious elements integrally into the machine itself, into the technology of the system. Hence we can see the perfectly ordered, mechanized process in seeming union with the casual, playful, tensionless child-world of the clown.

The drive-in window may serve as a case in point. The window is a common piece of fast food design in many McDonald's as well as most fast food vendors. It allows for a maximum casual encounter, speed, minimum of customer effort, in a machine-limited interaction. We can remain in our metal bubble while accepting nourishment through the portal. The window becomes our mouth, the first opening of the digestive tract. As gas stations are for cars, so McDonald's are fuel stations, or pit stops, for people whose automobile has become an exoskeleton. The situation describes a McLuhanesque world of projection and counter-projection: humans are like machines and machines are like humans. It is a world where man is pacified and precariously at home in a technological womb. It is a seeming contradiction that, while allowing the height of informality and relaxed encounter, the drive-in window really perpetuates the American speed syndrome responsible for the hectic pace of life. This is a compromise between *l'homme machine* and his biological/psychological limits. Speed means we can get something or somewhere as quickly as possible. It means escape from the necessity of waiting, of being patient. In our fast moving society, where waiting can demand determination and perseverance, escape from "wasted" time is deliverance, relief, or happiness. Speed may be preferred because it promises a future in which more things can be done in less time. The value of experience becomes a measure of its quantity and intensity. The measure of McDonald's success is in the quantity, the billions of hamburgers sold, the intensity of happiness (" . . . fun, folks and food.") it can offer. Ultimately this is the therapy we buy, the carefully designed commercial relief from cooking and waiting.

The mortuary industry has taken a cue from other popular American business and is offering a "drive-in funeral home." Mourners in New Roads, Louisiana may now view the remains of their relatives through a five-by-seven foot window at the Point Coupee Funeral Home. Owner Alven Verette says the new feature allows mourners to pay their respects without getting out of their cars. Explains Verette: "We wanted something for people who didn't have time to dress."

Admittedly, the fast food encounter is qualitatively different from the mortuary experience. The example serves only to illustrate the pervasiveness of the American preoccupation with speed and informality and to make clearer its effect. With the foot on the brake, there is hardly time to view the remains through an antiseptic pane of glass before the machine demands we be carried away. The drive-in window gives us a picture of the distant corpse bathed in a metallic blue neon light. The machine-limited encounter separates us from the experience. In much the same way, the mechanized, ritualized McDonald's process minimizes the possibility of relating to anything but categories or species of situations.

This limitation is an essential ingredient of an efficiently run operation like McDonald's. But, it would be enervating if the unindifferentiated series of exchanges between members was nothing more than mechanical. If the customer feels he is nothing more than matter in its place, he will not know the thrill of the McDonald's experience. Hence, the machinery must be imbued with a mysterious life. This is accomplished by advertising campaigns which give significance to the ritual around which the McDonald's experience turns.

Dr. Kottak, a Univ. of Michigan professor of anthropology, addressed the 1976 annual meeting of the American Anthropological Association. His claim: that McDonald's has become a virtual religious experience for millions of Americans. Kottak believes that McDonald's eateries, much like churches or temples, offer uniformity in an otherwise chaotic world. He says: "From the rolling hills of Georgia, to the snowy plains of Minnesota, with only minor variations, the menu is located in the same place, contains the same items and has the same prices." According to the professor, "We know what we're going to see, what we are going to say, what will be said to us and what we will eat." From that first request for a Big Mac to the final "Have a nice day!", every move is ritualized much like a religious service.

But the religious experience of McDonald's goes deeper than ritual. McDonald's is the Messiah carrying the new theology into a world of chaos; the Messiah whose Golden Arches are symbols heralding the new age of Yankee fast food technology. Eateries which are the same everywhere destroy the artificial boundaries of local custom and become a unifying force, bringing together all believers in a common brotherhood of those who have been cured of a Big Mac attack. This applies to the people of Europe and the Orient as well as Americans, because everyone must have a chance to believe. It is understandable why Steve Barnes, head of McDonald's International Operations, says of the European campaign, "It's corny, but I feel like a missionary over here."

The McDonald's canon is one of basically Puritan values: law and order, cleanliness, purity, hard work, self-discipline and service. The jingle, "We do it all for you," is meant to characterize the selfless aspect of the religious McDonald's. Cleanliness is a personal fetish of Ray Kroc's. It is well known among franchise owners that Kroc is a self-assigned, plain-clothes policeman who patrols his empire on periodic inspection tours in order to catch deviants. He once walked into a Canadian McDonald's and roared cantankerously. "There was gum on the cement patio, cigarette butts between the wheel stops for the cars," he relates. "There was rust on the wrought iron railing, and the redwood fence needed to be restained. I went in there and said to the manager: 'You get somebody to mop this goddamned floor right now! And if you don't, I'll do it myself!' "

McDonald's accepts the beleaguered and hungered modern into its fold and nourishes him. Many find the cheerily bland atmosphere reassuring. It is designed to neutralize anxiety. At this level McDonald's is able to ally the mystery of the computer circuit with the mystery of religious peace. The Golden Arches become symbol as well as sign. Obviously the arches form a letter M for McDonald's. But they also resemble cathedral arches which have been the architectural equivalents of man's ethereal aspirations.

Inspiring values of power, dominance and mastery which produce kingdom, McDonald's is the perfect embodiment of American military prowess. Accordingly, McDonald's has captured the suburbs and, in the language of *Time* magazine, conquered the country. Advertising *campaigns* are waged to win the populace and deliver lethal blows to the competition (Jack-In-The-Box, Whataburger, etc.). Armed with a variety of "secret" sauces and jingles, the fast food brigadiers engage in pitched battle for a bigger cut of the market. The artillery is in the form of jingles, musical ammunition which lodges in the psyche of the consumer and prods him continually. As Bill McClellan writes: "It is Orpheus in alliance with Pavlov working on the Whimpy in all of us." The roots of this mobilization and expansion are at the heart of the American movement itself, the exploration and colonization of the remaining frontiers. It is Commander Kroc who leads the fast food army into fertile territory, current exploitable American preoccupations, winning the natives with Ronald McDonald straws and napkins.

McDonald's has not swept Europe as it has America. Suburban Europe is not as mobile as suburban America. When they moved to the city they found extremely high rent cut their profits substantially, a problem that Kentucky Fried Chicken and Whimpy were able to minimize because of their decreased overheads. Speed does not seem to be as important in Europe as in the United States. Britain's Whimpy and Switzerland's Movenpick do better with slower service. The Germans and Swiss are more likely to remain at home in the evening rather than go out again. So McDonald's has had to depend on weekend shopping crowds for most of its profits.

The McDonald's phenomenon is not necessarily a sign of declining culture. It is more a reflection of basic American values and as such may be a symptom of stresses. Centuries from now, when historians and anthropologists sift through twentieth century artifacts, they will try to make sense of a hamburger joint that inspires religious fervor. If we could hold it up to ourselves like a mirror, we might experience a moments astonishment. But almost as quickly we might see the signs of hamburger addiction; the gaunt, harried look that precedes a Big Mac attack. Like Faust before the Mater Gloriosa, an irresistable power draws us on and we may find ourselves in the sanctum of a McDonald's kitchen. Although we may not genuflect after receiving the great beef cure, we may feel the urge to glance skyward, giving thanks that we do not need to leave a tip.

Bibliography

"Not For Export," *Forbes*, October 15, 1975.

"The Burger That Conquered The Country," *Time*, September 17, 1973.

McClellan, Bill, "Hamburger War Broils Over As Tactics Change," *Phoenix Gazette*, January 9, 1976, Sec. C, p. 1.

Can Mama Mac
Get Them To
Eat Spinach?

by Maryellen Spencer

Why? Why is the Big Mac the symbol of American food preference? Why, in the midst of what many of us like to think of as an era of interest in food as a creative art form is the most popular food one that requires no thought and promises no surprises? Why, in a time of fervent interest in nutrition, is there so much comsumption of food which is generally recognized to be nutritionally suspect? Why has McDonald's had a greater impact on American eating habits than have all the hard-working, hard-talking nutritionists?

Until I was asked to write this article, I had never eaten at McDonald's. I had spent fourteen years in the food profession—developing recipes, writing cookbooks, and serving as home economics director for a public relations agency—without eating where everyone else was eating. I had eaten in many fine restautants where you need either a lot of money or an expense account. I'd eaten in lots of character-ful country restaurants and diners. I frequently bought frankfurters with sauerkraut from street vendors. I kept graham crackers and peanut butter in my desk drawer. But I never ate at McDonald's; so lately I've been working diligently to correct that lamentable gap in my gastronomic experience.

On my first McDonald's trip cautious selections were the quarter-pound hamburger with cheese, french fries and black coffee. The food was surprisingly decent. It was tasty, tidy, and very filling. I'm never going to like those thin flat burgers that seem sort of pre-chewed, the soft rolls, or the catsup and raw onion, but the burger concoctions do have a certain homogenized integrity. The french fries are really first-rate, thin, crisp and non-greasy. I couldn't judge the coffee because I'm normally a tea-drinker (McDonald's doesn't serve tea). In later expeditions, I found the fillet of fish burger discouraging—it's difficult to tell where the soft bread stops and the fish starts, and the tartar sauce is vinegary. The apple pie surprised me. Piping hot, the fruit filling is very good and the pastry wonderfully crisp. The pastry is also very salty, and I swear that I couldn't help thinking of an apple egg roll. The Egg McMuffin is a splendid invention imaginatively named, but I just wish the muffin was toasted and the egg a bit runny. Of course, then the food would require special handling and couldn't be pre-prepared and ready to go the instant one steps in the door. When I met the Big Mac, it won. Ingenious it may certainly be, but refined it ain't. It is rock 'n' roll food, noisy and harsh. And popular.

But however much one may complain about the lack of esthetic refinement in McDonald's food, we are honor-bound to recognize its resourceful and practical nature. The pies are individual turnovers that require no cutting and no forks. The Egg McMuffin is a ham and egg breakfast in sandwich form, all put together, ready to go and easy to eat. There are also small embellishments that add style and an element of care. The Big Mac definitely has panache of a sort; it is an assemblage, however far it may be from Tournedos Rossini.

In 1973 *Time* asked four food writers and critics for their comments on McDonald's fare. They generally praised with faint damning. Craig Claiborne thought the french fries excellent but wanted more pickle on his hamburger. James Beard liked the efficiency, cleanliness, and insulated packaging, but not the shakes. Gael Greene expressed an extravagant passion for both the Big Macs and the shakes. Julia Child liked the french fries but not the Big Mac, and then raised the question of nutrition when she stated, "It's not what you would call a balanced meal; it's nothing but calories."[1] No, it's not a balanced meal. But neither is it "nothing but calories;" there is honest food value. But how *do* McDonald's foods rate in terms of nutrition?

If people ate at McDonald's occasionally or once in a while, the nutritional quality of the food wouldn't matter much. But many people eat there with astounding frequency, and thus "fast food" comprises a significant part of the collective American diet and of the diet of many individuals. McDonald's foods are by no means ideal as a total or frequent diet. They tend to be especially high in calories and fat and very low in vitamin A (see Table 1). They tend to deserve the most frequent criticisms of our popular eating pattern—too much fat and cholesterol, too many calories, not enough fresh fruits and vegetables, too much sugar and salt.

One way of evaluating the nutritive value of a diet or a meal is in terms of the RDA's or U.S. RDA's. The RDA's are the Recommended Daily Dietary Allowances, amounts of nutrients for persons of various ages and sizes, recommended by the Food and Nutrition Board of the National Research Council and considered adequate for maintenance of good nutrition in healthy people. The U.S. RDA's are amounts of nutrients established by the Food and Drug Administration as standards for nutritional labeling.[2]

If we assume that one-third of the day's mutrients should be consumed at each meal, then we can evaluate the nutritive value of a meal in terms of the percentages of one-third of the U.S. RDA's it provides. Two McDonald's menus were calculated in terms of percentages of one-third U.S. RDA's: one meal of regular burger, french fries and soft drink, and another meal of regular burger, french fries and strawberry shake (see Table 3). The meal of burger, fries and soft drink is low in all nutrients—extremely low in calcium and vitamin A and too low for comfort in iron, thiamin and riboflavin. The meal with the shake brings the level of nutrients up to a much more generous level, but vitamin A is still very low.

It is generally agreed that the desire for quick and easy eating that has contributed to the great success of McDonald's restaurants has perhaps also contributed to poor food choices and poor eating habits, and consequently poor diets.[3] Although there is much controversy as to exactly what our diet should be and what should be done to improve it, there is sufficient national concern about the state of the American diet to bring about the establishment of the U.S. Senate Select Committee on Nutrition and Human Needs. In February 1977 *Dietary Goals for the United States* was published as that committee's report.[4] The report states that the over-consumption of fat, especially saturated fat, along with cholesterol, sugar, salt and alcohol have been related to six of the ten leading causes of death, and that our eating patterns represent as critical a public health concern as any now before us.

To act on that public health concern, the Senate Committee suggested that major changes in eating habits are necessary to implement the goals it recommends for improving the state of the American diet and consequently the health of the American people. The goals include an increase in complex carbohydrate consumption along with decreases in the consumption of fat, saturated fat, cholesterol, refined sugar and salt. And the suggested changes in our food selection and preparation are:

1. An increase in the consumption of fruits and vegetables and whole grains.
2. Consumption of less meat and more poultry and fish.
3. A decrease in consumption of foods high in fat and substitution of polyunsaturated fat for some of the saturated fat.
4. The substitution of non-fat milk for whole milk.
5. Decreased consumption of butterfat, eggs and other high cholesterol sources.
6. Decreased consumption of sugar and foods high in sugar content.
7. Decreased consumption of salt and foods high in salt content.

Many people are of course not pleased with the U.S. Senate report, and some nutritionists have quarreled with the degree and type of change recommended. The goals have already been rejected by the American Medical Association and by the National Dairy Council. But, as D. Mark Hegsted, Professor of Nutrition in the Harvard School of Public Health, says, "The thing that everyone should realize is that nobody planned the American diet. We did not have evidence that increased consumption of meat, fat, cholesterol and sugar would help us. This diet is simply the result of our affluence. We know that the risks associated with this kind of diet are high. Everything we know indicates that a more moderate diet would be beneficial. The important question, therefore, is not, 'Why should we change our diet,' but 'Why not change it?' "[5]

McDonald's foods did not result from planning in terms of nutritional needs. They do not comprise a planned diet. McDonald's foods are as they are because of the objectives and limitations of fast-food marketing, and because of the consumer's desire for fast, tasty, rather indulgent foods. Nutrition had little or nothing to do with it.

McDonald's foods have seductive qualities—rich, filling, unctuous, sweet, salty—that appeal to our gastronomic moral weaknesses. Somehow or other, we tend to think of indulgent foods as wicked and immoral, and of good-for-you, healthful foods as moral. That may well be the source of the resistance to good-for-you eating. We eat food that we think will make us happy, not food that we think will make us healthy. There is a tendency to carry the Puritan ethic right into food and nutrition, presenting nutritional ideals in a moral, self-denying context which immediately makes them unappealing. Anyhow, we thought it would be interesting to compare the nutritive value of an indulgent and seductive McDonald's meal with a Moral meal, with a menu of foods that could be considered more Moral counterparts of the McDonald's items.

For the Indulgent McDonald's Feast we chose a quarter-pound burger, french fries, apple pie and vanilla shake. For a menu of Moral counterparts we chose a plain grilled lean burger with roll, a baked potato with margarine, a fresh apple, and a glass of skim milk. We made both food-to-food comparisons and meal-to-meal comparisons of the nutritive values (see Tables 2 and 4).

All in all, the big differences are in calories, fat and carbohydrate. The Moral meal actually has more food or weight—766 grams as opposed to 584 grams for the McDonald's meal. But the McDonald's meal has 65% more calories, 104% more fat and 62% more carbohydrate. It also has 32% more sodium, in spite of the fact that we allowed generous amounts of salt for both the plain grilled burger and baked potato in our Moral menu. McDonald's menu has 22% more calcium, but the Moral meal has 147% more Vitamin A (because of the fresh apple and the margarine added to the baked potato, and still far from an adequate amount), and 185% more Vitamin C (also because of the potato). Although the baked potato is superior to french fries in nutritive value, it's interesting to note that there is more fat with a large baked potato topped with a tablespoon of margarine (margarine because of its lack of cholesterol) than with a serving of french fries, all notions of grease to the contrary. The fresh apple has it all over the apple pie, being much lower in calories and essentially free of fat and sodium. Moral *is* better in this case.

If we accept then that the McDonald's diet is not ideal in terms of nutrition, and that most of us *know* it is not ideal, then why do people flock to McDonald's? Poor people accept communism not because they agree with or even understand its doctrine, but because it feeds them. And herds of the hungry go to McDonald's not because it's good or bad for them, but because it feeds them. And it feeds them in a clean, wholesome, efficient and convenient fashion. Day in and day out, most of us like for our food to be familiar and comfortable. Maybe McDonald's format, consistent both in food and physical surroundings, is a substitute for love, a secure suggestion of home.

We know that food has a psychological, even physiological, association with love. Obesity is very much an emotional problem. Over-eating is self-pampering, something many people do when they feel unloved. We know there are "reward foods" and "bribe foods." If you're a good boy I'll give you a piece of candy. Stop crying and you can have a cookie. There are also "comfort foods," soft and creamy custards and puddings associated with the protective cocoon of childhood. And mama generally fixes the food the same way all the time, and nobody cooks like mama. Except McDonald's. At Mama Mac's everything is always the same, safe and cozy. But without restraints or table manners.

Children have been telling me they like to eat at McDonald's to get away from the food at home. That remark is probably partly in imitation of the television commercial that says exactly the same thing, and partly the straight truth. McDonald's and the food there are a lark. No broccoli, no tablecloths, and no forks. Sheer bliss. The same sentiments are bound to remain in the adult, however sublimated. And because McDonald's is a thoroughly respectable family restaurant, grown-ups can go there and satisfy their juvenile cravings with socially acceptable thrills and no one will be the wiser.

At the same time that McDonald's can be seen as a substitute for home and love, it is also an impersonal, no-involvement experience. Millie's Diner with its camaraderie and cooked-to-order service demands a certain confidence and aplomb of its customers. Unless you're a regular, the individual diner or restaurant is an unknown experience. You don't know the menu, you might not be comfortable with whoever takes your order, and you must maintain some sort of stance or attitude while waiting for your meal. McDonald's doesn't require that the customer demonstrate any individuality or "perform" in any way—it's all very cut and dried.

Cut and dried like a baby's formula. Many people confess that they would just as soon take a pill as fool with a meal. Eating is a nuisance need, not a savored experience. So they go off to McDonald's for a formula fuel stop.

What should we do about the gap between ideal nutrition and McDonald's food? *Should* we do anything about it? Do we try to get McDonald's to change those phenomenally successful foods, or do we tell people to stay away from the foods they like? What would happen if restaurants as efficient and appealing as McDonald's served imaginative foods that were also possessed of noble nutritional qualities? My own experience with restaurants that serve "health" or "healthful" foods has been a mixture of pleasure and disappointment. Many of the salad, soup and sandwich restaurants that have sprung up in New York City in recent years have delightful menus and promise delicious and healthful eating. But frequently the quality varies drastically from visit to visit, the prices are high, the hygiene leaves something to be desired, service is poor and slow, and you just plain don't get your money's worth. That type of management will never produce good-nutrition restaurants that can compete with McDonald's.

At the same time, we certainly can't expect carefully managed establishments that feed for profit to endanger their fiscal health with attempts to sell unpopular good-nutrition food. But we do have requirements for anti-pollution devices on automobiles, and safety standards for children's toys. Should we have nutrition standards for restaurants? Why not? And why not subsidies or tax incentives for restaurants that conform to especially ambitious and innovative standards for good nutrition in fast food? Even small changes would help. McDonald's could surely offer raw vegetable relishes as an alternative to french fries, and whole fresh fruit as a dessert choice. Non-fried chicken burgers are another possibility.

Convincing the public may be another matter. Instead of fighting Mc-Donald's, nutritionists should perhaps be taking lessons from them. All of the skills of advertising and marketing need to be applied to nutrition crusades. We need to spend millions, even billions, of dollars developing creative communication programs and innovative good-nutrition food merchandising. It could be done, if anyone really wanted to do it. Not by preaching, but by providing. Good food can't be a moral good-for-you issue; it must be made accessible and exciting. We'll probably have to create nutritionally ideal fast-food meals, sell them in the guise of exciting fun foods, and keep the nutritional benefits a secret. It's easier to sell fun than it is to sell nutrition.

Notes

[1]"The Burger That Conquered the Country," *Time*, September 17, 1973.

[2]For an explanation of RDA's and U.S. RDA's, see *Nutritive Value of Foods*, Home and Garden Bulletin No. 72 (Washington, D.C., Agricultural Research Service, United States Department of Agriculture, 1977). A copy may be ordered for $1.05 from the Superintendant of Documents, U.S. Government Printing Office, Washington, D.C. 20402.

[3]For discussion of nutrition and fast food, see: "The American Dietetic Association Position Paper on nutrition education and fast food service," *Journal of The American Dietetic Association* 65:54, 1974.

David L. Call, "The Changing Food Market—Nutrition in a Revolution," *Journal of The American Dietetic Association* 60:384, 1972.

Coleen P. Greecher and Barbara Shannon, "Impact of fast food meals on nutrient intake of two groups," *Journal of The American Dietetic Association* 70:368, 1977.

[4]*Dietary Goals for the United States* is available from the Superintendant of Documents, U.S. Government Printing Office, Washington, D.C. 20402. Substantial excerpts from the original report are reprinted in *Nutrition Today*. September/October, 1977. The Senate Select Committee on Nutrition and Human Needs was disbanded on December 31, 1977, after it revised the *Dietary Goals* in an effort to "update, clarify and elaborate" upon the first edition. See *Nutrition Today*, January/February, 1978.

[5]"Forum's Forum on Dietary Goals for the United States," in *JC Penney Forum*, Fall/Winter, 1977.

Table I
NUTRITIVE VALUE OF McDONALD'S FOODS

Food (1 serving)	Weight (g)	Calories	Protein (g)	Fat (g)	Carbohydrate (g)	Calcium (mg)	Sodium (mg)	Iron (mg)	Vitamin A (I.U.)	Niacin (mg)	Vitamin C (mg)
Egg McMuffin	127	312	18	11	35	167	1130	2.5	460	3.1	4
Hamburger	97	249	13	10	28	53	542	2.6	165	3.7	4
Cheeseburger	111	309	16	14	30	137	821	2.3	317	3.9	4
Quarter-pound hamburger	157	414	27	19	33	66	690	3.8	263	6.5	3
Quarter-pound cheeseburger	186	521	31	28	36	234	1173	3.9	395	7.2	5
Big Mac	183	557	26	32	41	161	1064	3.8	213	6.3	5
Fillet of fish	136	406	15	22	37	94	759	1.6	85	2.9	2
French fries	69	215	3	10	28	9	117	.4	0	2.4	9
Apple pie	84	265	2	15	30	16	395	.6	0	.3	2
Chocolate shake	269	317	11	7	52	408	296	.8	0	.4	0
Vanilla shake	274	322	11	7	55	355	274	.3	0	.4	0
Strawberry shake	267	315	10	8	50	362	267	.3	0	.6	0

Figures from RCALL Food Selection Guide, Computer Assisted Instructional Program in Family Resources, Extension Division, Virginia Polytechnic Institute and State University Publication 642, Revised 1975.

Table II
NUTRITIVE VALUE OF SELECTED McDONALD'S AND NON-McDONALD'S FOODS

Food (1 serving)	Weight (g)	Calories	Protein (g)	Fat (g)	Carbohydrate (g)	Calcium (mg)	Sodium (mg)	Iron (mg)	Vitamin A (I.U.)	Niacin (mg)	Vitamin C (mg)
McDonald's quarter-pound hamburger	157	414	27	19	33	66	690	3.8	263	6.5	3
Quarter-pound hamburger with roll and 1/8 teaspoon salt	125	305	27	12	21	40	549	3.8	20	6.0	0
McDonald's french fries	69	215	3	10	28	9	117	.4	0	2.4	9
Baked potato with 1 tablespoon margarine and 1/8 teaspoon salt	216	247	4	12	33	17	436	1.1	470	2.7	31
McDonald's apple pie	84	265	2	15	30	16	395	.6	0	.3	2
Fresh apple (3'')	180	96	0	1	24	12	2	.5	150	.2	7
McDonald's vanilla shake	274	322	11	7	55	355	274	.3	0	.4	0
8 ounces skim milk	245	88	9	0	12	296	127	.1	10	.2	2

Figures from:

RCALL Food Selection Guide, Computer Assisted Instructional Program in Family Resources, Extension Division, Virginia Polytechnic Institute and State University Publication 642. Revised 1975.

Catherine F. Adams, Nutritive Value of American Foods In Common Units, Agriculture Handbook No. 456, Washington, D.C., Agricultural Research Service, United States Department of Agriculture, 1975.

Barbara Kraus, The Dictionary of Sodium, Fats, and Cholesterol, New York, Grosset and Dunlap, 1974.

Table III
PERCENTAGES OF ONE-THIRD
U.S. RDA'S PER McDONALD'S MEAL

	Hamburger French fries Soft drink	Hamburger French fries Strawberry shake
Protein	82	138
Calcium	20	122
Iron	59	69
Vitamin A	3	24
Thiamine	64	84
Riboflavin	56	154
Niacin	75	90
Vitamin C	80	80

Figures from Rebecca M. Mullis, **Foods and Nutrition Newsletter** No. 16, August, 1977, Co-operative Extension Service, Virginia Polytechnic Institute and State University.

Table IV
NUTRITIVE VALUE OF A McDONALD'S MEAL AND
A "MORAL" MEAL OF THE SAME BASIC FOODS

	McDonald's Quarter-pound burger French fries Apple pie Vanilla shake	"Moral" Quarter-pound burger Baked potato Fresh apple Skim milk
Weight	584 g	766 g
Calories	1216	736
Protein	43 g	40 g
Fat	51 g	25 g
Carbohydrate	146 g	90 g
Calcium	446 mg	365 mg
Sodium	1476 mg	1114 mg
Iron	5 mg	6 mg
Vitamin A	263 I.U.	650 I.U
Niacin	7 mg	9 mg
Vitamin C	14 mg	40 mg

Based on figures from:

RCALL Food Selection Guide, Computer Assisted Instructional Program in Family Resources, Extension Division, Virginia Polytechnic Institute and State University Publication 642, Revised 1975.

Catherine F. Adams, **Nutritive Value of American Foods in Common Units,** Agriculture Handbook No. 456, Washington, D.C., Agricultural Research Service, United States Department of Agriculture, 1975.

Barbara Kraus, **The Dictionary of Sodium, Fats, and Cholesterol,** New York, Grosset and Dunlap, 1974.

Hamburger University

by Sarah Sanderson King and Michael J. King

The ubiguitous nature of McDonald's restaurants has made the Golden Arches synonymous in the minds of some with the "Red-White-and-Blue," "American way," "All-American,"[1] Mom and apple pie approach to patriotism. As of March 1977, there were 4,200 world-wide stores—3,700 in the United States and 500 in 24 countries and territories outside the U.S.[2] including Canada, Japan, Australia, Germany, New Zealand, Okinawa, and the largest McDonald's in the world in Guam. During the second quarter of 1976, the Smithsonian Institution in Washington, D.C., opened its Bicentennial exhibition, "A Nation of Nations," with a McDonald's outdoor sign in Japanese and a multi-product illustrated menu in German to reflect American activity outside the United States.[3] During our study, one astute customer, when asked if he would participate in a survey about McDonald's, replied, "It is about time someone did a survey *about* McDonald's; it is becoming so much a part of our culture, a standard, that we should look at it."

This paper will investigate this phenonmenon of a segment of our culture—McDonald's—which is very American in its attempt to provide the same services for all people in the same way. The hypothesis was that just as McDonald's attempts to create an image distinctly MCDONALD'S through standardization of its food, packaging, preparation techniques, and computerized equipment, so does McDonald's hope to augment and polish this image by creating a working staff through training that will be the same throughout the world. Questions included—"What is the image McDonald's hopes to convey to the public?," "How is it polished?," and "What is the rate of success at determined by McDonald's personnel and customers?"

Methodology for this study included—

A. field research in at least three geographical locations to determine the extent of the standardization of the training—Illinois (home state of Corporate Headquarters at Oak Brook and of Hamburger University at Elk Grove); Hawaii (about as far geographically as you can get from Corporate Headquarters and still be in the United States); and West Virginia (the only franchise operations in our survey, not as far as Hawaii but still some distance both geographically and culturally from Corporate Headquarters).

94

B. a survey of the McDonald's image as perceived by McDonald's manager, employees, and the public. Three different McDonald's sites in each state were chosen for the survey—Ala Moana Center, Kailua, and Waianae in Hawaii; Aurora, Oak Brook, and Evanston in Illinois; University and Downtown Morgantown and Fairmont in West Virginia. Fifty customers at each site, plus all working employees and managers were asked questions 1 and 2—

1. "What is your image of McDonald's?" (or if an employee or manager, "What image do you believe McDonald's is trying to convey to the public?")
2. "What factors have contributed to this image? (or "Where did/do you get your image?" or "Why do you have this image?")

Customers only were asked question 3.

3. "How many times a week do you eat at McDonald's?"

We will discuss the history of Hamburger University; the McDonald's formula for success which is also, in part, the preferred McDonald's image; the training programs of the three regions and stores which we visited; and the image of McDonald's as perceived by managers, employees, and customers plus the factors perceived by them as contributing to this image.

Corporate Headquarters or "Hamburger Central" rises eight stories high, overlooking the suburb of Oak Brook, west of Chicago. From Corporate Headquarters all business flows—including the negotiations with franchise operations (licensees); the decisions about new food products to be tested in McDonald's stores (such as chicken, salads, saimin, onion rings) and new products on the open market which are McDonald's oriented (Remco McDonaldland Playset and Character Toys and Fieldcrest McDonaldland sheets, pillow cases, blankets, rugs, bedspreads, and towels); the rigid specifications for McDonald's products; the field supervisors who check on the adherence of stores to McDonald's fast-food policies of QSE and V (Quality, Service, Cleanliness, and Value); the training materials for Hamburger University and all hardware and corporate-made software available to corporate and licensee stores for in-house training.

Ray Kroc, founder of the McDonald's chain as we know it now, predicted in 1955 that the "Hamburger Science" of McDonald's was a system that could be reduced to a formula that would govern all aspects of the operation and could be taught to unskilled people with impunity. In 1961 the codification of institutional training for managers was taking place in the basement of a McDonald's store in Elm Grove. From the first graduating class of three students, the enterprise grew and as more Bachelor degrees in Hamburgerology were awarded, a Dean and expansive curriculum became part of the enterprise. The first McDonald's training film was made and distributed in 1964 which represented a new and serious step toward the utilization of audio-visual aids, resulting in an ever-increasing library of videotapes, films, and slides for training purposes.

By July of 1966 Hamburger University had graduated over 1,400 students and was introducing the new and improved basic operations manual. It was apparent that a new facility was needed. In 1968 the new look in the corporate logo with its modernized Golden Arches was "run up the flagpole in front of the new half million dollar building for Hamburger University in Elk Grove, a self-contained school with the latest in innovations of education and training."[4]

At present, Dave Gerfen,[5] Dean, operates the training program with a teaching staff of eleven, supplemented by supervisors and field consultants of McDonald's stores and a communication consultant, a Ph.D. from University of Wisconsin. The main purpose is to conduct an Advanced Operations Course for owner-operators of McDonald's stores who first spend two weeks working in a McDonald's store, and for managers, in both corporate and franchise stores, who have spent a minimum of four to six months in their managerial positions.

We visited Hamburger University on February 25, 1977, a comfortable ivy-covered white building with huge oriental wooden doors carved with multiple Golden Arches. Arriving at the same time were the members of the new class, each carrying a copy of the corporate bible, the approximately 300 page loose-leaf binder notebook[6] that would carry them through cold drinks, fries, controls, refrigeration, personnel, maintenance, marketing, shakes, stat report, store control, grill-toasters, training. The class we visited had 104 registered, 60 percent of whom were licensees and 40 percent company. By the time these persons get this far in the McDonald heirarchy, they are well steeped in Hamburger Science and need only the fine tuning and polishing that the University can give to them. They are there for the finer points of technology and management training.[7] We sat in a classroom with 60 students for a lecture covering the Multiplex Drink System, one of which was resting on a table in the front of the room. The instructor, who not only knew all the students by name but seemed to know the type of machine and equipment they had or would have in their stores, talked enthusiastically about the parts of the machine. His lecture/discussion was punctuated by the use of slides projected by rear-screen projection on two huge screens to the right front of the room and by the utilization of an overhead projector to the left front of the room. If he had wished, he could have utilized closed circuit video on the four TV monitors in the room, written on the blackboards in back, or referred to the model. This course is an intensive two weeks, culminating in a graduation ceremony with the awarding of a Bachelors degree in Hamburgerology.

Hamburger University is not the total answer to McDonald's attempts to "make its licensees [at least 70 percent of the stores], restaurant managers, and burger slingers seem as standardized as its machines and cuisines."[8] From Corporate Headquarters come the training materials and from Hamburger University come the trained personnel to utilize these materials in basic operations training (BOC) in their home stores. Each store is equipped with a LaBelle, cartridges of training films, and rear-projection screen which can be utilized by store personnel on breaks or for in-store training sessions. In addition each store has a Training Coordinator or the equivalent for Crew Training. Each region has its own Training Coordinator and offers training programs as well as individual guidance for each store in the region.

Although the same basic principles of equipment, products, and procedures are contained in all training materials, the three areas we visited (Illinois, Hawaii, and West Virginia) employed different methods in "getting the material into the heads of the trainees."[9] Each, however, adhered to the McDonald's formula originally codified by Ray Kroc into a kind of fast-food religion—QSC, Quality, Service, and Cleanliness. "V" for value was added to the formula approximately one year ago. "It is equivalent," said Denis Detzel, "to a democratic distribution system and is price-related—'how much of this can we do for how many people.' " Quality, or "good food," as many of our interviewees put it, is guaranteed by the rigid specifications for products, the computerized equipment, and the holding time for products after which they cannot be sold to the public—for example, 7 minutes for fries, 10 minutes for hamburgers, 30 minutes for coffee, 90 minutes for pies. One of the manuals dictates—"Talk more in terms of quality, rather than yields. The employee should be concerned with customer satisfaction." The abundance of large colorful trash cans in McDonald's stores and in the parking lots attests to the dedication for cleanliness. There is always at least one person assigned to keeping the dining area tidy, the bathrooms clean, the spills mopped up, etc. There is much emphasis on service, with McDonald's six window steps for serving customers starting with "Greet the customer (eye contact)," and ending with "Thank the customer."

Training for the Illinois stores follows what might be called the "traditional" or "solid corporate based" approach. According to Ron Maurice,[10] Regional Manager for the three stores we surveyed, there is little deviation or addition in training materials from that which comes from Corporate Headquarters. The "buddy system" is the strategy used to introduce the new employees to the store and to the different routines they will have to follow in learning to work at each station (fries, grill, window, etc.) in the store. The employee is teamed with the manager or a management-team member. Each store has one or two people in charge of training and updates information once a quarter for all employees. The principle, says Maurice is, "sticking to basic concepts and doing them well."

Patrick Kahler,[11] General Manager of McDonald's in Hawaii, utilizes all the training films sent from Chicago and adheres to the standard operating procedures of the McDonald's dictum. The training program, however, is geared for making it easier for "trainers in Hawaii to train" and "trainees to learn."[12] A hefty training manual, similar in format to the Hamburger University Notebook, has been prepared for Crew Training.

Our approach to Crew Training is a simple consistent "Modular Training" program. It is a step-by-step approach segmented into 6 basic categories.

I. INTRODUCTION TO STATION (conducted on the floor)
II. STATION INFORMATION (conducted in the classroom)
III. ON-THE-JOB TRAINING (on the floor with Crew Trainer)
IV. FIRST MANAGEMENT OBSERVATION CHECKLIST (conducted on the floor by Crew Trainer)
V. WORK EXPERIENCE (experience necessary to meet qualifications)

VI.SECOND MANAGEMENT OBSERVATION CHECKLIST (conducted on the floor by management)[13]

Dwain Thompson, Training Coordinator, saw Hawaii's isolation as an advantage for being able to follow-up and control the results of the training by
organizing and spelling it out to the letter.

The West Virginia stores are part of the "Pennsylvania region," a conglomerate of 260 stores with an anticipated 300 by the year's end. Seventeen or 7
percent of the 260 stores are company owned. (The overall policy of Corporate
Headquarters is to keep approximately 30 percent of the stores company
owned in which to try out new products, procedures, etc.) There is multi-level
training program in this region.[14] The objective is to create "behavioral change
back at the store." There is (1) a quarterly one-week training program for operators to upgrade and refresh owner operations; (2) middle-management seminars; and (3) seminars for store managers conducted two weeks monthly called
F.M.E. (Fundamental Management Effectiveness) for the purpose of upgrad-
ing the Basic Operations Course. Programmed note-taking formulas are utilized. The F.M.E. seminars are for those managers or operators who have
attended Hamburger University and want a brief "brush-up" course or for
those who are hoping to go to Hamburger University at some later date but desire more immediate refinement or training.

A. Baker Nicholson and Peter Pifer,[15] the owner/operators of the three
stores we visited in West Virginia, have, like Hawaii, gone beyond the required
in their local training programs. As the only licensees in our survey, we were
interested in their degree of proprietorship and pride in their stores and in
being part of McDonald's (not too dissimilar from that of Pat Kahler in
Hawaii). Two supplemental positions have been added to the West Virginia
stores by their owner/operators—a Training and Personnel Director (Ed
Keffer, a former Burger King man) and a Promotions and Community Relations Man (Ed Shockey, a retired Assistant Athletic Director at West Virginia
University). The Training Director made a Crew Trainer out of one crew person
from each of the three stores. The team would concentrate on a certain area of
training, moving each three days to a new store. This teamwork went on for six
months and morale was high. The Fairmont store has the lowest turn-over that
we know for any McDonald's—30 percent.

The employees of all stores agreed that their image of McDonald's came
from "training," "experience," "management," "other employees," and "promotions" in advertising. Managers added "company standards" as a
significant source. For a more comprehensive breakdown of all areas cited as
the source of image of McDonald's for employees and managers, see Table 1.

Of the 27 Managers and 89 employees surveyed, 35 percent were men and
65 percent were women. There was no attempt made to get a balanced number
of male/female respondents for managers, employees, or customers. They surveys were conducted both at breakfast and lunch periods with whoever hap-
pened to be present. The ages of employees and managers in West Virginia and
Hawaii were between 17 and 34; in Illinois, the range was from 16 years (13
percent) to 55-plus (7 percent) with one employee being 71.

In verbalizing what they believed to be the image that McDonald's was trying to convey to the public, both the employees and the managers followed the party line of QSC and V. High precedence was given also to "fast," and "friendly," "family," and the "reactions of the customers" which would shape the reaction of the employees to them. "Fast" did not rate as high in Hawaii as it did in Illinois and West Virginia but this may be because speed is not a value or premium in Hawaii as it is on the Mainland. The only "stand-up" McDonald's in our survey (the Evanston store) had the highest premium for "fast" with 7 out of 10 employees mentioning it as part of their image. See Table 2 for those elements of the image which were included by at least 15 percent of the employees and managers surveyed, with percentages by location.

Of the 450 customers surveyed, 47 percent were men and 53 percent were women. (See Table 3.) In answer to the question, "How many times a week do you eat at McDonald's?," the most frequent response in all three states was 2-3 times a week. Hawaii had the highest percentage of customers reporting to eat at McDonald's seven or more times a week. The highest single response was 20-25 times per week (a female in Fairmont, W. Va., between the ages of 35-44 whose children liked McDonald's) and the lowest was zero (a family visiting Illinois from Holly Springs, Missouri where there is no McDonald's).

The response from customers was significantly higher for the formula than for other areas with the exception of the naming of products (such as "Big Mac," "apple pie," "coffee") and of "fast." "Value" was included by only 7 percent of those surveyed but "inexpensive" was included by 15 percent. Since quality was a major factor in the image building, we reasoned the value ("your money's worth") and inexpensive (not extravagant, "cheap") might be synonymous in the minds of the respondents. Only 5 of the 100 respondents who listed either "value" or "inexpensive" duplicated themselves by saying both. As with the employees and managers, "fast" received its highest rating at the "stand-up" McDonald's in Evanston, although Ala Moana in Hawaii and the Fairmont and University stores were only a few customers less. "Cleanliness" as an image factor was highest at the Hawaii and W. Va. stores, "Convenience" seemed to be an important part of the image for customers in Hawaii and W. Va. but not in Illinois perhaps because fast food restaurants and drive-ins are not as prevalent in Hawaii and W. Va. as in Illinois. "Place to eat" (including "good place to eat," "another place to eat") seemed to be a popular phrase in both Illinois and West Virginia but almost non-existent in Hawaii. See Table 4 for those elements of the image which were included by at least 10 percent of the customers surveyed, with percentages by state. The two percent who perceived McDonald's as "All-American" were among the most enthusiastic of respondents.

According to the percentages for QSC and V (if you put value and inexpensive together), the Ala Moana store in Hawaii and the Fairmont store in West Virginia are perceived by customers as being most exemplary of the party line. What do we know about the customer who believes that the image of McDonald's is QSC and V? This customer (see Table 5) would have a nearly equal chance of being either male or female, of being in the 20-34 age group, and of being a customer at McDonald's 2 to 3 times a week.

The customers reported that they formed their image of McDonald's first (66 percent) from their experience in the stores and second (31 percent) from promotions—television and radio commercials. Employees and managers also found promotions a significant source for their images.

In summary there is an attempt by McDonald's to provide the same kind of service to the public at all of its outlets—be they company or franchise operations. Although the organization may be a carefully controlled one even to the location of the stores, the exterior and interior design, the computerized operations for handling food, and the rigid specifications for food and supplies, the normally uncontrollable factor—human beings—is involved also. This humanistic element cannot be mechanized, only standardized. Through a broad range of training programs which includes Crew Training and Basic Operations Course at the store level, F.M.E. and management-level courses at the regional level, Advanced Operations Course at Hamburger University, McDonald's hopes to develop the most important resource—the managers and employees who represent McDonald's to the public. From Hamburger University come the trained owners/operators and managers and from Corporate Headquarters come the training materials—the basic operations manuals, the videotapes, the film cartridges for the LaBelle. Of the three geographic areas listed, Illinois has the most traditional training program; Hawaii has a highly innovative, locally oriented state-wide training program supplemented with its own manuals and materials; and West Virginia has gone beyond the minimum also by hiring a Training and Personnel Director who has an innovative approach to structuring training.

According to the managers and employees, McDonald's hopes to present an image of quality, service, cleanliness, and value to the public. According to customer responses, McDonald's is perceived as having an image that does include Q,S,C, and V—at least in Illinois, Hawaii, and West Virginia. As the results of our survey would indicate, McDonald's is succeeding more in Hawaii and in West Virginia than in Illinois. This may be due to that extra attention paid to training which goes beyond the minimum required or suggested by Corporate Headquarters.

Through a desire for equality of service to all, the equating of the Golden Arches with the democratic American way becomes reinforced in the minds of some. But for the majority, the equation is $M = Q + S + C + V$.

Table I

Factors Contributing to Image of McDonald:
Responses of Employees and Managers

		Training	Experience	Management	Employees	Promotions	Cus. Reaction	Attitude	Company Standards	Exp. / Customer
		Employees								
Hawaii	%	28	55	31	24	31	3	10	0	0
Illinois	%	7	43	33	20	37	17	10	13	7
West Virginia	%	33	33	33	30	40	17	17	10	10
Total: Employees	%	22	44	33	25	36	12	12	8	6
		Managers								
Hawaii	%	25	50	25	13	38	13	13	13	0
Illinois	%	10	30	20	30	20	20	20	40	0
West Virginia	%	22	11	33	33	22	11	11	44	0
Total: Managers	%	19	30	26	26	26	15	15	33	0

Table II

Image of McDonald's:
Responses of Employees and Managers

		Quality	Service	Cleanliness	Fast	Value	Friendly	Family	Kids	Cus. Reaction
Employees										
Hawaii	%	55	55	34	21	3	24	10	3	14
Illinois	%	60	57	30	50	33	20	20	10	13
West Virginia	%	47	50	53	40	7	33	13	3	17
Total: Employees	%	54	54	39	37	15	26	15	6	15
Managers										
Hawaii	%	60	60	50	25	13	13	25	13	0
Illinois	%	80	80	50	60	40	10	30	20	10
West Virginia	%	56	67	89	22	11	33	22	11	22
Total: Managers	%	67	70	63	37	22	19	22	15	15

Table III

NUMBER AND SEX OF SURVEY RESPONDENTS

	Hawaii Sex			Illinois Sex			West Virginia Sex			Total Sex		
	No.	M	F	No.	M	F	No.	M	F	No.	M	F
Customers	150	47%	53%	150	53%	47%	150	40%	60%	450	47%	53%
Managers	8	38%	62%	10	60%	40%	9	44%	56%	27	48%	52%
Employees	29	21%	79½	30	30%	70%	30	43%	57%	89	31%	69%
TOTAL	187	43%	57%	190	49%	51%	189	41%	59%	566	44%	56%

Table IV

Image of McDonald's
Customer Responses

		Quality	Service	Cleanliness	Fast	Value	Products	Inexpensive	Atmosphere	Convenient	Place
Hawaii	%	36	24	30	29	8	25	19	7	16	1
Illinois	%	23	16	11	33	5	25	16	9	7	10
West Virginia	%	25	25	21	36	8	36	11	15	16	18
Customers	%	28	22	21	32	7	29	15	10	13	10

Table V
Customer Profiles for Responses—QSC, V, and I
(Quality, Service, Cleanliness, Value and Inexpensive)

	Age							Times a Week/Eat at McDonald's						
	Under 13	13-16	17-19	20-34	35-44	45-54	55/over	Less/1 a month	Once a month	Twice a month	1 a week	2-3 a week	4-6 a week	7/over
Quality														
(50%) Male	2%	11%	13%	41%	3%	17%	14%	0%	3%	13%	14%	42%	14%	14%
(50%) Female	5	14	16	33	10	14	8	2	11	13	22	30	10	13
Total	3	13	14	37	6	16	11	1	7	13	18	36	12	13
Service														
(48%) Male	0	0	15	43	17	17	9	6	4	8	11	40	21	11
(52%) Female	2	8	26	30	10	14	10	2	10	10	30	26	14	8
Total	1	4	21	36	13	15	9	4	7	8	21	33	18	9
Cleanliness														
(45%) Male	0	5	12	32	15	15	22	10	0	5	12	34	17	22
(55%) Female	2	8	12	39	12	16	12	4	5	6	31	30	10	12
Total	0	7	12	36	13	15	16	7	5	5	23	32	13	15
Value														
(50%) Male	0	6	0	44	6	19	25	6	0	0	13	38	25	19
(50%) Female	6	0	19	44	6	25	0	0	6	13	19	63	0	0
Total	3	3	9	44	6	22	13	3	3	6	16	50	13	9
Inexpensive														
(47%) Male	0	3	19	59	6	3	9	3	0	19	6	50	13	9
(53%) Female	0	14	14	44	17	8	3	3	14	11	25	28	6	14
Total	0	9	16	51	12	6	6	3	7	15	16	38	9	12

Notes

This paper was prepared to be read at the Popular Culture Convention, Baltimore, Maryland, April 28-30, 1977. Without the cooperation of McDonald's Corporate Headquarters this study would not have been possible. We would like to thank the following people for their assistance—Denis Detzel, Director, Corporate Social Policy; Barbara Ford, Corporate Communications Supervisor; Cindy Williams, Administrative Coordinator, Corporate Social Policy; Patrick Kahler, General Manager of McDonald's Hawaii; A. Baker Nicholson and Peter Pifer, Owner/Operators of McDonald's, Morgantown and Fairmont, West Virginia; Ron Maurice, Regional Manager, Illinois; Steve Nicholas, Regional Manager, and Bob Silzle, Training Coordinator, Cherry Hill, N.J.; Dave Gerfen, Dean, Hamburger University; and the employees, managers, and customers who so willingly took part in our survey. We want to thank Laurie Sanderson, Linda Sanderson, Cathy Pace, and D. Louise Fukano who helped us conduct interviews.

[1]Comments made by interviewees during the survey about McDonald's. Hereafter unless such comments in quotations are identified otherwise, they are from the survey.

[2]Interview with Denis Detzel, Corporate Social Policy, McDonald's Corporate Headquarters, McDonald Plaza, March 10, 1977. Further information supplied by Cindy Williams, Secretary, Corporate Social Policy Office.

[3]McDonald's Corporation, *Report for the Second Quarter for the Six Months Ended June 30, 1976*, p. 1.

[4]*McDonald's Twentieth Anniversary, April 1975*, McDonald's System, Inc., pp. 24-25.

[5]Interview with Dave Gerfen, Dean, Hamburger University, Elk Grove, February 25, 1977.

[6]"Hamburger University Notebook," loose-leaf binder with training modules. The particular notebook we had to study was from Advanced Operations Class, #210, November 10 through November 20, 1975.

[7]"Making the Grade at Hamburger U," *Newsweek*, September 25, 1972, p. 78.

[8]"The Burger That Conquered the Country," *Time*, September 17, 1973, p. 84.

[9]Telephone interview with Bob Silzle, Training Coordinator, Cherry Hill, New Jersey.

[10]Telephone conversation with Ron Maurice, Regional Manager, McDonald's, Illinois, April 4, 1977.

[11]Interviews with Patrick Kahler, General Manager of McDonald's in Hawaii, December 14, 1976 and December 23, 1976. McDonald's in Hawaii (26 stores) has only one franchise store and it is located Kona on the Big Island.

[12]Telephone conversation with Dwain Thompson, Training Coordinator for Hawaii, December 27, 1976.

[13]"McDonald's Hawaii: Training Manual," loose-leaf binder with training modules, p. MT-1. The particular notebook we had to study was up-to-date for December 1976.

[14]Telephone interview with Steve Nicholas, Regional Manager, and Bob Silzle, Training Coordinator, Pennsylvania Region, Cherry Hill, New Jersey.

[15]Interviews with A. Baker Nicholson, owner/operator of three McDonald's sites in Morgantown and Fairmont, March 22, 1977. (Peter Pifer was not in town at the time of our visit. We had, however, spoken with him and Mr. Nicholson in January 1977.)

Empires of Popular Culture:
McDonald's and Disney

by Margaret J. King

Beginning in 1955, McDonald's family restaurants have grown at a breath-taking pace and have emerged as a cultural institution in American life. McDonald's holds the first-ranking position among "fast food" outlets, through a vast network of roadside, suburban, and urban establishments under the direction of the central organization. But McDonald's has also crea-ted a realm of order—a total environment—and a small-scale standard of life at marked variance with what many have seen as the decline of modern (Ameri-can) civilization, especially in such respects as "urban decay." Although Mc-Donald's itself is often cited as a contributing cause or prominent symptom of this decline of the West, it has added much to a resurgence of certain values felt to be disappearing from social relations.

In any discussion of popular culture empires, an archetypal case in point for logical comparison is the Disney Corporation. The empires of McDonald's hamburgers and the Walt Disney Corporation—particularly in the aspect of the Disney theme parks—have been unavoidable features of everyday life in America since the mid-1950's. Both were founded by a self-made man with a flair for business, creativity, and innovation. Both made innovative use of the concept of "place," supported by a strong basis in fantasy and various types of need and wish-fulfillment. Both grew out of an ideology which is easily identi-fiable with a middle-class ethos. Both have applied unique and distinctive solu-tions to various problems and concerns in American life having to do with family life, television, leisure, mobility, and collectively-felt needs for cleanliness, order, safety, relaxation (accompanied by mild stimulation), effi-ciency, standardization, patriotism, and a particular type of uniform beauty and stability.

Walt Disney was a product of the Protestant Ethic. His empire of inter-locking systems of films, television, and amusement centers was built on novel concepts setting it apart from others by its imaginative premises. Tireless energy and an upbringing in the cradle of Americanism, the Midwest, made Disney what his biographer Richard Schickel calls an original American type—"the midwestern go-getter."[1]

Popular journalism usually based its acolades of his work on his Horatio Alger career, which proved the validity of the American Dream, as a symbol of the American middle-class and its aspirations, including political conservatism. Disney was a master of the powers of positive thinking and of an optimistic attitude toward his "guests" (as visitors to the theme parks are called). These traits tend to create a stance of assertive good will about the state of the nation as the land of economic opportunity in the form of free enterprise, which emerges as patriotism. Disney worked as filmmaker for the American cause with the Department of Defense during World War II, and had congenial relations with the power elite as a whole.

Disney was a figure of public influence and achievement far exceeding the usual parameters of "business." His enterprise created far more an institution of popular culture than a business in its effect on public behavior and the quality of American life through the beliefs and values propagated—consciously as well as sub-consciously—by the unique "medium" of film and theme park.

These beliefs include those of pragmatisim, scientism, collectivism, consumerism, the "social ethic," specialization, centralization, and a wholehearted dedication to technological progress—as an extension of "Yankee ingenuity" of an earlier American era—to solve the problems of modern living and to create new styles of life. But overshadowing this list is a firm commitment to the idea of an energetic individualistic leader with a vision, able to lead and to develop the talents of others in a close-knit family-style business team of the antiquarian pre-corporate sort. And to guarantee the perpetuation of the Disney ethos ad infinitum even beyond its studio tradition, Disney enterprises founded a conservatory, the University of Disneyland.

Disney demanded full control and authority over his business, insisting that distributors or franchisers of the company name comply closely with a strict code of business ethics to incorporate into the esprit de corps of the organization. Self-determination, made possible because there was no hindrance from "outside" stockholders, for example, is what allowed Disney to take chances in trying out new, innovative, controversial strategies.

* * * *

McDonald's impact, since 1972, has been as profound. It has not been just a multi-million dollar business but a billion dollar-a-year enterprise; it is the largest meal-serving company in the country, just surpassing the U.S. Army in 1972,[2] and more recently going far beyond that record. On the average, one new outlet is built every day somewhere in the U.S. or abroad in some 22 countries. This year McDonald's marquees announce "24 Billion Sold."

Various mind-boggling statistical images have been concocted to convey a sense of the volume of McDonald's business to the present: the millennia required for one person to consume the number of hamburgers sold at McDonald's since its first sale (114); the number of cattle sacrificed to the cause (enough to fill an area larger than Greater London); the size of a pyramid constructed of all hamburgers sold (783 times larger than Snefru's).[3] These gargantuan images have since increased in magnitude and have every reason to continue to rise. Currently at the three-billion dollar stage, the corporation hit the billion dollar mark in its 22nd year of business, compared to the record of

IBM and Xerox, which reached the mark in their 46th and 63rd years of business respectively, and such giants as Polaroid (founded 1937), which have not yet "arrived."[4]

The early 1950's saw an intensification of trends toward blandness in food. Motivation Researcher Ernst Dichter explained this "de-excitation" of food as the result of "the social tensions of our times and the emphasis on the slim appearance."[5] Besides the lowered calories in a whole new breed of diet foods, this "lite" revolution took to "lightening-up" everything, replacing dark syrupy rum with a lighter type; dark beers gave way to light ones (and currently "light" denotes "low calorie" beer); consume replaced fullbodied soup; breads got lighter and lighter, both in weight and in taste. James Vicary, an early "depth researcher" for marketing these foods, saw these innovations in food and drink as food substitutes, promising a "bland new world."[6] Into this stage setting of mild-mannered eating entered McDonald's.

These trends in popular cuisine were consistent with the dominant melting-pot ethic of the time because they facilitated an amalgamation of various ethnic tastes.[7] This was accomplished by the process of elimination—one by one excluding each too-distinctive strong taste group. In casting out pungent seasonings and sauces, McDonald's, among others, created a low-profile food with a penchant for low-level if not nonexistent seasonings geared to the largest common denominator—the bland Northern European palate. (Burger King attempts to refute this taste trend by urging "Have It Your Way.") In this way—Middle-American, middle-class, mid-western—McDonald's brought the "mildness epidemic" to its apex as the great Middle Way of American eating.

Even though McDonald's is clearly identified with its innovative menu items such as the Big Mac, *how* McDonald's produces its food and drink may be even more significant that its food wares. Serving methods (including the design and coordination of kitchen, preparation stations, counter, and seating areas) are just as important to the McDonald's eating "system" as ingredients and their assemblage. McDonald's reputation for maximum efficiency of food preparation is well-deserved. Their commitment to fast—in fact, almost instant—service[8] has made it worthy to lead in fulfilling the promise of fast food for "instant eating" for the millions. In addition to the customary indoor counter, many stores have now installed drive-through windows for highway traffic.

But the concept of fast turnover, the basis of fast food, had to struggle for acceptability. Early in his career, as a salesman for Lily paper cups, Kroc had to go to great lengths to persuade Chicago's busy Walgreen's lunch counter manager that a take-out business for malts (using disposable cups) was a workable concept which could increase sales volume many-fold. Obviously thinking big for the times, Kroc envisaged a system of production and service to support the many-fold multiplication of customers. But Kroc's vision was an idea of the future in the 1920's. In the Walgreen case as well as later with McDonald's, Kroc had to fight to innovate within the atmosphere of more conventional notions of food dispensing based on the leisurely, formal, family sit-down meal; going on a second sense about what would work, Kroc prevailed and Walgreen's take-out business flourished. He recalled: "I was green as grass, but I sensed that the potential for paper cups was great—that I would do well if I could overcome the inertia of tradition. It wasn't easy."[9]

Inspired by F. W. Woolworth's idea of selling commodities at low fixed prices, Kroc applied Henry Ford's lessons of the assembly line and of efficiency studies to "strip down" the process of receiving, cooking, warming or freezing, packing, and serving to their barest possible components. Harvard Business School's Theodore Levitt calls McDonald's procedures a "supreme example"[10] of technological know-how, creating a system so finely-tuned as to use human beings only as part of its machine. The ultimate in "total design," the grills, friers, warmers, freezers, and mixers turn out a uniform product every time in the fewest possible (identical) seconds. To master the "machine," franchise operators attend training courses at McDonald's Hamburger University in Elk Grove, Illinois, to graduate with a "Bachelor of Hamburgerology," and a minor in French Fries (Master's and doctoral degrees are also available). The University stresses a professionalism unique among fast food giants.[11]

The operating motto at McDonald's is "Q, S, C, and V"—"Quality, Service, Cleanliness, and Value," a rough paraphrase of Freud's formula of "cleanliness, beauty, and order" as the basis for civilized life. This high level of asceptic hygiene was unheard of for roadside restaurants, much less for drive-ins. One of the first differences which set even the original McDonald's apart from other drive-in stands was the absence of trash and flies, and the fresh white paper hats of the crew, who cleaned as they worked. "Even the parking lot was kept free of litter."[12]

Order is next to cleanliness in the McDonald's catechism. An assembly-line mentality is absolutely essential to the feeding of millions of daily patrons. Efficiency—cooking each pre-weighed 1.6-ounce hamburger patty exactly the same number of seconds (a signal light on the grill tells the operator when to flip them over); ordering supplies from butcher, baker, and dairy in customized unit sizes and containers; cybernetic french frying, and scientifically-measured doses of ingredients—is the key to the sense of stability and the futuristic style of total control. The exactitude of measurements and ordering for the kitchen is so precise that pilferage can be spotted immediately. Customers' orders are taken down not on a blank order pad but as a series of pencilled check-marks on a permanent list of all possible choices and combinations of choices (recently orders go directly into the register for instant price total). The interior layout of McDonald's outlets, though not identical, has certain similarities in materials, furniture type, and relationship of seating space to ordering counter, kitchen, and restrooms, so that there is assurance of predictability from city to city and state to state. Prices, too, are a known quantity as one moves across country, with no unpleasant price surprises or hidden costs.

Order, predictability, stability—all lend an aura of certainty and a feel of an eternal nature amidst the rapid flux of changes which traumatize people and nations with "Future shock." As much as they are futuristic, McDonald's are a hedge against the disequillibrium of change. And for those who bemoan the disappearance of standards, the rigorousness of McDonald's demands on itself could be an inspiration.

But the notion of Progress is also included in the McDonald's creed. Expansion to and with the west—mainly in California during its boom years in the early 1960's—was also the watershed of McDonald's outsized growth, propelled by its high-powered program of national television advertising, now one of the largest accounts in the industry (number two in 1973).[13]

This outlook of Manifest Destiny, for a corporation which began as a small-time supplier for another business, recreated for big business the classic American success story. A rags-to-riches hero who had a vision of big possibilities through hard work, perseverance, some canny business sense, loyal co-workers who were able to share in his vision, Kroc (and a number of his franchise operators, administrators, and his secretary) became millionaires or multi-millionaires. Among the collection of Kroc's "sayings" are his metaphor for work ("the meat in the hamburger of life");[14] his adage about growth as the ultimate priority in business life ("As long as you're green, you're growing; as soon as you're ripe, you start to rot");[15] his favorite epigram (part of the official decor of every McDonald's office), is that of Calvin Coolidge: "Press on. Nothing in the world can take the place of persistence."

Kroc's allegiance to the values of self-reliance, hard work, fair play, and conscientiousness about service, despite the vast properties of his business, link him closely with a traditional, but moribund, breed of businessman epitomized by Disney: the self-made, rather autocratic, individualist born of hard times, who works himself as hard if not harder than those who work for him, and prides himself on being the guiding conscience, manager, and "idea man" for his company.

Criticism of McDonald's, usually from the ranks of the artistic/intellectual elite, takes the stance basic to other attacks on popular culture in general: hurling first the damning epithet "plastic," followed by a string of invectives against "dehumanization" (read: mass-produced, standardized, assembly-line, etc.). McDonald's without its critics—including those among them who are nevertheless regular patrons—is almost unimaginable.

So heavily is the balance of power weighed against popular culture in intellectual circles as the repository of "bad taste" that for the popular culture researcher to illuminate his subject, even if merely to show its importance as a part of "real" culture, the vow of objectivity is not enough. One must consider McDonald's contribution to the general quality of life in America. To detect positive cultural influences—even a humanism—at McDonald's may at first seem an absurd challenge. But several aspects of its outlook and operations are suggestive; these center on (1) McDonald's concern for the customer; and (2) this concern as worked out within the scheme of large-scale service for its vast clientel.

First, serving large numbers does not automatically make an institution impersonal and alienating; its design and intentions must be weighed against other factors in its social context. It is a triumph for any institution, public or private, to serve crowds. The more and larger the crowds, the more difficult this service becomes, and the more engineering is required. McDonald's is an example of an organization of mammoth scale that has managed to maintain,

to renovate, or to invent, novel ways of dealing with the inherent human problems of socio-engineering in a mass society. The break-through made possible
by McDonald's production-line approach to service is in the way service is
thought of: i.e., not in the conventional terms of discretionary (therefore, uncontrollable) activities on the part of agents for a business, but of the business
itself, emanating from all of its activities as an inevitable outcome. Thus, Mc-
Donald's is both a production and a service business. Instead of being artifi-
cially divided, as these categories are in the taxonomy of business, McDonald's
functions are so closely interrelated as to be indistinguishable. So much is service a product of McDonald's that there is effectively no choice for its workers
about whether or not to deliver clean, quick, courteous service. It is the end-
product of the system—a literal "code" of honor.

Community service is a company-wide policy, extending to each local franchise, which is required to "tithe" a considerable percent of its profits to community causes, from supplying hamburgers to unwed mothers to fund-raising
for muscular dystrophy research.[16] McDonald's size is tempered by the
company's interest in the small out-of-the-way town detached from the super-
highway system and without industrial centers or shopping complexes: "They
are important: to us, the heart of America is still in the boonies."[17]

For a nationwide chain whose *modus operandi* is by any standard of franchise business highly centralized and coordinated, there is considerable
encouragement to "localize" outlets with unique local or regional motifs and
atmosphere in an individual style integrated with that of the larger community
setting. The new Corrales store near Albuquerque is a museum showcase of
local Indian culture, complete with baskets, pottery, blankets, sand paintings,
and Kachina dolls. Campus-related outlets use the school colors and insignia as
the decorating theme as has the DePauw University location in Indiana, with
its overwhelming green and gold atmosphere. One Hawaiian store, in addition
to the "aloha" uniforms unique to the 50th state franchises, has an Oceanic
motif in abstract plexiglass panels in addition to Guaguin prints, and "local
color" paintings and photographs by various state artists.

Menu items may also be tailored for regional tastes. Tokyo's McDonald's
has a thriving market for the tangerine shake, designed both to take advantage
of and to help relieve Japan's large surplus of the fruit. The Filet-O-Fish
"burger" was developed in a Cincinnati outlet in response to demand from the
large Catholic sector there. Some menu items evolved directly from competition: the Big Mac (a double-decker sandwich, the most popular McDonald's
offering) was launched in Pittsburgh in response to the larger-than-life hamburgers at Burger King. In Hawaii, with the most Oriental of all American
subcultures, McDonald's menus cater to the special requirements of the Ja-
panized palate by featuring rice, a noodle soup called "saimin," and another
ethnic favorite, Portuguese sausage. McDonald's has granted exceptions to
their usual prohibition on alcohol to allow German and French McDonald's
their national beverages: beer and wine.[18]

Although the golden arches of McDonald's stores soon became a cultural
icon permanently imprinted on the mind of modern America, Kroc gradually

became concerned about the physical appearance of McDonald's as the original design and color scheme—golden arches surmounting the red and white tile building—became too garish for the more muted community-planning style of suburban taste. Although Kroc was attached to the prototypic structure, he began to realize that design continuity was important to city planners and zoning boards as the chain began to move into California-style shopping centers around the country. In the mid-60's, the low-profile brown brick structure with shingled mansard roof, looking like a tasteful bank or real estate office (except for the reduced logo of arches at the entrance), became the standard model, capable of fitting in quite unobtrusively into any environment. McDonald's faithful critics were suddenly forced to switch the grounds of protest from "grotesque, gaudy, and glaring" to "bland; accommodating; blends into the suburban landscape."

Modifying building appearance to fit community standards is one indication of McDonald's awareness of its place in the public landscape. The corporation has already put into action its crisis program to dispense free coffee and hamburgers in the event of natural disasters (one's "breakfast" after the Holocaust may well be Big Mac). The Kroc Foundation, begun in 1969, supports a wide range of medical research programs and provides funds to increase popular awareness of environmental issues. McDonald's containers and cups bear the legend "Please Put Litter in Its Place." And on the cultural scene, McDonald's sponsors such public service television programming as "Once Upon A Classic." But it is in the day-to-day relations of McDonald's with the public, both as customers and as members of McDonald's communities, that its real impact is felt.

Kroc's response to criticism of McDonald's as super-efficient, de-humanizing, and impersonal is to point to the final ends of his innovative techniques, which is serving the customer—as quickly as possible and with maximum value for the dollar. Realizing that ultimate efficiency would theoretically produce just a row of vending machines, he cautions, "McDonald's is a *people* business, and the smile on that countergirl's face when she takes your order is a vital part of our image."[19] The perpetual courtesy of the staff is a new tradition in the world of fast food, and is thought of by the company as reviving some faded graces in human relations.

Three basic principles emerge from a study of the McDonald regime. First, McDonald's most significant contribution is not only in what it added to American highway and shopping center architecture, nor in its contribution to fast food cuisine such as the Big Mac and nonpareil french fries, but in those institutions which it consciously or inadvertently displaced. First and most obvious of these "traditional" establishments is the local diner or greasy spoon, catering to local trade and, until the nation-wide freeway system pervaded travel patterns in the 50's, also to transients. Second, such "specialty" eateries as the local soda fountain and roadside tavern were in some measure shunted off to the sidelines of development and popular interest by McDonald's convenience, low cost, democratic appeal, and general "classlessness." The homogenized mildness and blandness of McDonald's made it acceptable to a broader range of ages, classes, incomes, and tastes. Part of the often-cited "plastic" quality of McDonald's is exactly, in fact, the key to its success in outranking other food-oriented sociability centers which have more "spice."

Second, its innovations in building design, location, operations, and business-customer relations amount to a complete philosophy of food service and of "eating out," one which has significantly modified public tastes and expectations to the point that McDonald's can be said to have created a new standard against which other centers of eating and socializing are now being judged and are also judging themselves. The current fast-food successes such as Burger King (second in hamburger sales to McDonald's), Burger Chef, and the up-and-coming Wendy's are based on the lessons of McDonald's. In fact, the appeal of Jack-in-the-Box, in their television advertising campaign of 1973, was based on McDonald's success, issuing the challenge, "Watch Out, McDonald's!"

Third, McDonald's outlook and style have repercussions which extend far beyond the limited scope of food consumption to make various statements about the contributions to values, attitudes, and beliefs about life; specifically, about life in America as lived on the "mass" level of concentrated urban culture.

In a recent paper given at the annual Association of American Geographers meetings in Salt Lake City,[20] cultural geographer Yi-Fu Tuan suggested that suburbia now serves as the sacred sector of our lived space, as a modern extension of protected space-use in more traditional cultures. Given the atmosphere of hostility and the threat of crime in the inner city on the one hand, and the sparsely-inhabited countryside and uncivilized wilderness at the other extreme, these sacred areas—those dedicated to child-raising, leisure, cleanliness, the regimen of home improvement, and the status symbols of house, landscaping, and car—represent the zone of care and safety in modern life. This sacred space is protected by the supervision of its "priesthood" of housewives who are its guardians during most waking hours.

The high standards of cleanliness and order at McDonald's restaurants have extended the special character of suburbia into shopping centers and, more recently, into the inner downtown areas, creating an archipelago of islands of security (each flying the McDonald's flag like an embassy of sanctuary) in an insane world of traffic and the fast-moving life of urban America. Through this diffused system of highly recognizable icons and architecture which function as havens of security and certainty under their golden arches, McDonald's has created an entire network of reassuring predictability. It provides a definite "known," for both travelers and for local patrons, in an uncertain cosmos. In fact, more significantly, McDonald's is a system of landmarks, creating a sense of place in the placeless sea of newly-built suburbia, or to mark off on our mental maps the centers of suburban neighborhoods or the areas between neighborhoods as the local church spire used to do in serving as town center and orientation point in traditional towns.

For Americans traveling abroad, McDonald's plays a similar role as embassies of American popular culture (in fact Kroc uses the term "hamburger diplomacy" in discussing his foreign outposts), which serve as refuges giving temporary relief from culture shock away from home. These shelters offer familiar surroundings and, operating as an ad hoc club, a logical place to encounter fellow-countrymen over a malt and a Big Mac.[21]

McDonald's tranformation of the diner echoes Disney's more instantaneous metamorphosis of the amusement park. Disney's impulse was to replace the sleaziness and low-life atmosphere of an older form—the amusement park— with the values of safety, wholesomeness, cleanliness and ultimately, patriot- ism of a family form—the theme park. In 1955, the same year McDonald's was born and began to expand, Disneyland emerged as a bold experiment; a proto- type of the new "safe" amusement center to replace the risk-taking, danger, morbidity, and the sexual and mercenary overtones of the midway, carnival, and even the county fair. Very quickly the prototype presented by Disneyland proved to be the most popular entertainment center on earth. For both Disney and McDonald's, faith in the drawing power of wholesomeness as an environ- mental concept which could be styled to structure an entire cosmos of ideas and icons was richly rewarded as an idea whose time had come.

The Middle Way, with its trinity of Middle American, middle-class, and mid-western taste, was used in the transformation by both Disney and Kroc of interesting, colorful, gamy, spicy, food and entertainment with "character"— into asceptic, cleaned-up versions acclimated to bourgeois "civilized" taste. By wiping off the dust, removing the grime, and expurgating the associations with lowlife and roadlife (with their insinuations of sex and violence), both empires de-classified their productions, making them anonymous, impersonal, region- less, classless, clean, and relatively association-free in terms of their historical flavorful antecedents (local color and taste), as in the style of the earlier individually-owned roadside diner and drive-in stand. Just as Disney completely redesigned the parks in every aspect to conform to his own specifi- cations, McDonald's refuses to allow such elements of game-hall and arcade origin as pinball machines, and goes so far as to ban vending machines, juke boxes, and pay phones from its premises on the grounds that these "down- grade the family image," encourage loitering and "unproductive traffic," and have roots in the underworld of crime.[22]

Public perceptions of fast eating have been altered forever by McDonald's new approaches. In his introduction to Kroc's autobiography, Paul Paganucci of the Dartmouth School of Business Administration claims that McDonald's "changed eating habits throughout the world . . . by rais[ing] expectations . . . Who among us is not now less tolerant of slow service, overpriced meals, soggy french fries, or a lack of cleanliness in eating places?"[23] In the same way, the brightness of Disney's parks has cast a shadow on carnival, circus, and fairground to make them look even more tawdry and shady than in the pre- Disneyland era.[24]

The Disney theme parks, as the largest visitor attraction in the U.S. and in the world, can be said to be the popular culture capitals of America. The

Disney parks are, like McDonald's, products of the booming auto industry and nationwide freeway culture. Both are heavily symbolic of American belief systems of a now distinctive kind: middle-American Protestant. Technologically, these are avant-garde total realms of controlled fantasy, making both restaurant and park archetypes from which imitators have freely taken inspiration.

Disneyland was consciously created to be a living laboratory of public engineering, one of the earliest places in which humane solutions to pressing urban problems were explored. The banning of the car, the extensive use of old-fashioned non-polluting modes of transportation, quiet and comfortable mass transit systems (among them the monorail), the values of pedestrianism, sight-seeing, and the sociability of "people-watching" at the parks' activities are built into one after another of the Disneyland and Disney World facilities. Thus the parks go far beyond being simply entertainment centers.

The Disney lands offer a "familiar experience" prepared for by television previews of life in the parks, their wide popularity and reputation, and the highly-recognizable popular images within their gates. Disneyland has thus superceded the carnival, old-fashioned amusement park, and the big-tent traveling circus (which went out of existence as part of the American scene almost the same year Disneyland appeared).

McDonald's, similarly, has created an instant "field of care"; that is, a place where people feel they know and understand the ambience and feeling of a place by having made it an integrated part of their lives. In the McDonald's case, however, this feeling emanates out from within the minds of the public rather than being a native (intrinsic) feature of each store unit itself. Older-style fields of care—the corner drugstore, neighborhood bar, and local coffee-house or restaurant, are now being replaced by fast-food outlets—often a McDonald's.[25]

Although under persistent fire from academic and intellectual social critics as "plastic," both institutions can be seen to be humanizing the concept of the crowd. The Disney parks are capable of managing up to 70,000 visitors a day without a sense of pressure which would accompany such numbers in other situations. McDonald's advanced socio-engineering of food service allows its staff to serve with civility and prompt politeness even in the packed lunch hour rush.

The appeal of both McDonald's and Disney for families, and the role of these corporations in family life, is critical. Family orientation, supported by the wholesomeness ethic, might be considered a major humanistic force. Just as Disney productions are now the mainstay of the vanishing family film, and the Disney parks are the equivalent as media entertainment centers, an important part of the McDonald name is the "family" in "Family restaurant." As has been noted by observers of the family film genre, of course, the adjective "family" is best read as "children's," since what is suitable for family patronage must ipso facto be designed for its lowest common denominator, the child. Thus it appears that the last bastions of family entertainment and dining outside the home are joined together in these two "last stand" empires of wholesomeness.

This appeal to children and to the child taste and mentality strongly links Disney with McDonald's. The comic fantasy characters of Mickey Mouse and Ronald McDonald are the iconographic mascots. Their fantasy lives, as rich with the promise of instant gratification in the almost-instantaneous delivery of fantasy and food, are closely allied. But fantasy is all too often understood to be associated narrowly with the imagination of childhood. Imagination itself seems to be tied to concepts of youth and inexperience, not to adult thought or experience.

But this index of child-related phenomena is deceptive. For, as Riesman, Glazer, and Denney observed in *The Lonely Crowd*, children may simply be the willing but unconscious middle-men for advertisers and business in their efforts to "sell" adults; it is often through children that even major household purchases are decided.[26] Thus, adults are led or badgered by their children to pay visits to Disneyland or to eat at McDonald's. It appears to be by indirect or second-step persuasion that parents find themselves at the golden arches and at the head of Main Street, U.S.A. in Anaheim or Orlando. However, the ratio of adults to children at the Disney parks is a startling four to one; we might ask if the parks are really designed primarily for children, or whether it may be that children supply the culturally obligatory alibi for adults to let themselves experience the parks without embarrassment about being there as adult "intruders."

If children are not the ultimate targets of the Disney and McDonald's "experiences," a highly active principle of popular culture is in action, as it is on so many other fronts of popular life. This principle might be seen as an extension of the mechanism of "shapeshifting" in which creatures or objects in folklore undergo a metamorphosis so that gods or ghosts turn into men, men turn into animals, and animals become men or ghosts. This concept can be useful in describing the intractable and often bewildering behavior of popular institutions (and, for that matter, many of our elite institutions): somehow their impact on the culture at large does not necessarily conform to their ostensible purposes or intended meaning; in this misfiring of purpose, their ultimate impact may be far removed from that which is assumed in formal definitions.

Shapeshifting can be perceived in McDonald's and the Disney parks. Is McDonald's basically a place to eat Big Mac's, Filet-O-Fish, french fries, a malt? Or is it something above and beyond a fast food franchise? In addition to fast food and drink, could McDonald's be performing such a momentous cultural role as symbolic landmark, reference point in America's mental image of its travel arteries, an island of safety, sanity, order, and middle-American values, where one can experience a feeling of respite and a sense of being taken care of?

Disneyland and Walt Disney World are ostensibly "entertainment centers"—yet perhaps entertainment, as usually thought of in terms of diversion, excape, and the margin around central concerns of life such as work, is their *least* important aspect. In many very demonstrable ways, they function as sacred centers for the U.S. (one West, one East)—as the popular culture capitals of the nation. By contrast, the official capital at Washington with its aristocratic and cerebreal overtones is rather formal, historical, and forbidding, living in a symbolic atmosphere outside the shared experience and probably also outside the imagination of most Americans. The Disney "capitals," on the other hand, are replete with images of America that Americans can really understand. These images play an active and comtemporary role in American life: the "received" folk and fairy tale (in Fantasyland), popular images of other lands (It's a Small World), images of turn-of-the-century small town America (Main Street, U.S.A.), the frontier and Manifest Destiny (Adventureland, Frontierland, New Orleans Square), and the American commitment to science and technology (Tomorrowland). The Disney worlds provide an intelligible, familiar, fun, living museum of American myth and experience; the core of American consciousness; America reflecting on America; by contrast, Washington, D.C. is the nation's mind; Disneyland is where the heart is. (Jerry Rubin had a canny awareness of the mythic importanct of Disneyland for Americans when he led the Yippie "takeover" of the heart of America in the late 60's.)

The Disney parks have shifted shape so completely as to assume a religious dimension. Like the Greek cities under the guardianship and spirit of a deity, the Disneylands are permeated by the guiding spirit of Walt Disney and his "disciple" organization men. The parks serve as Meccas, sacred centers, to which every American must make his double pilgrimage, first as a child (for whom the Disneyland experience is a focal point), later as an adult with his own children. The power of the Disneyland imperative in this role is demonstrated by the litany of question and answer in our society, beginning with the question "Have you been to Disneyland yet?" A "yes" answer leads to recounting of the experience. But if the answer is "no," an explanation seems called for: either in the form of a promise or intention to go, or in a statement of outraged good taste. "No, we haven't been, and we're not planning to go." In either case, a strong response is felt to be required and is invariably given.

Disneyland has presented all generations of Disney-raised children—and adults—with a larger pilgrimage as an extension of the minipilgrimage routinely made as family groups attend Disney films at local theatres (or gather at home in the Sunday-night ritual of watching Disney's television program *en famille*). McDonald's presents a converse case of place following mythic fantasy constellation: while Disney made apt use of his film and television productions to plug the parks, McDonald's began as a place-network and afterwards launched a hefty television advertising program which produced the fantasy character of the clown and the humanoid food-items to reinforce McDonald's-consciousness.

If Disneyland serves as a Mecca, McDonald's has become a neotraditional interfaith religious order. It has been observed that the golden arches insignia and sculptural symbol (a stylized portrayal of the letter M) have a deeper significance as metaphorical "gate to heaven," of like design and with a symbolic impact as strong as the Gateway Arch in St. Louis (were McDonald's golden arches in fact inspired by Eero Saarinen's "silver" one of 1948?) This religious reading of McDonald's is very telling, part of that process in a secular society in which other institutions and individuals take over the sanctified roles of church and priesthood which have begun to recede in cultural importance.

McDonald's does in fact offer a sanctuary—from the mad pace of highway or from the distresses and pressures of the nuclear family in urban or suburban home. Served by a staff of underling priests, presided over by the "managing" (local head) priest, and under the guiding spirit of the values of order and efficiency symbolized by the golden arches above, the customer is nourished, rested, reassured, and refreshed. Each of these sanctuaries has a similar inconography along with an identical view of life, with its ritual of order and of service, and the litany is prescribed: smiles, thanks, and "Have a nice day" are the fixed gestures and scriptures.

Kroc was amazingly candid about his dedication to his organization as something far more than a hamburger business: "I speak of faith in McDonald's as if it were a religion. And without meaning any offense to the Holy Trinity, the Koran, or the Torah, that's exactly the way I think of it. I've often said that 'I believe in God, family, and McDonald's—and in the office, that order is reversed.'"[27]

Both McDonald's and the Disney parks provide places high in the ethic of family life as compared with other institutions geared for adolescents, young adults, or the adult crowd. Clearly they are both consciously attempting this image. For both, providing a clean and attractive haven for families as a barrier against the corruption of the outside world gives them the defensive quality of temples dedicated to preserving a sense of safety and certainty—even dignity—in a darkening urban world.

Notes

[1]Richard Schickel, *The Disney Version* (N.Y.: Anchor Books, 1968), p. viii.

[2]"The Burger That Conquered the Country," *Time* (September 17, 1973), p. 84.

[3]*Time* (September 17, 1973), p. 84.

[4]Paul Paganucci, Associate Dean, Amos Tuck School of Business Administration, Dartmouth College, Introduction to Ray Kroc, *Grinding It Out: The Making of McDonald's* (Chicago: Henry Regnery Co., 1977), p. 3.

[5]Ernst Dichter quoted in Vance Packard, *The Hidden Persuaders* (N.Y.: Pocket Books, 1958; originally published by David McKay, 1957), p. 85.

[6]Vance Packard, p. 85.

[7]In *Portnoy's Complaint*, Philip Roth alludes to the wicked glamour which the serving of milk and meat together might hold for Jews, for whom McDonald's might represent the ultimate in goyisch non-Kosher eating, with its symbol of hamburger and shake joined together in unholy matrimony. Perhaps the ultimate in *tref* eating was the original fast food chain of "pig stands" in the South.

[8]According to a story in *McPeople*, the trade magazine for the McDonald's Albuquerque franchises, the standard of "fast" has been accelerated in customer consciousness to take on the meaning and expectation of "instant." The 1976 story cited cases in which customers complained if their order was not filled the moment they asked for it.

[9]Kroc, *Grinding It Out: The Making of McDonald's* (Chicago: Henry Regnery Co., 1977) p. 24.

[10]Theodore Levitt, "Production-line Approaches to Service," *Harvard Business Review* (September-October, 1972), p. 44.

[11]Mary Alice Kellogg, "Making the Grade at Hamburger University," *Newsweek* (September 25, 1972), p. 78.

[12]Ray Kroc, p. 7.

[13]"For Ray Kroc, Life Began at 50. Or Was It 60?" *Forbes* (January 15, 1973), p. 30.

[14]Ray Kroc, p. 15.

[15]Ray Kroc, p. 6.

[16]*Time* (September 17, 1973), p. 90.

[17]Ray Kroc, p. 162.

[18]Kit Smith, "A Touch of the Islands Added by 28 Restaurants in Hawaii," *Sunday Star-Bulletin and Advertiser* (Honolulu, Hawaii: January 1, 1978), p. A-17.

[19]Ray Kroc, p. 167.

[20]Yi-Fu Tuan, "Sacred Space: Exploration of an Idea," paper presented at the 73rd annual meetings of the Association of American Geographers, Salt Lake City, April 24-27, 1977.

[21]On field study in Tokyo to explore the impact of Walt Disney productions in Japan in 1976, I could always count on seeing plenty of Americans at the McDonald's near International House in Roppongi.

[22]Ray Kroc, p. 80.

[23]Paul Paganucci, Introduction to *Grinding It Out*, p. 3.

[24]Is it any accident that Chicago's Riverview, a classic thrills-and-chills amusement park, faded shortly after the rise of Disneyland?

[25]Joseph Morgenstern, "The Roadside Gourmet," *Newsweek* (September 25, 1972), p. 78.

[26]David Riesman, with Nathan Glazer and Reuel Denney, *The Lonely Crowd* (New Haven: Yale University Press, 1961 edition; originally published in 1950), pp. 96-97.

[27]Ray Kroc, p. 126, Kroc continues, "If you are running a 100-yard dash, you aren't thinking about God while you're running. Not if you hope to win. Your mind is on the race. My race is McDonald's."

The War Between the Hamburgers

by Kathryn Grover

American travelers, no matter how harried and frugal they've become, always need a roadside restaurant that they can trust. Fifteen years ago, most of them felt Howard Johnson's was that sort of place. It was relatively inexpensive to eat there, there were thousands of them, and the traveler could rest assured that the food would always be above suspicion. The HoJo Cola you bought on Cape Cod would be the same as the one you bought in Ohio.

But now, instead of HoJo Cola, we think of McDonaldland thick shakes, the Big Mac, the Super Shef, the Whopper and all of their scaled-down counterparts, one of which, at least, will be affordable and all of which can be ready within seconds. As the pace of life has accelerated, fast food has replaced Howard Johnson's as the repository of faith for the American traveler.

The steadfast virtues of uniformity and speed predominate the visions of fast food's great minds. The founders of McDonald's saw that consistency and uniformity were the firm's main assets. The corporation permits a few variations to accommodate regional tastes—regular hamburgers don't come with mustard on Long Island, but in Memphis they come with lots of mustard and not so much ketchup—but generally it will allow little experimentation with menu or decor to its 3200 franchisees. McDonald's feels such discrepancies would unsettle Americans on the road.

Analysts of the fast-food phenomenon have tended to take a mildly cynical view of this uniformity. In *Newsweek*, Joseph Morgenstern observed that it is not only what is best about "pop" restaurants, but also what is worst about them. "You're not going to get the epicurean experience of a lifetime," he cautioned, "but you're not going to get poisoned either." For *Esquire*, Daniel and Susan Halas did an analysis of the 15 fast-food places on Indianapolis' Pendleton Pike, which runs northeast out of the city. "Quality in the traditional sense is not the key to the popularity of franchised food, which is popular because it is standardized and partakes of all the guarantees that come with quality control. It may not be splendid," they say, "but it is always the same."

Those who have followed the rise of the fast-food empire closely would concede that the food is always nearly the same regardless of time and place of consumption. But they have often overlooked the fact that quality is very

120

much in the minds of fast-food entrepreneurs. Sameness is relative to the chain in question. Between chains, there are great differences in the quality of food, especially from management's point of view. These differences seem to be felt with particular strength where menus are virtually identical.

Kentucky Fried Chicken, the leader in the fast-food market in terms of gross revenue, would provide the best illustration of this thesis, if only it had competition. KFC has long been the frontrunner principally because Colonel Harlen Sanders' mythic frying recipe is a secret guarded with religious dedication. But with a shift of focus to the bountiful and expansive field of hamburgers, a meaningful comparison can be made. Here, McDonald's is the leader, and the Burger King chain is its stiffest competitor.

Of all the hamburger places—Burger Chef, Red Barn, Jack in the Box, Gino's, and Hardee's, for example—Burger King is most like McDonald's. Compare menus. At McDonald's, you can get four different sizes of both hamburgers and cheeseburgers, a fish sandwich, french fries in two sizes, a hot apple or cherry pie, McDonaldland cookies, soft drinks, three flavors of milk shakes, coffee, milk and hot chocolate. At Burger King, you can get five different sizes of hamburgers and cheeseburgers and everything else McDonald's offers except the cookies and the cherry pie. There are a few minor items at McDonald's that you cannot get at Burger King. The converse is also true. And management will insist that even those food items which are ostensibly comparable are not equivalent. There is a constant pressure to introduce items which will be similar enough to the most popular features on the opposition's menu to compete with them, but somehow original and exciting enough to divert the public's attention away from those saving graces.

Beneath this struggle, two more basic differences are responsible for the intense localism each company feels and which structure the competition between them. First of all, McDonald's uses a grill to cook its burgers, while Burger King uses a "chain broiler," cooking the product over flames. Secondly, McDonald's puts its condiments on the burgers immediately, operating on the basis of market research which indicated what most people in America like on their hamburgers. Burger King, on the other hand, waits for the customer's order before it begins slathering away; this approach is encapsulated in the corporation's "have it your way" philosophy and is considered the chain's prime selling point.

Management at each institution claims that its firm's approach to burger preparation is the superior one. Burger King people think burgers taste better broiled and think the customer has a right to be asked about his condiments. This seems a generally more republican view of the consumer than that which prevails at McDonald's, where the tack is more in tune with democratic principles. Kathy Henry at McDonald's district office in Detroit says, "McDonald's has tested and found that its condiments are the type of thing most consumers want on hamburgers. There aren't that many people who want a special order, we find." But it is true that those who do have to wait, while special orders don't upset anyone at Burger King, as anyone who watches television knows.

The sense of distinction that these differences in approach have imparted to each firm have also placed constraints on the items each introduces for competition with the other. McDonald's major recent innovation is its breakfast menu, which started in 1974 with the Egg McMuffin—a poor man's Eggs Benedict. The idea was to capture people who wanted a quick breakfast, but the Egg McMuffin didn't have enough singular appeal to accomplish this on its own. So the company introduced hotcakes and sausage. Although these items account for five to ten per cent of the revenue in the franchises that serve them (about half do), McDonald's has been trying to generate more clientele with scrambled eggs. You can also get an English muffin, a Danish pastry, assorted donuts, a citrus cup and various fruit juices. In some parts of the country, you get a free cup of coffee if you buy an Egg McMuffin.

In much of its advertising, McDonald's capitalizes on the breakfast menu, because Burger King can't duplicate it. Tim Clayton at the Detroit regional office of Burger King points out that these breakfast items are cooked on a grill, which Burger King doesn't have. "We've tried microwaving scrambled eggs," he says, "but it doesn't work."

In the McDonald's breakfast ad, the sun rises in the background behind a unit somewhere in America as a female employee opens the glass door and invites us all in to join them (the staff?) for breakfast. Factory workers, a businessman, a jogger, lovers and farmers run in, as if they'd been shivering through the dawn in Buicks, Volkswagens, semis and pickup trucks in the parking lot, waiting for the place to open. Everyone smiles and has a great time.

Yet for all that, McDonald's has failed to come up with anything comparable to the Whopper, Burger King's original feature and still its most popular item, a quarter-pound hamburger on a five-inch sesame seed bun with lettuce, tomatoes, mayonnaise, ketchup, onions and pickles. You can get a Whopper, a Double Beef Whopper or a Whopper Junior with all of these condiments, any combination of them or none of them. For five cents extra in every case, you can get one with cheese. Burger King also has normal hamburgers and cheeseburgers available in one- or two-patty versions.

Burger King personnel are quick to point out that the Whopper was around long before the Big Mac, the most massive piece of food on McDonald's menu, and both managements admit that it's no competition for the Whopper. The Big Mac is two burgers, three pieces of patty, lettuce, onions, pickles and McDonald's enigmatic "special sauce." This last quantity may have been an attempt to get back at Colonel Sanders and his secret recipe, but many people are uneasy about the special sauce and like to know exactly what they are getting on their big burgers.

The simple and frank formula at Burger King has always been an asset to the firm. McDonald's first real attempt to come back was called the QLT, which translates into a quarter-pound hamburger with lettuce and tomato. The QLT is still a test product, and, according to Burger King's Clayton, it is a "miserable" response to the threat the Whopper poses. Several months ago in San Diego, McDonald's began to test out another item for this particular battle in the war called, predictably, the McFeast.

Although breakfast is out of the question for Burger King, the company's broiling method has allowed it to do two things McDonald's hasn't done. It makes onion rings — they were introduced in April, 1974 — and a hot ham and cheese sandwich, called a Yumbo. Onion rings, Clayton says, do very well, but the Yumbo only does "all right." He adds, "If they would change the name it would probably do a lot better. I think that was the trouble with the Big Plain too. People didn't know what the hell it was."

The Big Plain is an interesting failure in Burger King's food experiments. Introduced in the spring of 1973, it was a quarter-pound hamburger with nothing on it. Believing there was a market for an ungarnished hamburger of that size, the corporation mounted a sizable advertising campaign on its behalf. I remember clearly the first time I saw a television commercial for the item. A friend witnessed this event with me. When the spot ended, we looked at each other and said, "Big *Plain?*"

Our interest was piqued. The next day we went to the nearest Burger King to see how the new hamburger was being received. The interesting thing about the Big Plain was that it cost 90 cents, while a regular Whopper cost 85 cents. There is no difference at all between these two items except the condiments, which at Burger King, we must remember, can be eliminated immediately at the customer's whim. My friend went through this argument step by step with the girl waiting on him. "If someone can get a Whopper with nothing on it," he asked, "why would he get a Big Plain and pay five cents more for the same thing?" Apparently, this was a point of logic with which she felt unequipped to deal. "I can't answer that," she said. "Ask the manager." She took the rest of our orders down with smoldering restraint. In any event, others must have caught on to this paradox, since the Big Plain died a quiet death soon after the advertising push stopped.

Burger King and McDonald's people alike seem surprised when asked if they really believe their products are superior to the competitor's. "McDonald's is a very high-quality corporation," Ms. Henry points out, "though we try to keep away from the corporate image. You're proud to work for such a very personal organization. Each store is an individual operation, and we pay a lot of attention to the customer." She explained the company philosophy — Quality, Service and Cleanliness — neatly symbolized in the acronym QSC. "I know that our food quality is just superior. It's better meat than you can buy in a grocery store," she says. "It's got less fat."

Ms. Henry shies away from admitting that McDonald's competes directly with Burger King, and she thinks the issue between them is the condiments on the burger, not the bigness of it. But Clayton does not think the situation is one of simple personal preference; he thinks the public is unaware of the differences between the two places, and that it is generally fickle to boot. He notes that when a Burger King locates near an existing McDonald's, the Burger King tends to do a better business for a while than its rival does. But when a McDonald's locates near an existing Burger King, the same thing occurs. "People like to try out new places, and then they develop loyalties," Clayton says. "Besides, McDonald's units are generally newer, since they had to build additions for seating. Remember, they used to all be drive-ins before Burger King was on the scene," he notes.

Clayton points out that McDonald's greater number of units allows a greater volume of advertising. "That's why," he says, "you can't watch television for an hour without seeing one of their commercials." This fact contributes to McDonald's ability to stay on top in terms of profits, even though to Clayton's way of thinking Burger King's product is far superior. "I always have thought that," he says. "The only problem is persuading the public. For instance, the drinks we serve are 12, 16 and 24 ounces. McDonald's serves 11, 15, and 22 ounces. But you ask people on the street, and they don't notice the extra ounce. We get ten patties per pound, while McDonald's gets twelve. But people don't know the difference."

Until, or if, Burger King catches up with McDonald's, each can probably be counted on to expand menus in existing units to further boost their enormous sales, which have grown in steady leaps and bounds even during the recession. Both companies seem to be looking towards a future which sees the decline and fall of Kentucky Fried Chicken. McDonald's is testing a $1.10 chicken plate in Dayton; Burger King is testing chicken in Florida. Even Jack in the Box is testing a product it calls Judge Tibbs' Chicken and Ribbs. How well chicken will do is debatable at this point. Clayton points out that hamburgers have more general appeal and that Kentucky Fried Chicken may not be a very desirable item in cities and college towns. Morgenstern has noted that there is some degree of "sales resistance" to the Colonel's pressure-cooked product. Its appeal does seem to be more highly variable from region to region than the hamburger's. My own experience has shown that some New Englanders have tended to look askance to Kentucky Fried Chicken outlets, especially when there is a McDonald's nearby. They seem to suspect the product, and I think this suspicion has roots in the North's general distrust of anything Southern, particularly of anything Southern fried.

Even if chicken doesn't work, Burger King is thinking of introducing a salad resembling the one the Red Barn features, and McDonald's is thinking of a roast beef sandwich such as can be found at Arby's. Whatever comes next, Burger King will thrust its broiler in McDonald's face, and McDonald's can be expected to retaliate with its grill. And whatever emerges from the struggle, you can be sure, will emerge quickly.

Berger vs. Burger:
A Personal Encounter

by A.A. Berger

I am interested in Ronald McDonald's world not only because it is full of hamburgers, but full also of symbols and signifiers which reflect many things about American culture and society. Often they take on personal meaning. At the same time a hamburger is an *artifact*, fit subject for anthropologists now and archeologists later. There is a deeper significance to one of Ronald's hamburgers than the functional one—being eaten. I want to speak of these deeper things; but first, let me tell you about my first McDonald's hamburger.

I ate it in 1964, while teaching at the University of Minnesota. The newly-opened McDonald's near the campus had two huge golden arches and a sign telling how many millions of people had purchased burgers before me. No Berger was part of a mighty army.

I was struck by the organization and the ritual. Of course, the company was turning out an endless stream of hamburgers at low prices. But it was doing much more. For a long time I thought it. Then I went home and wrote an article called "The Evangelical Hamburger." It began: McDonald's offers the hamburger without qualities for the man without qualities. It must be seen as more than a gaudy, vulgar oasis of tasteless ground meat, a fountain of sweet, syrupy malted milks in a big parking lot that caters to students, snack seekers, and hard-up hungers who grind its bloody gristle through their choppers at fifteen cents a shot.

I went on to draw parallels between my experience and organized religion, suggesting that the hamburger was a kind of "new, improved wafer" leading to a "kind of communion" with all the other Ronaldites who had also partaken.

Although the chain's function involves serving food, the spirit of McDonald's still strikes me as essentially evangelical and religious. It has spread round the world with a passion that is frenzied and pietistic. One of the things that bothers me most about all this is its uniformity. The hamburgers themselves are standardized products and compared to the competition (from Burger King, Burger Chef, Jack in the Box, etc.) they are relatively good. McDonald's has excellent quality control and has done enough time-and-motion studies to turn out the most efficiently handled product in the fast food industry. (The Big Mac carton was phased out when it was discovered that foam shells could be filled a split-second faster by countermen.)

125

But there is something about mechanization of food that bothers me. At McDonald's we cannot (without disrupting things and having to wait) get hamburgers the way we want them. We have to accommodate ourselves to what McDonald's gives us and that step, though seemingly a small one, is symbolically important.

McDonald's means organization, rationalization and specialization, carried to the point of perfection so that the consumer can have a hamburger with the minimum delay at the cheapest price possible. The restaurant works on a continuous flow format, like an automobile assembly line, with hamburgers being cooked and everything else being at the ready, so that orders can be filled almost at once.

McDonald's has hired statisticians who have figured things out so that at any given moment in time a hamburger at a McDonald's is moving towards a customer who is moving towards that McDonald's. Does Ronald have everyone's number? Does it mean anything to have lost the human touch when we eat?

By now McDonald's has sold 5 billion hamburgers and who knows how many packets of french fries. Everything comes wrapped in paper, to be thrown away. The packaging industry has made studies of consumer beliefs and preferences and has found that individual packaging, putting hamburgers (like Big Macs) in their own cartons, gives people a sense of "value received" or "added value."

But everything is finally thrown away into a trash can, and I think that eating mass-produced hamburgers wrapped in paper napkins or foam boxes is ultimately depersonalizing and dehumanizing. In a throw-away culture we cannot escape wondering whether we, too, will be "thrown away" when we are no longer functional or useful—in the moral equivalent of one of McDonald's trashbins?

A recent book about fuel foods argues that in some restaurants you don't get food that is enjoyable and which made eating a pleasure, but food which can be thought of as *fuel*, providing calories and carbohydrates to keep your body functioning. In many respects I would characterize McDonald's as being a fuel food restaurant: a place in which food has lost its identity. Is McDonald's a gasoline station for hamburger eaters?

McDonald's spends millions of dollars a year for advertising, so the McDonald's hamburger is one of the most heavily advertised product in America. These advertisements are often consummate achievements in the art of persuasion and play an important role in making Ronald not just a clown chain but part of our lore. McDonald's has, in just a decade, become a quintessential American pop icon, and is now part of what might be called pop-Americana, along with Mickey Mouse, Snoopy and Coca-Cola.

Not only has Ronald been deeply imbedded into the American collective consciousness (is there anyone in America who has never heard of him?), but ads have often profoundly affected our psychic equilibrium. In a single McDonald's commercial, "Quick Cuts," there are some 65 different shots. This quick cutting technique has a tendency to stimulate us and make us feel we're living an exciting life while it also confuses us and evades our rational decision-making capacities.

In our psyches we tend to feel that Ronald is connected with excitement and good living, so that we become, in effect, programmed by the commercials. Then, there is the matter of incremental repetition so that we all become "McDonald's-ized" by the ubiquitous commercials.

There is something ironic about the fact that an enormous rationalized fast-food franchise like McDonald's, which turns out machine-tooled hamburgers, advertises "You—you're the one . . ." for what McDonald's deals with is not individuals with particular preference but the mass stomach. The Corporation understands the mass stomach and has waged a powerful campaign to convince everyone that individual taste preferences are old hat. Speed is more important than tastes and the price of speed is homogenization of tastes.

And so McDonald's spends millions to bombard us with hamburgers and various foods that go with them. We all have a McDonald's consciousness now: sales figures show it.

Marxists theorists frequently talk about the problem of *embourgeoisement*—which involves dissipating working class consciousness (and protest) by making working class people think they are members of the middle class. From this point of view the basic function of Ronald's hamburger is *mystification*.

In America people eat more meat than ever before. But statistics show that we are eating less steak and other prime cuts and more hamburger, so in truth our standard of living (in this respect) has gone down. The fast-food industry and its franchise arrangements is the last hope of the so-called "little" American to rise in the world. Most of the growth in the American economy is in the service industries, but there is now so much proliferation that the hamburger no longer guarantees wealth and success. All too often, on both the individual and social level, hamburgers lead only to heartache and heartburn.

There are now some 4000 McDonald's restaurants and another 4000 are projected for the next decade. Someone has estimated that it is possible (that is, profitable) to have one fast-food franchise for every 7000 people, which means we can look forward to some 30,000 fast-food outlets in America. The thought staggers the imagination.

Life is now so expensive in America that more and more women find it necessary to work, which means they do not have time to cook. So we have become habituated to going to fast-food chains, which means we need more money and must work more. Once caught in the cycle, only indigestion, alienation, ulcers and death (by becoming too bored with the limited menus to eat) remain. This is a frivolous and fanciful notion, but not too far-removed, from the situation in which people find themselves. We now eat one of three meals out in America and the fast-food people and other restauranteurs plan on making it two out of three.

If Ronald McDonald has his way, will the home-cooked meal be something we read about in history books? Will it be perpetuated by antiquarian societies and those root-crazy ethnics? Is McDonald's the future? Is this what progress is all about? Is equal access to fast-foods the proof of our democratic pudding?

Are the arches (which in their earliest manifestations suggested portals to me) breasts, symbolically speaking? And what effect does eating chopped meat, which can be shaped and molded, have upon the people? Do people who "do it all for you" end up "doing it all *to* you"?

These thoughts come to my mind as I think about all that is contained in the deceptively simple world of Ronald McDonald. Not the hamburger itself but everything behind it is of interest. To understand McDonald's, the most important of our fast-food franchises, is to understand a great deal about the American mind, the spirit and psyche—as well as stomach.

In *The Waning of the Middle Ages* Huizinga quotes Saint Irenaeus, who said, *"Nihil vacuum neque sine signo apud Deum,"* "In God nothing is empty of sense." Then Huizinga writes, "So the conviction of a transcendental meaning in all things seeks to formulate itself." Secularized, this means that commonplace and seemingly trivial things often contain a great deal of meaning.

So it is with the irresistible Clown, and all that Ronald's world represents.

What Can We Learn From Ronald?

by Michael R. Steele

n the beginning, Man stole fire from the gods. Man (and Woman) cooked food, and it was good. And Man said: Let there be spices for this food. And the New World was found. Man said: Let cooked spiced food be refrigerated. And yet again: Let this cooked spiced and refrigerated food be served under a golden rainbow. And McDonald's was created. And Man saw all the things that he had made, and they were very good. And Man now resteth for man deserveth a break today.

Few in the last quarter of the twentieth century will ever completely realize the revolutionary impact of McDonald's on all aspects of modern life. It is not facetious to include McDonald's as the fourth wonder in the history of our relationship to food. Just as the controlled use of fire made man a more successful omnivore, and just as the European penchant for spices drove restless spirits to find the other half of this earth, McDonald's is an equally important development (mutation?). We may not be able to make a complete prognosis as to the nature of McDonald's significance for the future, but we can be certain that the surface phenomenon signifies much deeper changes in the organization of human behavior.

The study of this entire phenomenon is not a frivolous undertaking. The essays here are an important step in the proper description and analysis of this culinary colossus. McDonald's is a culminating point of several crucial human developments. The technological line of movable parts producing a uniform product runs clearly and directly from Gutenberg to Ford to Kroc. Economically, McDonald's stands at the pinnacle of franchising capitalism (even though its basic product is not franchised). Mythically, McDonald's has created and disperses an entire cast of characters that have replaced other such fantasies which have been on the scene for decades or more. And Ronald McDonald did this in less than ten years.

Man is what he eats. Writing about the French anthropologist, Claude Levi-Strauss, Bob Scholte amends this to say that "Man is what he thinks he eats."[1] This may be the most important aspect of our study. No human activity takes place in a socio-cultural vacuum. No single human act is only what it *seems* to be. Accordingly, the study of Ronald's World must go far beyond the enumeration of the staggering production figures and cost-per-unit analysis. In Scholte's rephrasing of Feuerbach, the "thinking" precedes the eating. It is at this point of departure that the popular culturist's study is immensely important. No one buys a Big Mac for the simple reason of eating it. Instead, the behavior is part of an entire *gestalt* in which the consumer participates on a subliminal level. The purchase of a Big Mac involves a "deep" interior perception of self, family, country, and socio-economic status. Along with his Big Mac, the consumer "buys" a vision of himself at leisure on a well-deserved break; a vision of family cohesiveness and family role models; a vision of a particular type of patriotism; and a vision of his participation in a socio-economic process that is growing at an exponential rate. It is this deep structure which is contained in the *gestalt* of the McDonald's phenomenon that helps make a repetitive, uniform experience avoid a degeneration into dullness to become a longed-for break from other routines. Yet McDonald's is now almost as routine as any other shared experience on the human scene. The basic product is essentially the same from one year to the next, and from one place to another. But all the other routine behaviors in our experience cannot claim the interior sense of change that accompanies a brief stop at a McDonald's.

E pluribus unum. Out of many restaurants one. We might also say, "out of one comes many." For each McDonald's customer, there is a private experience of differentiation which somehow derives from a seemingly rigorous conformity. Similarly, the Catholic Latin Mass provided a universal, orderly experience for a worshipper in the midst of the multifarious demands of the secular world. Again, though, both experiences allow for interior differentiation. Man worships a private image as well as a public one. At McDonald's, the consumer becomes what he thinks he eats in the midst of a universal, orderly experience which relieves him from the multifarious demands of the rest of the secular world. In this respect, then, McDonald's has become a secular religion replete with vestments, ceremony, a sense of cycle, icons, and a communion. We should not be surprised to learn that more people go to McDonald's in a month than attend church.

America and the world will never be the same thanks to a middle-aged milk-shake machine salesman from Illinois. At the end of the arch we will find it necessary to go beyond the implied pot of gold in search of all the true keys to Ronald's success.

The search can begin with our own students—or our own personal experiences. In my case, the experience began when I was a high school student in the early 1960's.

A local drive-in, I well remember, was "off-limits" to all of the high school's students during the regular school day. It was just a block or two from the school. Then, (in 1963 as I remember) came the golden arches—on the other side of town. Like the steel ax mentioned by McLuhan which completely destroyed the social and cultural fabric of an aboriginal village,[2] McDonald's brought its own message to Winter Haven, Florida, in 1963. That message was, at first, more modest and less threatening than the steel ax which gutted the aborigines' society. First of all, the high school cafeteria found that students were abandoning the bland government surplus food served there for those mass-produced burger and fries served at the red and white glassed-in hamburger stand which advertised, at that time, about 450 million sold. There was a sense of identity among those of us who preferred Ray Kroc's burgers to the institutional high school food.

We liked to watch the progress found in the exponentially increasing sale of hamburgers. We watched the signs whenever we were in Lakeland, just ten miles away, in order to see that the totals were right. I think that we felt a subliminal sense of competition with the Lakeland McDonald's. We watched that sign in Winter Haven like people watch the Census Bureau's demographic clock or the Commerce Department's GNP totals. And the rest of America watched along with us whenever they passed their local golden arches.

We did not know it then, but that other drive-in, far on the other side of town from McDonald's, was in trouble. No one then thought to study the effects of that little glassed-in hamburger stand on the other eating establishments in town, not to mention such diverse areas as traffic flow patterns, the hiring of youth, and the host of reasons why the place attracted people almost magnetically. Nor did my fellow students think to observe our own behavior patterns at McDonald's. (The *teachers*, as far as we could tell, simply never entered the place.) It never crossed our juvenile minds that, unlike the pit stop down the road, we were unable to listen to Martha and the Vandellas or Dell Shannon or that tinny English music sung by something called the Beatles. No—we simply drove up, got out, ordered, paid, received, and went back to our cars. We loved it. But we couldn't use a telephone to call in a lie excusing us from school or baseball practice; we couldn't call up someone for a date. We couldn't rip off plastic utensils or condiments. We couldn't burn holes in padded plastic seats. We couldn't carve our initials in table tops. We couldn't play pin ball machines or shoot pool. We couldn't buy chewing gum. We couldn't cruise around the parking lot watching our peers in their souped up '57 Chevies or latest Bonnevilles. There was no space-age intercom system to be used for ordering. There was no waitress wearing a frilly little mini-skirt and rolling up to our cars on roller skates while confidently balancing a tray of food to be hung precariously from a car window. There wasn't even a printed menu. We simply paid, left, and ate.

That was an "American Graffiti" year. Life was different then. And, not surprisingly, life in more recent years is also different. For instance, an entirely new childhood fantasy/myth has appeared on the world scene thanks to McDonald's. Ronald McDonald and all his cartoon cronies have, for children, overtaken in popularity such stalwarts as Mickey Mouse, Donald Duck, Terry and the Pirates, Snoopy, and even the Easter Bunny. The Big Mac rapid-fire jingle of a few years ago became a folk-art on school playgrounds, Kids can buy McDonaldland cookies instead of more mundane animal crackers and they can color in Ronald's coloring books instead of Disney's. McDonald's has, in fact, gone far beyond the mere culinary impact of its message to become a pervasive phenomenon in almost all aspects of our lives—especially the lives of our children. It cuts across demographic maps, generation gaps, and sociological classifications in making its influences felt.

McDonald's is an incalculably rich source of study for our students. Besides the fact that it is now serving food in high school and college cafeterias (thus replacing the government surplus food that I rejected fifteen years ago)—our students can use their numerous visits to McDonald's, this social, mythical wonderland, to achieve a clearer understanding of the society that spawned the phenomenon and, more importantly, a better perspective on themselves.

For instance, can students understand properly the middle quarter of the twentieth century without realizing the socio-technical implications of the fact that McDonald's and the interstate highway system were begun within months of each other? As the interstate system marched across America (a technological wonder designed not only for tourists but also for Army tanks and personnel carriers), McDonald's kept in step. The interstate system, a vestige of the Cold War, came to stand in symbiotic relationship to the golden arches which traced its progress. From the Cold War, America grew into a fast moving, fast-spending society based on throw-away mobility. An interstate system, which would have never existed but for Henry Ford's Promethean genius, spawned thousands of oasis-like McDonald's which, in turn, employ a modified version of Ford's assembly-line procedures. In fact, McDonald's may be the ultimate in assembly-line technology since it uses all phases that Ford refined but produces a product that is not reusable. I've owned some second-hand Fords but I've never even seen a second-hand Big Mac or chocolate shake. So, our students should be able to see the completed cycle—magnificent highways which were a technological response to advances in automobile engineering—McDonald's which took advantage of the increased mobility *and* the very technology which produced the cars and roads in the first place. Gutenberg brought to technology the principle of using moving parts to create a static, uniform product; Ford expanded this so that the assembly line moved and the people did not. Ray Kroc went another step with his golden-arched units: the assembly line is stationary and *we*, the consumers, are the movable parts.

The technological advancements that culminated in McDonald's present ample opportunity for meaningful investigations. But there are many more facets of McDonald's that one could study. We all know that McDonald's menu is highly standardized. The company is proud of the fact that its products are uniform from coast to coast. Given this fact of rigorous standardization, students could be given the task of investigating the reasons why McDonald's patrons are so loyal to the product. Part of the answer is to be found in the *gestalt* spoken of before. Part of the consuming decision is the result of advertising. The icons that one sees in the television advertisments and in cartoon books are also what the consumer buys. McDonald's is now one of the largest purchasers of television advertising time. With such a heavy promotional emphasis, students have countless opportunities to investigate the nature and appeal of the iconic statements to which a potential consumer relates. The students will be able to compare the corporate vision of what it means to deserve a break today with the reality of that break. They will probably learn that the surface appearance is accompanied by a differing, internal perception of the consuming act.

After an investigation of the advertising, the students will have a solid base for further study within the hallowed edifice itself. This will provide students with the opportunity to observe the methods by which the corporate engineers control human movement from the moment the customer's car leaves the highway, through the ordering and purchasing ritual, the secular communion with the Big Mac and shake, to the (usual) act of neatness as refuse is disposed. Almost all aspects of this hamburger ritual have been learned by Americans within the last twenty years—and certain behaviors have been learned since the corporation changed architecture to the family-oriented mansard roof units. In addition, students can speculate on the use of interior decoration from one unit to the next—from the cathedral-like stained glass window in an Ann Arbor McDonald's to the more secular celebration of the champion Portland Trailblazers in Beaverton, Oregon.

Especially interesting to students should be the values-creating process that helped form their lives as they grew up in this wonderland McDonald's. Today's students are members of the first generation which grew up watching the expansion of McDonald's via advertising and various promotional campaigns. This experience is today a nationally shared experience. However, there is a generation gap which exists between those who grew up Before Ronald and those who grew up After Ronald. I suspect that the interior nature of the consumer's behavior is different according to which McDonald's generation one belongs to. People who are over twenty-two or so simply cannot relate to Ronald and his friends as children do. This dimension of McDonald's experience is a most important one and one that is readily available to our students. They thus have themselves to study—not to mention their parents and younger siblings.

We can also learn from *Grinding It Out*, the autobiography of Ray Kroc. The language of Kroc's book reveals metaphorically some of Kroc's values and perspectives. Three metaphorical patterns are repeated throughout the book: religious, sports and war. For example, Kroc was fascinated when he first saw Mac and Dick McDonald's french fries operation. Ultimately, the lavish preparations for McDonald's french fries would become "sacrosanct" and a "ritual to be followed religiously." The sound of the salt shaker over the golden fries reminded Kroc of a Salvation Army girl's tambourine.[3]

As he gaped at the marvel of the brothers' hamburger stand, Kroc could feel himself "getting wound up like a pitcher with a no-hitter going," (Kroc, p. 8). He continues his baseball talk—as we might expect from a man who has followed baseball from his time as a spectator in the stands when Ruth "called his shot" to now being the owner of the San Diego Padres—when he says that salesmen must "pitch" like baseball pitchers who never throw the same way to different batters (Kroc, p. 18).

More important than religious and sports metaphors is Kroc's use of war metaphors. When he is intrigued or awed, he slips into religious diction. When he wishes to show intensity and drive, his language is from the playground and ball park. But Ray Kroc is nothing if not a combative personality. He is a socio-economic throwback to the social Darwinists when he speaks of capitalism and interpersonal relationships. At these moments, Kroc's war imagery flows. In 1955, at that critical juncture when he knew instinctively that he was on the verge of something truly great, Kroc reminisces that he was "a battle-scarred veteran of the business wars, but . . . was still eager to go into action," (Kroc, p. 13). In 1966, Kroc knew that a proposed change in McDonald's architecture would mean "a big battle" with Harry Sonneborn, his trusted business partner (Kroc, p. 143). In 1972, Kroc was persuaded to make a pitch for the unexploited breakfast trade. "We went after it like the Sixth Fleet going into action. . . . It was exhilarating to see the combined forces of our research and development people . . . all concentrating on a program," (Kroc, p. 165).

There is internal consistency in this pattern. America, and Americans —especially very successful Americans—may be said to share in the values and perspectives of religion, sports, and war. As a "chosen people," Americans have always been able to see themselves in a religious light. And the super-rich, the "chosen of the chosen," almost naturally turn to religious language in order to explain their revelations to lesser mortals. Kroc, unwilling to give much credit to his fellow man for his success, has only religious language to turn to at certain moments. Likewise, sports play a disproportionate role in this country. Perhaps as an outlet for energies thwarted by the closing of the frontier, sports have come to serve as a metaphor for the mythical American adventure—competition rather than cooperation, the brilliant solo performer rather than the beauty of teamwork. Of course, these categories exist on a continuum, but Kroc is typical of American success stories when he perceives and employs the polarities rather than the continuum.

Finally, the logical extensions of a sense of religious, metaphysical manifest destiny and the rugged individualism of the American hero-athlete are the language and values of war. War is the secular confirmation of America's role in the world as a self-anointed chosen people—as well as being the ultimate playground for the athletic rugged individualist. Kroc succeeds in sublimating all of these idiosyncratic American values in what he like to refer to as "hamburger diplomacy," (Kroc, p. 190).

Ray Kroc, winner of a Horatio Alger award, was known to his family as "Danny Dreamer" in his youth. He asserts that "each man makes his own happiness and is responsible for his own problems," (Kroc, p. 5). He tells us that "Work is the meat in the hamburger of life," (Kroc, p. 15). He believes that "the history of McDonald's corporation is a dramatic refutation of all who believe that risk takers will no longer be properly rewarded," (Kroc, p. 1). Kroc, who distrusts highly educated people who cannot act expeditiously in daily life, nevertheless quotes the ill-fated Brutus of Shakespeare's *Julius Caesar* before Chapter One of *Grinding It Out:*

There is a tide in the affairs of men,
Which, taken at the flood, leads on to fortune;
Omitted, all the voyage of their life
Is bound in shallows and miseries.
On such a full sea we are now afloat
And we must take the current when it serves
Or lose our ventures.

Brutus as an incipient Ray Kroc? It is very likely that the American hamburger magnate would have never hired the noble Roman—another thinker who failed as a doer. Yet there are similarities between the two. Both eagerly took advantage of a situation in order to exploit a preferred chance. And both may ultimately be charged as failures in human relationships—Brutus for doing the right thing for the wrong reasons and in the wrong way—and Kroc for the cavalier manner in which he disposed of two wives as he clawed up the sides of the mountain of success. Both would admit that it is lonely at the top of that mountain. Each man's larger destiny led to failure in the smaller human relationships which helped to compose that destiny.

Kroc chooses not to quote Brutus's line which immediately precedes the above quotation: "We, at the height, are ready to decline." Kroc's book is marked by unbounded optimism and enthusiasm—and equal measures of egocentricity and pomposity. These are perhaps the ingredients of the American hamburger success recipe.

The list of learning activities could go on *ad infinitum*. The inescapable fact is that McDonald's presents students with a subject matter that pervades all aspects of their lives. The unexamined life is not worth living. As the corporation grows towards its saturation point, students should be given the chance to develop a coherent body of knowledge about the interaction between McDonald's and the culture that helped create it. In doing this, our students will be able to study *themselves* in a context never before available.

We all deserve such a break.

Notes

[1] Bob Scholte, "Levi-Strauss's Unfinished Symphony," *Claude Levi-Strauss: The Anthropologist as Hero*, ed. E. Nelson Hayes and Tanya Hayes (Cambridge, Mass.: The M.I.T. Press, 1970, p. 148.

[2] Marshall McLuhan, *Understanding Media: The Extensions of Man* (New York: The New American Library, Inc., 1964), p. 37.

[3] Ray Kroc, *Grinding It Out: The Making of McDonald's* (Chicago: Henry Regnery Company, 1977), p. 10. Additional references will be cited in the text.

MAO AND MAC:
A Cultural Perspective

by Sarah Sanderson King and Richard A. Sanderson

"Modesty helps one to go forward, whereas conceit makes one lag behind."
"The world belongs to you; the future of China belongs to you."
                                        . . . Mao Tse-Tung[1]

"Nothing recedes like success. Don't let it happen to you or us."
"The world belongs to those who aim for 110%."
                                        . . . Ray Kroc[2]

For the "All-American" McDonald enthusiasts, it may seem incongruous and even unAmerican to attempt to include in one article an examination of any part of one of the most successful of all private American enterprises—McDonald's—with a system based on collectivism, the very anathema of American individualism—the People's Republic of China. It is much easier to attempt to answer the question of "how transferable is China's experience with development communication"[3] by comparing it to India or the Tasadai rather than the United States or some aspect of it.[4] But through an in-depth study of communication in Mainland China and communication in McDonald's, some answers to the question emerge inviting a comparison between the two.

Granted there are basic differences in philosophy and purpose between the approaches of Ray Kroc, founder and Chairman-Elect of McDonald's (hereafter referred to as Mac), and Mao Tse-Tung, founder and leader of the Communist Party of the People's Republic of China (Mao). However, there are enough similarities to make the hypothesis that an effective system is an effective system, regardless of the political or ideological base, provided there is a person with vision to enforce it.

The effective systems for both Mac and Mao are their communication systems, "guiding and motivating the people in conformity with the policies of the . . . leaders."[5]

The ways in which communication is used, the networks through which it flows, the structures of the media system, the regulatory framework for the system, and the decisions of the people who operate it, are all the outcome of communication *policies*. Policies are the principles, rules and guidelines on which the system is built and may be specifically formulated or remain largely implicit.[6]

In this article we will examine the communication strategies employed by both McDonald's and Mainland China in the development and maintenance of their organizations. We will consider if this transferability of modes has been intentional and has proven feasible. We will consider also the objectives and philosophical base for these strategies.

It was during the Cultural Revolution that the "little red book" of Mao's thoughts—*Quotations of Chairman Mao*—was printed. Frederick Yu, scholar at the East-West Center, compares this little book with Confucius' *Analects.* The force of the *Analects* lies in their brevity, randomness, easy use, multiple interpretations, simplicity, informality, and intimate nature.[7] Mao's quotations appear everywhere; in newspapers, on the sides of buildings, on pipes, machinery, and bridges, and on large character poster boards encouraging workers to work harder for the development of their country.[8] Although there is no "little red book," there is an "annual motto"[9] that comes from Ray Kroc and graces the walls of Hamburger Central, corporate headquarters of McDonald's now located in Oak Grove, Illinois. The 1977 motto is "Yesterday is gone/Let's work for the world of tomorrow." The literature that comes from corporate headquarters emphasizes points with quotations[10] and corporate personnel will often punctuate their speech with quotations from Kroc or Fred Turner, President-Elect: "Knowing when policies apply is what management is," or "no matter what it is, it's not good enough."[11]

Both Mao and Kroc placed their emphasis on the concept of the will of humankind—persistence and determination—as the factors for success. "The people, and the people alone, are the motive force in the making of world history."[12] The Great Leap Forward, although a disaster in the minds of many, was based on Mao's "betting on the human spirit and man's will," an attempt to "raise the consciousness of his people and to ignite their enthusiasm."[13] Ray Kroc borrowed from Calvin Coolidge the motto that in later years "bedecked his empire—scrolled, framed, and hung on the walls of Hamburger Central, the doors of Hamburger U., in the tiled kitchens of McDonald's and the clubhouse of the San Diego Padres."[14]

> Press On
> Nothing in the World can
> take the place of persistence.
> Talent will not;
> Nothing is more common
> than unsuccessful men
> with talent. Genius will
> not; unrewarded genius
> is almost a proverb—
> Education alone will not;
> The world is full of educated derelicts.
> Persistence and
> determination alone are
> omnipotent.

"We are in the people business," said Fred Turner. "I never saw a machine that could turn out a hamburger," said Jim Schindler.[15]

Decentralization is one of the keys to organizational structure for both China and McDonald's. Under the communist government, the villages of China are organized into communes. These communes are virtually independent, especially in determining their capabilities—crops they will grow, quotas they will meet—and in choosing their own leaders. Each village is organized into work teams which form brigades. A collection of brigades then makes up the commune. Each brigade elects its own leader who works with other brigade leaders under the general guidance of the commune director. China has a centrally-planned economy and all communes and factories work within the plans laid down by the ministries in Peking. Directives are sent down from Peking to the communes, but recommendations are also sent up.[16] Decentralization for McDonald's with a move to the establishment of regional offices proved to be an important step in improving communications by placing the company near the restaurants. As one official pointed out—

All of the day to day activity is planned and takes place in the region. Company function became policy making. The region goes out and buys the real estate, they build the buildings, they find the operator and once the operator is in, they feed all of the training orientation, everything he needs to operate.[17]

"Grass-roots" activity is stressed; the prime responsibility of the various departments of McDonald's is to help owners and operators and provide back-up services for them. Guidance for store operations is provided by the *McOpCo Policies and Procedures* notebook provided by Corporate Headquarters.[18]

Just as the training for the members of the Brigades takes place in the village itself so does the majority of the training for McDonald's take place in the region in which the store is located. BOC (Basic Operations Training) takes place in the home store, guided by basic training materials from Corporate Headquarters that have been adapted for and by the needs of the particular region and by cartridges of training films for in-store projection.

Training which cannot be obtained in the home offices can be obtained in technical colleges established throughout China for this purpose. Staff examinations help determine entry but most important is the selection by members of their own village, commune, factory, or military unit to attend. Hamburger University, the technical college for McDonald's—began operations in 1961 in Elm Grove, Illinois—the result of Kroc's codification of "Hamburger Science" into a system of institutional training for managers. In attendance are managers who have spent at least six months in that position as well as owners-operators after spending two weeks in practice in a nearby store. The approximately 300 page corporate bible[19] which covers all operations from drinks to fries is held in as much esteem at McDonald's as Mao's *Quotations* is in China. From Hamburger U. come the trained personnel to not only manage and operate the stores but to handle the BOC at home. In addition to the store Training Coordinator, each region has its own Training Coordinator and offers training programs and individual guidance for each store in its region.[20] Not only have 90 percent of the personnel at Corporate Headquarters been through Hamburger University but all of them have worked in a store.

The May Seventh cadre schools may be now the most well-known of Mao's techniques for improving communication and advancing the Revolution. These institutions are designed primarily for professionals, for people who sit behind a desk, including managers and teachers. . . . The idea is to get the office manager into a rural setting where he works like a peasant.[21]

Created in 1968, the system permits the urban personnel to spend part of their time in a rural setting. Hopefully they go back to their offices healthier, happier, and with a better understanding of the person who works in the fields. "It is well known," said Mao, "that when you do anything, unless you understand its actual circumstances, its nature and its relation to other things, you will not know the laws governing it, or know how to do it, or be able to do it well."[22]

To encourage communication between employees, restaurants and customers, McDonald's initiated National Store Day during which corporate employees left their offices to work in the restaurants. This experience not only refreshed the employee's knowledge of basic restaurant operations, but also gave them the opportunity to meet McDonald's customers.[23]

Twenty five hundred McDonald's office employees from across the country left their desks to join the ranks of crewpeople packaging fries, cleaning tables and waiting on customers. The day ended with a rap session, giving a recap of the day, thus giving home office employees and crewpeople an opportunity to exchange reactions.[24] This was in 1976 and the plan is that in 1977 two days will be spent in the stores by office employees with Corporate Headquarters shutting down for the occasion.[25] "Roll up your sleeves and go to work. Start from scratch and learn every facet of your operation. Most important, get out where the customers are."[26]

The Chinese know how important it is to know every facet of one's operation. In the early 1960's the Sino-Soviet split with the departure of the Soviet specialists with their plans, blue-prints, skills, and in several places irreplaceable parts, strained the nation's resources and its people. Each factory is now complete down to the fuses it needs to run its machinery and the technicians to repair it. Hamburger U. doesn't go as far as making technicians of every student but it does make them acquainted with all the equipment and what to look for in case of trouble. Stores are encouraged to carry parts for equipment, especially those that are known to fail. Each store is as complete as McDonald's can make it.

The rap sessions held at McDonald's around the nation during "Store Day" were but an extension of McDonald's Open Door policy. "Criticism and Self-Criticism" is a separate section in Mao's quotations emphasizing the importance of this concept in Mainland China.[27]

Conscientious practice of self-criticism is still another hallmark distinguishing our Party from all other political parties. As we say, dust will accumulate if a room is not cleaned regularly, our faces will get dirty if they are not washed regularly. Our comrades' minds and our Party's work may also collect dust, and also need sweeping and dusting.[28]

The criticism, said Mao, was not to be personal but to be political and organizational. "Place problems on the table," "Do not talk behind people's backs," "Exchange information,"

This is of great importance in achieving a common language. Some fail to do so and, like the people described by Lao Tzu, "do not visit each other all their lives though the crowing of their cocks and the barking of their dogs are within hearing distance of each other." The result is that they lack a common language.[29]

Mao's policy on open communication is explicit in its directions regarding the open exchange of questions, answers, and information with feedback going in both directions—"be a pupil before you become a teacher; learn from the cadres at the lower levels before you issue orders."[30] Following Ray Kroc's dictim that "when you're green you're growing, when you're ripe, you rot," rap sessions are held in all McDonald's stores and in all departments at Corporate Head-quarters and its extensions. The Open Door Policy is exemplified in Head-quarters office design with Task Response Modules (low wall enclosure, no doors, pastel colors) which create an "open-space" environment. June 1977 MESSENGER, the employee publication, reported on "Open Door Day," an attempt to emphasize the policy "that any employee has access to his or her supervisor, the supervisor's supervisor, and on up regardless of rank or title.[31] One employee handbook of McDonald's states "your problems are ours."

> We know that you will have problems on the job from time to time. We believe these problems can best be resolved by immediate attention to them in open and frank discussions. Help us resolve these problems—call them to our attention when they occur. Also, take advantage of crew meetings, rap sessions, and any other opportunity to speak out and be heard when things are bothering you.[32]

The idea was that at the first sign of complaint, the source of the complaint must be brought into the open.[33]

The well-being of the worker is considered important in both systems. In China the health and education of the people receive high priority in the budget. Medical clinics are part of every village with free preventative and immediate treatment available. Eliminating illiteracy is the focus of the schools. "Cultural palaces" are established for the recreation of the workers who dance, sing, and play together at their places of work as well. Baby-sitting and nurseries are established for working mothers. Intra-group compe-titive games such as basketball, ping-pong, etc., are established between worker "brigades."[34] All full-time employees at McDonald's have life insur-ance, medical insurance, dental insurance, and vacations. Educational assist-ance can come after six months of employment as well as long-term disability. Employees are urged to play together by the scheduling of many activities each week—diversified enough to satisfy any taste—and publicized by bulletin boards, newsletters, and word of mouth. Plans are underway for a recreational facility for Corporate Headquarters workers—a gym, track and possibly a pool. At the moment although there are only scattered site day-care systems for working mothers, discussions are being held to determine the need and feasibility of more facilities.[35] Competition is a keyword for McDonald's with its All-American crew teams, its awards (President's Award, President's Bonus Award, Outstanding Achiever in Department), its Ronald Award for operators who do the most in developing the public image of McDonald's, and its performance reviews and ratings each six months in which one is in competition with oneself. One wall in Corporate Headquarters is framed by statuettes of awards won by the All-American McDonald sports teams which are sponsored by the fervor Kroc has for athletic activities.

In China under Mao other modes of communication included loudspeakers in the villages which might carry information or partyline propaganda; bulletin boards or "diazi bao" which report the latest information or party line items; regular group meetings for discussing policies and events; radio, television and newspaper entries supervised by Party Headquarters; and party literature in the form of newsletters and books passed down to brigades for distribution. Those who could not read were read to, often by the younger members of the village who were attending or had learned to read in their local schools.[36] An internal Party journal was published by the Central Committee in an attempt to promote nationalism.[37] At McDonald's the *Newsletter* which was started in 1955 became a sophisticated tool in the company structure for relating news items, advertising events, and sales volumes of stores. What was not covered in the *Newsletter* would be covered for those individually involved through memorandum within the organization. Not to be overlooked as a factor for workers as well as the public were the television and radio advertisements which contributed to the image McDonald's wanted to convey to the public.[38]

Those communication strategies which we found shared by both McDonald's and Mainland China (Mac and Mao) have some of the same basic underlying philosophies—equality, democracy, and development of the individual for the betterment of the whole:

1. Dissemination of philosophy of the leaders through the use of slogans and quotations printed in books, newspapers, or posted on bulletin boards and other available spots in public places.
2. Emphasis on the concept of the "will of man" with communication efforts directed toward raising the consciousness of people and igniting their enthusiasm.
3. Decentralization of organizational structure with regional offices which improved communications by placing headquarters closer to the workers.
4. Establishment of a substantial amount of training in regions rather than sending everyone to school elsewhere, thus building pride in regional abilities.
5. Establishment of more technical facilities in central locations for training beyond regional capabilities that permit easy access by workers even though they must travel to them.
6. Initiation of a system which insures that the bureaucrats (office workers, scholars, administration) spend part of their time with the workers in the fields or the stores in an effort to improve communication and understanding between employees in all levels.
7. Encouragement of communication of all facets of operation and of each worker's knowledge of these facets.
8. Exchange of information so that a common language can be achieved, and learning can be two-way.
9. Practice of criticism and self-criticism, not of a personal nature, but political and organizational so that problems can be taken care of when they arise.
10. Consideration of the well-being, health, education, recreational, family; creating a climate of concern for people as well as for production.

11. Encouragement of competition by the establishment of an award and reward system for hard work and diligent loyalty for all members of the system.
12. Design and implementation of various modes of communication for disseminating information and for morale—newsletters, bulletin boards, slogans, radio, television and newspaper coverage.

The constant review and evaluation of these communication strategies gives for a viable system of monitoring the organization. We doubt if any of this transferability of communication modes from China to McDonald's was done consciously. It was, as we said before, that an effective system is an effective system, regardless of the political and ideological base. Especially when the system is created or adapted by a person with strong beliefs and the will to overcome obstacles.

Notes

[1]*Quotations from Chairman Mao Tse-Tung* (Peking: Foreign Languages Press, 1967), p. 237. *Jen Min Jih Pao* (People's Daily), February 5, 1973.

[2]Letter from McDonald's Corporation, July 25, 1977.

[3]Wilbur Schramm, Godwin C. Chu, and Frederick T.C. Yu, "China's Experience with Development Communication: How Transferrable Is It:," *Communication and Development in China*, Communication Monographs, Number 1 (Honolulu: East-West Communication Institute, September 1976).

[4]Sarah Sanderson King, *Communication Strategies in Social Action and Development* (Honolulu: Hawaii Open Program, U. of Hawaii, 1975), pp. 49-53.

[5]E. Lloyd Sommerlad, *National Communication Systems: Some Policy Issues and Options* (Honolulu: East-West Center), p. 9.

[6]Sommerlad, p. 7.

[7]Frederick T.C. Yu, "Tao of Mao and China's Modernization," *Communication and Development in China*, p. 56.

[8]Richard A. Sanderson (Producer) and Sarah Sanderson (Research and Script), *Life in China: Industry*, motion picture film distributed by Ohio State University, 1972.

[9]Letter from McDonald's Corporation, July 25, 1977.

[10]*McDonald's Twentieth anniversary*, April 1975, McDonald's System, Inc.

[11]Interviews with Denis Detzel, Corporate Social Policy, McDonald's Corporate Headquarters, McDonald Plaza, March 10, 1977 and June 6, 1977 (latter by telephone).

[12]*Quotations*, p. 118.

[13]Stephen Uhalley, Jr., "Chairman Mao: The Teacher-Communicator in Revolutionary Development," *Communication and Development in China*, pp. 70-71.

[14]Max Boas and Steve Chain, *Big Mac: The Unauthorized Story of McDonald's* (New York: E.P. Dutton and Co., 1976), pp. 7-8.

[15]*McDonald's Twentieth Anniversary*, p. 36.

[16]Richard A. Sanderson (Producer) and Sarah Sanderson (Research and Script), *Life in China: Agricultural Worker in the Commune*, motion picture film distributed by Ohio State University, 1972.

[17]*McDonald's Twentieth Anniversary*, p. 30.

[18]*McOpCo Policies and Procedures Manual*, McDonald's Corporation, the manual we had to work with was dated July 1972.

[19]"Hamburger University Notebook," loose-leaf binder with training modules. The particular notebook we had to study was from Advanced Operations Class, #210, November 10 through November 20, 1975.

[20]Sarah Sanderson King and Michael John King, "Hamburger University and Its Affiliates: The Polishing of McDonald's Image," a paper presented at the Popular Culture Convention, Baltimore, Maryland, April 28-30, 1977.

[21]Stephen Uhalley, Jr., p. 80.

[22]*Quotations*, p. 210.

[23]*The McDonald's Way of Life: Annual Report 1976*, p. 4.

[24]*McDonald's Messenger*, May 1977, p. 1.

[25]Telephone interview with Denis Detzel.

[26]*McDonald's Twentieth Anniversary*, p. 39.

[27]*Quotations*, pp. 258-267.

[28]*Quotations*, p. 25.

[29]*Quotations*, pp. 108-109.

[30]*Quotations*, p. 109.

[31]*McDonald's Messenger*, June 1977, p. 1.

[32]"Employee Handbook: McDonald's of Morgantown and Fairmont," n.p.

[33]Godwin C. Chu, "Communication and Group Transformation in the People's Republic of china: The Mutual Aid Teams," *Communication for Group Transformation in Development* edited by Godwin C. Chu, Syed A. Rahim, and D. Lawrence Kincaid, Communication Monographs, Number 2 (Honolulu: East-West Communication Institute, September 1976), p. 160.

[34]Sanderson, *Life in China* films.

[35]Telephone interview with Denis Detzel.

[36]Sanderson, *Life in china* films.

[37]M. Rejai (ed.), *Mao Tse-Tung on Revolution and War* (Garden City, N.Y.: Anchor books, 1970), pp. 328-333.

[38]King, "Hamburger University . . ."

And You Thought Big Macs Were Fast Food
When they're made for TV commercials such delicacies can take hours to create*

by Lisa See

Bring on the hero," the director yells. Ten technicians are still fussing with the camera, adjusting the lights, removing the stand-in.

Lila Gilmore, one of Hollywood's top "stylists," rushes over with the hero. Today, it's baked cod with hollandaise; it gets the star treatment. A perfect, glistening lemon slice, a sprig of parsley with a few drops of water and glycerine, a soupcop of paprika for color, oil on the cod to make it shiny.

But wait.

The cinematographer isn't happy. The white plate, white fish and white sauce look a little too much like what they are.

Not a problem for Lila. She's ready with a wooden skewer to "texturize" the cod by poking it until it fluffs up into sweet dignified, fishlike flakes.

Food stylists—mostly women trained as home economists—make food appear luscious, delicious, beautiful, appetizing for commercials. They pridefully protect their secrets of how to make colors vibrant, to make ice cream last under hot lights and butter melt on steamy corn on the cob. They're hired for their aesthetic eye and persistence. For $225-300, Hollywood stylists work 12 hours a day over a hot stove in a trailer on location, in a temporary kitchen on a sound stage, or at the special McDonald's built just for shooting commercials. Most important, they're hired for their fierce integrity regarding the "marbles-in-the-soup" episode.

In 1970 the Federal Trade Commission discovered that Campbell's soup had been using marbles at the bottom of the bowls in its commercials to make the vegetables protrude above the soup. The FTC considered this practice deceptive. Food stylists cannot change or adulterate a product being advertised. (Or at least that's true for a "foreground" food. A "background" food—candied yams in a ham commercial, for instance—can have anything done to it.)

I talked to Elizabeth James, the "Big Mac" queen, to Nona Baer, known especially for her pizza work, who once scrutinized 75 boxes of cornflakes to find the perfect bowlful, and to Lila Gilmore, 15 years in the business, who has seen the changes since the "marbles-in-the-soup" affair and the advent of fast food. She has "styled" every food from ice cream and cookies to taco-flavored chips and turkeys.

McDonald's probably makes more food commercials than any other company. A Big Mac is just a hamburger, right? Wrong. A Big Mac takes time. Elizabeth James, who has made Big Macs look juicy for three years, can spend two hours just looking for ingredients.

"I look for the perfect hamburger patty," says James. "My assistants and I will cook maybe a hundred standard McDonald's patties to McDonald's specifications. Then I have to find one that meets my standards. No rips. No unsightly corners. It can't be symmetrical, but it has to be a good shape. Not too dark, not too light. Not curled. I look for the perfect bun with the perfect amount of sesame seeds. I pick out the exact amount of lettuce pieces. They have to be white and green and have a nice size and shape. I look for the prettiest pickles, too."

The Big Mac goes together in a certain way. The Heel, toasted bun, sauce, lettuce, cheese and patty. The club (or that middle piece of bread you always wondered about), toasted bun, sauce, lettuce, pickles and patty. And finally, the Crown, with its perfect sesame seeds. The sauce goes on with the special McDonald's sauce gun. The Big Mac can't be too tall or too short. To be a Big Mac—and not just another American burger—it must fit into the precise standards found in the McDonald's manual.

"McDonald's pays me to paint a picture," says James, who also does other foods for other companies. "Although I can make a Big Mac in my sleep, it's always a challenge and very rewarding. I try to make the best Big Mac every time."

If it takes two hours to prepare a hamburger for a close-up, what about a traditional Christmas feast? Nona Baer—the woman who hunted down the quintessential cornflakes—describes her recent holiday-dinner shoot for a grocery store. "The first day, I went to a production meeting with the director and the guys from the agency to find out exactly what they wanted. The second day, I made a list of ingredients and amounts—a combination of by-guess and by-gosh, multiplied by two. I spent four hours shopping. Then I went home and unpacked. I had to store 10 turkeys. The third day was a prep day for anything that would keep—raw vegetables and gelatin molds. I made 10 molds. Usually they're lit from behind, like Garbo, so that they will glow. They have to be made layer by layer so the fruit will show evenly throughout the mold. Its time-consuming. The next morning I got up at 5 to pack and load my car. As soon as I got to the set, I prepared the stand-ins so the crew could set their lights. I made the heroes—the dishes they actually shoot in the commercial. Then, it was a matter of using an artist's eye. Did the food look real? Tasty? Was it beginning to wilt, crinkle, die? We were using a snorkel camera that goes in and around and up and over, just inches away from the food. That snorkel is *very hot*. I had 10 pounds of broccoli and it died a lot faster than I anticipated."

Whether it's a hamburger or a feast some foods are more cooperative than others. The stylist needs to pace turkeys, gelatin, lobster, not only to last under hot lights but to withstand the blunders of actors and hand models. (The beautiful manicured fingers that grasp the jar of salad oil belong to a hand model.) The food stylists' tricks of the trade keep the hero alive, not dead. Remember, these can be 12-hour days.

Pizza is easy, until the cheese becomes hard. A fried egg lasts forever. Cereals are a breeze. Pour the cereal and show it, at least once, with toast, orange juice and milk as part of a "balanced breakfast." Lemon wedges crinkle. Parsley wilts. Ice cream lasts only one take before it melts. It usually starts out frozen solid enough to qualify as a lethal weapon. (Lila Gilmore uses mashed potatoes with strawberries and red food coloring for her strawberry ice-cream stand-ins.) Cakes and pies are difficult. The cake cannot have tunnels or holes or crumbs in the frosting. Pies? Depends on whether it's apple or lemon meringue. The apple filling has to be firm and not slither off the spatula or all over the plate. Cookies, on the other hand, just sit politely. Chocolate candies melt. But candy-bar commercials— where the chocolate pours in elegant ribbons over coconut or caramel—are helped by the cinematographer's special effect, "overcranking" the camera to create caloric sin in luxurious slow motion.

Steam is critical for soup and coffee. The food stylist is positioned right next to the camera, armed with her microwave or stove, reheating the product for each shot. A special "steam light" helps to capture the vapor on film.

Meat has special problems. If it is cooked too long, it will appear too dark on camera. But it can't look raw either. Blemishes disappear with soy sauce. A little paprika gives meat a "warm feeling." One legendary stylist lacquers her turkeys, but most just use oil for the shine. If the turkey is part of a larger display, it's cooked only a couple of hours. If it has to be sliced, then it has to be cooked until it's golden on the outside, juicy and tender on the inside. If it is sliced, how many turkeys will the models slice before they get that first slice right? The answer: 10 to 20.

Human beings are the food stylists' bane, the vegetarian actor who's been hired (his first job in months) to eat pepperoni pizza, the little boy who has to eat ham all day and spends half the time throwing it up, the model who has to break an egg into the batter but doesn't know how to crack eggs without crushing them.

So once again: *Lights! Camera! Action!*

A "restaurant" under blazing lights, surrounded by a vast stage. It's 3 on a Friday afternoon and the producer wants to call it a wrap at 5:45. Lila Gilmore and her daughter, Kelly, must make a low-calorie supper menu look sumptuous. On long tables, ingredients vie for space, together with a scale, toaster oven and a fishing-tackle box filled with brushes, skewers, can openers, aspirin, tongs, soup ladles, cotton swabs, eye-droppers.

After its half hour of fame, the cod has been chucked into the trash. The foods still to be shot are chicken marinara, spaghetti and veal, and tuna salad.

The chicken is next. Kelly Gilmore trims away a stringy fringe from an already excessively neat breast, then pops it into the microwave. Lila pours on an exact measurement of marinara sauce while Kelly prepares celery slices. Then, all's quiet on the set as 10 people tape the sound of satisfied customers: "Ah! Ah! Ah!"

Lila scrutinizes the ad executives' 8-by-10 glossies of the tuna salad. "It's too mushed. To me, its not appetizing," she says. Her daughter's salad has take-charge chunks of celery and tune. "*That* looks good," says Lila. "It's got some identification in it...." But the crew wants to shoot the veal first.

The veal dinner—barely browned veal patties, three ounces of spaghetti, parsley. Lila lovingly arranges each strand of spaghetti into art-nouveau patterns. She scoots around for a look through the camera before they shoot. It's getting late.

"Let me get that dark spot out of there."

The crew sighs. The cinematographer says, "Let Lila be happy, because she's always right."

She removes a rude piece of spice, swabs a pool of fat, adds new parsley, and spritzes it with water that drips down into the plate. She mops up the water with another swab and adds drops of glycerine. Will the sauce last? It does.

Decked out with lettuce and shimmering tomatoes, the tuna salad—a gorgeous rainbow of color and texture—goes before the camera, on cue. Ten minutes later the tuna's in the trash, it's 5:46. The production assistant yells, "It's a wrap."

Cloning Clowns:
Some Final Thoughts

by Marshall Fishwick

> *God may or may not be dead,*
> *but Ronald McDonald is*
> *immortal.*
>
> **Jon Carroll**

laire Fuqua, a little girl from Chicago, had her wish come true. She finally met Ronald McDonald! In an instant her future emerged: "When I grow up, I'm going to be Mrs. McDonald," Claire said, with a beatific smile on her face. "Then I'll do television commercials with Ronald."

Claire's electronic generation has come to believe not only in the reality of cloned clowns, but the possibility of marrying them and living happily ever after. We are reminded of the famous confession of Charles Dickens: "Little Red Riding Hood was my first love. I felt that if I could have married her, I should have known perfect bliss." In studying the uses of Ronald's commercials, we might factor in what Bruno Bettelheim calls *The Uses of Enchantment*. Dickens, he points out in his book, understood that fairy tales help children better than anything else in their most difficult and yet most important and satisfying task: achieving a more mature consciousness to civilize the chaotic pressures of their unconscious.

In most cultures there is no clear line separating myth from folk or fairy tale. This is particularly true in the electronic cultures, going through transformations which none of us yet understand. What this book indicates, I believe, is that these things interlock and merge in the World of Mickey Mouse, or of Ronald McDonald; we are only beginning to understand the implications.

What does seem clear is that places like Disney World and Ronald World are microcosms of America—perhaps of the emerging Global Village—as we move toward the final years of the 20th century. We have seen the future and it is Donald and Ronald. Go for Big Mac!

Not *just* monolithic Big Mac; fast food will surely diversify and localize in the days ahead. New Englanders will find new ways to handle their clams, New Yorkers their kosher hot dogs. Somewhere in the heart of Georgia a whole chain of stores will put peanuts in the batter and serve "Presidential Waffles" with a side order of peanut butter. Virginians will learn to speed up their hickory-cured hams, and rice will provide a new fast-food base in South Carolina. Mexican food will not be stopped by any immigration service. Ethnic groups everywhere are serving proudly what they once ignored or disowned. Nationalists will not surrender their taste buds nor cultural variations.

But, you ask, how can a company like McDonald's, which in 1962 developed a French fry computer that automatically adjusts the frying time, hope to keep variety in environment and products? One way is through architecture—especially interior decor. Great pains are taken to adjust the restaurant to a specific locale or historical period—what Ronald calls "theme restaurants." One in Saginaw, Michigan, for example (a former lumbering capitol and hang-out of Paul Bunyan) has actual lumbering tools inside, including a saw, wagon wheels and a pike pole. A Kokomo, Indiana, restaurant has an antique car motif that ties into the area's historic association with the automobile industry. A restaurant located in downtown Chicago features space art and plastic stalactite-type objects that serve as white columns in a futuristic setting, one close to the airport near Toledo, Ohio, allows anyone who so wishes to dine in an airplane seat, and one at the University of Michigan, invites reverence while eating and watching the sun shine through stained glass windows.

In order that McDonald's building architecture blend in with existing community structures, restaurant operators are provided with an exterior restaurant package which features a dozen variations of the standard mansard roof design, including Alpine, Bavarian, Colonial, Country French, English Tudor, French Quarter, Gaslight, Mediterranean, Old English, Spanish, Village Depot and Western. Thus does one find variety (of a sort) inside the larger, carefully manipulated consistency.

As for murals, that same kind of variety might be supplied by new techniques (developed by the 3M Corporation) featuring a computer process that constructs mural-size four color graphic with paints rather than photo-dye. A photo-electric sensing system transmits color information to micro-paint spray guns—so we have in effect "original" computer art.

This kind of individuation is still questionable, perhaps unworkable; but the "Ronald McDonald House" concept has demonstrated how there can be local variety within a monolithic structure. Each House, purchased, manned, and controlled by local residents, is set up on a non-profit basis to house families of children being treated for cancer, leukemia and other serious illnesses. Families can reside here while the child receives treatment at a nearby children's hospital. In some cases, such as when a child receives outpatient therapy, the youngster can spend time with his family in the non-institutional atmosphere of the House. A Ronald House is a temporary residence for families or family members—not a medical treatment facility, a hospice, hotel, motel or psychotherapy unit. But it is an idea whose time has come.

In 1973, Kim Hill, the seven-year-old daughter of Philadelphia Eagles football player Fred Hill, was being treated for leukemia at Children's Hospital of Philadelphia. Hill and his Eagles teammates became determined to do something to benefit families using Children's Hospital. They approached Kim's physician, Dr. Audrey Evans, head oncologist at Children's and indicated their desire to help. Dr. Evans expressed the need for a "home away from home" facility near the hospital and a search for a suitable home began. Ultimately this led to a joint fund-raising effort by the Eagles and Philadelphia area McDonald's restaurant owners to support the purchase and renovation of an older home.

The House, opened in 1974, was named for Ronald not just because of McDonald's support, but because of the love children have for the Clown. By 1979, ten more had been opened; and by the end of 1981 there were 32 Ronald McDonald Houses in operation. Thirteen additional Houses opened in 1982, 30 more were being renovated or constructed in the U.S. and Canada in 1983. Each new House gets a $25,000 gift from the Ray A. Kroc-Ronald McDonald Children's Fund, initiated on Kroc's seventy-fifth birthday.

McDonald's continues to stress its community role, not only with Ronald McDonald Houses but with support for youth organizations, Muscular Dystrophy Association and patriotic groups. As a sponsor of the XXIII Olympiad in 1984, McDonald's is funding a $4 million Olympic Swim Stadium, to be donated to the University of Southern California after the Olympics.

McDonald's cultivates many publics, makes a special effort to diversify its hiring policies (large numbers of minorities and teen-agers are hired), and tries to maintain a friendly image. Even the form letter one gets when he writes to corporate headquarters says, "Your letter has been carefully read," and explains that if the information you requested isn't enclosed, it's because "this information is not available in printed form or cannot be released for general knowledge." The letter goes on to suggest that you read *Grinding it Out* by Ray Kroc, and is machine-signed by Elizabeth McCollum, Supervisor, Community and Consumer Affairs.

Company spokesmen have been willing to attend scholarly meetings (such as the Popular Culture Association) and list their areas of special interest:

1. The social dynamics of operators of individual McDonald's and their customers.
2. The changing pattern of employment, and labor relations, brought about by Equal Opportunity laws and other mandatory regulations.
3. The relationship between the organizational structure of McDonald's and other companies—and other cultures.
4. Problems and prospects for McDonald's overseas. (A preliminary study might center on Japan, which has 66 units, including the "world's busiest McDonald's.")
5. The impact and ripple-effect of community involvement and advertising—particularly of Ronald McDonald.

As the fast foods business grows, so does the urgency of dealing with these matters. The 1982 figures on McDonald's international market, for example, showed dramatic changes since 1978:

	1982	1981	1980	1979	1978
Pacific	536	467	414	343	267
Canada	417	389	366	335	293
Western Europe	348	300	245	189	142
Central and South America	40	29	25	23	28
	1,341	1,185	1,050	890	720

Will the real imperialism of the future be not by the military but the media? Will the nation that feeds the people control the people? To visit Ronald and watch him prancing and dancing nevertheless raises serious questions. Just ahead lies 1984. What shall we say—eat your heart out, George Orwell; or eat a Big Mac? Might we not be entering the computerized Brave New World without even knowing it?

Behind Big Mac stands the mass-produced car which produced the endless highways, roadside stops, gas stations, honky-tonks, open road. All this took shape during the Great Depression, though (as essays in this book have shown) segments appeared even earlier. Drug stores gave way to drive-ins, which flourished first in the South, where year-round operation was easy. As early as 1921, R.W. Jackson's "Pig Stand" did well on the Dallas-Fort Worth highway; there were 45 "Pig Stands" by 1938. Few scholars or historians took them seriously then—just a few take McDonald's seriously forty years later. Our essays *have* tried to take fast foods seriously, and to make it clear *why* this should be done. If McDonald's is indeed a cultural microcosm, we must study it carefully. Only then can we understand the macrocosm.

Consider three arches: Virginia's Natural Bridge (of stone), St. Louis' Memorial Arch (of steel), McDonald's Golden Arch (of neon glass). The first celebrated a natural God, the second an industrial frontier, the third a mechanized American Dream.

And that is why millions visit Ronald day after day year after year.

Ronald is a funny fellow, but the company he represents is no joke. Man cannot live by burgers alone!: but for more and more people burgers are the staff of life. I speak not only of stomachs but also of attitudes; not only of money but mythology.

There he is, that charming ageless Ronald McDonald, clowning around, being cloned, inviting us in. Hold his hand, and you're half there.

A Burger Bibliography

Eugene L. Huddleston

I. On McDonald's

"Coloring Contest Cops Car Clan." *Sponsor* 19 (29 November 1965), 39-43. [McDonald's carry-out restaurants in Philadelphia and Washington, D.C., area focus TV promotion on tots in hopes of securing whole family.]

"Hamburger University." *Life*, 61 (21 October 1966), 100.

"Appealing to a Mass Market." *Nation's Business*, 56 (July 1968), 70-74. [Interview with Ray Kroc]

"McDonald's." *Volume Feeding Management*, 30 (February 1968), 26-28.

"McDonald's Makes Franchising Sizzle." *Business Week*, 15 June 1968, 102+.

"Mirror, Mirror, on the Wall." *Forbes*, 106 (1 November 1970), 21.

"America's Hamburger King." *Reader's Digest*, 99 (October 1971), 137-41.

"As American as McDonald's Hamburger on the 4th of July." *Time*, 4 July 1971, 4-5+.

"Beef Against Big Mac." *Time*, 98 (27 December 1971), 43.

"McDonald's Is Their Kind of Place." *Nation's Business*, 59 (March 1971), 20.

Lukas, J. Anthony. "As American as a McDonald's Hamburger on the Fourth of July," *New York Times Magazine*, 4 July 1971, 21-29.

"In Print: Ronald McDonald Travel Kit." *Motor Trend*, 24 (August 1972), 127.

"Making the Grade at Hamburger U." *Newsweek*, 80 (25 September 1972), 78.

"McDonald's for breakfast? We're working on it." *Advertising Age*, 47 (11 September 1972), 52.

White, C. and M. Kingman. "Hamburger? McDonald's Takes It Seriously." *Advertising Age*, 43 (22 May 1972), 3+.

Woodman, J. and J. Shoen. "I'm the Hamburger Man." *Institutions/Volume Feeding Management*, 71 (15 September 1972), 73-88. [Interview with Ray Kroc]

"Better Boys Burgers: McDonald's Franchise Nets Profits for Chicago Boy's Club." *Ebony*, 28 (March 1973), 63-6+.

"Big Burger Boss: Chief Executive F. Turner." *Time*, 102 (17 December 1973), 100.

"Bull in the Hamburger Shop: D. Fujita of McDonald's Japan." *Forbes*, 111 (15 May 1973), 130.

"Burger That Conquered the Country." *Time*, 102 (17 September 1973), 84-6+.

"Fight for All of McDonald's Business." *Business Week*, 17 February 1973, 24+.

"For Ray Kroc, Life Began at 50. Or Was It 60? What McDonald's Had the Others Didn't." *Forbes*, 111 (15 January 1973), 24-30.

"McDonald's Takes Fast Food Lead." *Advertising Age*, 44 (14 May 1973), 93. [Tables].

"Meaty Results at McDonald's." *Financial World*, 139 (2 May 1973), 12.

"While the Big Macs Sell Like Crazy." *Financial World*, 141 (29 May 1973), 25.

"Will Big Mac Meet its Match in the Land of the Rising Sun?" *Forbes*, 111 (15 May 1973), 118+.

Goldberger, Paul. "Buck Rogers in Time Square." *New York Times*, Magazine Section, no. 6, part 1, 26 August 1973, p. 8 ff.

"Academic Twist to Sale of Hamburgers: A Scholarly Detroit Trio." *Ebony*, 29 (October 1974), 64-6+.

"Burgers for Books: Promotion of Library Services." *American Library*, 5 (November 1974), 540-41.

"McDonald's Keeps Them Cooking." *Financial World*, 142 (28 August 1974), 45.

"McDonald's Readies Moves on New Full Breakfast Menu." *Advertising Age*, 45 (29 July 1974), 55.

"McDonald's: Will Wall Street Love Affair Last?" *Institutions/Volume Feeding Management*, 74 (1 May 1974), 48-9.

Briloff, A.J. "You Deserve a Break: McDonald's Burgers are More Palatable Than Its Accounts." *Barrons*, 54 (8 July 1974), 3+.

Sheraton, Mimi. "The Burger That's Eating New York." *New York*, 19 (August 1974), p. 35.

Maples, M.G. "McDonald's Invades UK via Bow of 3,000th Unit." *Advertising Age*, 45 (14 October 1974), 41.

Sasser, W.E. and S.H. Pettway. "Case of Big Mac Pay Plans." *Harvard Business Review*, 52 (July 1974), 30-32.

"The Fast-Food Furor." *Time*, 21 April 1975.

"If You Stop, They Might Catch You." *Forbes*, 115 (15 May 1975), 48-49.

"Is McDonald's Growth Formula Getting Stale?" *Commercial and Financial Chronicle*, 220 (7 July 1975), 1+.

"Jack v. Mac." *Time*, 105 (5 May 1975), 71-72.

"At McDonald's Big Macs and Quarterpounders Bigger." *Commerical and Financial Chronicle*, 220 (24 February 1975), 13.

"McDonald's Looking for the Perfect Chicken." *Commerical and Financial Chronicle*, 220 (5 May 1975), 5.

"McDonald's Managing Director Peter Comments on Expansion [in Australia]." *New York Times*, 11 August 1975, 37.

"McDonald's: A New Urban Image." *Interior Design*, 46, part 3 (September 1975), 168-171. [On San Francisco's Embarcadero Center store.]

"McDonald's: A Variation on the Formula." *Interior Design*, 46, part 2 (May 1975), 172-75. [On store at 966 Third Avenue, New York.]

Trillin, Calvin. *American Fried: Adventures of a Happy Eater*, New York: Doubleday & Company, Inc., 1975.

"Not for Export." *Forbes*, 116 (15 October 1975), 23-24.

"Painting Chicago Wall-to-Wall: Yankee Doodle Dandy Collection of Kids' Murals." *Chicago Tribune*, 16 December 1975, sec. 3, p. 1. [Includes Bicentennial mural on a wall facing an Archer Avenue McDonald's.]

"Smith Barney Eyes Other Big Mac." *Commerical and Financial Chronicle*, 220 (11 August 1975), 2.

Hightower, Jim. *Eat Your Heart Out: Food Profiteering in America*. New York: Crown Publishers, 1975. See "The McDonaldization of America," pp. 237-41.

Murray, T.J. "Millionaire Meatman." *Duns Review*, 106 (July 1975), 12-14+.

"Big Mac Goes to School: Lunch Program in Benton, Arkansas, High School." *Newsweek*, 88 (4 October 1976), 85.

"McDonald's Focuses Ad Attention on Mealtimes." *Advertising Age*, 47 (10 May 1976), 32.

"McDonald's Drops a Notch in Merrill Lynch's Estimation." *Commerical and Financial Chronicle*, 221 (31 May 1976), 3.

"McDonald's Has Entered Joint Ventures for Establishment of Units in Netherlands and Japan and Is Developing Units in West Germany and Australia." *New York Times*, 31 October 1976, 54.

"In McDonald's Offices, Everyone Is Out in the Open." *Office*, 84 (September 1976), 115-19.

"McDonald's Restaurant, San Francisco." *Architectural Record*, 159 (January 1976), 96-97.

"McDonald's Sales." *Insiders Chronicle*, 221 (2 December 1976), 14.

"Have It Your Way." *National Observer*, 21 August 1976, n.p.

"Where Will McDonald's Pop Up Next?" *Institutions/Volume Feeding Management*, 78 (15 May 1976), 19.

"New Jersey Assembleyman Scores $474,000 Loan to McDonald Corporation for Building of Two Hamburger Restaurants." *New York Times*, cartoon, 5 September 1976, XI, 32.

"North By East." *Down East*, 22 (April 1976), 29-31. [Among series of short articles is one on McDonald's use of historically incorrect trayliners.]

Boas, Max and Steve Chain. *Big Mac: The Unauthorized Story of McDonald's*. New York: E.P. Dutton, 1976. Reprinted: New American Library (paperback), 1977. Reviews: *Library Journal*, 101 (15 May 1976), 1199; *New York Times Book Review*, 4 April 1976, 24.

Chamberlain, Charles. "McDonald's Goes Fancy in Chicago Outlets." *Lansing State Journal*, 13 December 1976, D4.

Drill, H. "Big Macs Helped Make Elkran the Agency It Is." *Advertising Age*, 47 (15 November 1976), 30 +.

Duston, Anne, "Jukes: Eye Eateries." *Billboard*, 6 March 1976, 1, 30. [Fast-food outlets are shedding their hesitancies about installing jukeboxes . . . some researchers contend that McDonald's will eventually change its anti-music policy.]

Kroger, W. "Horatio Hamburger and the Golden Arches." *Business Week*, 12 April 1976, 14.

McClellan, Bill. "Hamburger War Broils Over As Tactics Change." *Phoenix Gazette*, 9 January 1976, sec. C, p. 1.

Root, Waverly and Richard de Rochemont. *Eating in America: A History*. New York: William Morrow Inc., 1976.

"Burger King-McDonald's Competition in Fast Food Business." *New York Times*, 13 March 1977, sec. 3, p. 1.

"Chairman Fred Turner Predicts 1977 Will Be Super Year." *New York times*, 6 May 1977, sec. 4, p. 9.

"Fast-Food Chains are Beginning to Cater to Urban Neighborhoods by Varying Architecture . . . New McDonald's and Burger King Designs Described . . ." *New York Times*, 20 April 1977, sec. 4, p. 13.

"The Fast-Food Stars: Three Strategies for Fast Growth." *Business Week*, 11 July 1977, 56-61. Includes "McDonald's Blends New Products with Savvy Merchandising."

"Fred L. Turner of McDonald's; Growth Company." *Forbes*, 119 (15 February 1977), 95.

"Still the champion." *Time*, 109 (25 April 1977), 77.

Fineman, Howard, "Quest for Hot Hamburger Raises Issue of 'Socially Useful' Use of Oil." *Louisville Couier-Journal and Times*, 14 August 1977, p. A1. On McDonald's switch from paper to plastic in packaging.

Gray, Paul. "Want Food Fast? Here's Fast Food." *Time*, 110 (4 July 1977), n.p. [Essay on the glut of outlets available.]

Kroc, Ray with Robert Anderson. *Grinding It Out: The Making of McDonald's*. Chicago: Henry Regnery, 1977. Reprinted: Contemporary Books (paperback), 1977. Reviews: *Booklist*, 73 (15 April 1977), 1226; *Book World (Washington Post)*, 5 June 1977, p. G6; *Kirkus Reviews*, 45 (15 March 1977), 326; *Library Journal*, 102 (1 May 1977), 1012; *Publishers' Weekly*, 211 (11 April 1977), 67.

Ruef, J.A. "Connecticut McDonald's Does It All for the Library." *American Libraries*, 8 (January 1977), 15.

Thornton, Susan M. "At Ronald's House: Open Doors for Sick Children." *National Observer*, 11 July 1977, p. 6. [McDonald's owners sponsor lodgings for parents with hospitalized children.]

Wallace, Jane Young. "Editorial: No, McDonald's, You Can't Be Queen . . ." *Institutions/Volume Feeding Management*, 80 (15 February 1977), 13. On appointing a vice-president in charge of individuality.

"McDonald's blends new products with savvy merchandising." *Business Week*, p. 56-60 July 1977.

"Restaurants; builders can do it for McDonald's. *Professional Builder and Apartment Business.* 42 (August 1977) 84-87.

II. Of Related Interest

"Drive-Ins Booming; with Data on Leading Restaurant Chains." *Financial World*, 116 (20 September 1961), 6.

Glenn, A. "Thriving Drive-Ins are the Hottest Thing in the Restaurant Business Today." *Barrons*, 41 (5 June 1961), 11 +.

Glenn, A. "Hottest Thing in Restaurants; Business Is Better Than Ever for Drive-Ins and Other Specialty Eateries." *Barrons*, 42 (31 December 1962), 11 +.

"Doesn't Anyone Cook at Home Any More?" *Printers Ink*, 289 (16 October 1964), 3.

"Franchise to Growth; with Data on Leading Restaurant Chains." *Financial World*, 124 (8 September 1965), 5-7.

Lynes, R. "Fast Food and Footloose Americans; Conference on the Problems of the Food Service Industries Held in Fontana, Wisconsin." *Harpers*, 232 (January 1966), 26 +.

"Proliferating Drive-Ins; with Data on Thriving Franchisers." *Financial World*, 127 (5 April 1967), 6-7.

"Franchisers Play the Chicken Game." *Magazine of Wall Street*, 122 (6 July 1968), 11-13.

Halos, D. and S. Halos. "Hamburgers, 18¢ Prole-Food Franchise Business." *Esquire*, 70 (July 1968), 80-82 +.

Louis, A.M. "Food-Franchise Boom." *Fortune*, 78 (October 1968), 207-208.

"Hangouts, U.S.A." *Madamoiselle*, 70 (November 1969), 158-59, 243.

Amann, F. "Experts Speak Out." *Vend*, 23 (1 July 1969), 22-23. [Convenience foods seminar at National Restaurant Show, Chicago.]

Elliott, J.R. "Speculative Bellyache? Fast Food Franchisers are Risking a Bout of Indigestion." *Barrons*, 49 (25 August 1969), 3 +.

Kendall, E. "Most, Least, Famous Boring Food in America." *Vogue*, 154 (1 October 1969), 258 +.

"Dining Out in America: How Old Ways are Changing." *U.S. News and World Report*, 68 (20 April 1970), 91-94.

"Guide to All-Star Indigestion." *Sports Illustrated*, 33 (12 October 1970), 88-101.

Weiss, E. B. "50 Corporate Giants, Conglomerates Will Control Restaurants by 1980." *Advertising Age*, 41 (11 May 1970), 61-2 +.

"Fast-Food Stands Sprout on the Ginza." *Business Week*, 16 October 1971, p. 41.

Elliott, J.R. "No Burned Fingers; a Handful of Fast-Food Franchisers Flourishes." *Barrons*, 51 (12 April and 26 April 1971), 3+ and 5+.

Tigert, D.J. *et al.* "Fast Food Franchise: Psychographic and Demographic Segmentation Analysis." *Journal of Retailing*, 49 (Spring 1971), 81-90.

"Design Census for Foodservice/Lodging Operators." *Institutions/Volume Feeding Management*, 70 (1 June 1972), 36-50. [See "Toward a Science of Design" and "Good Design starts with Economics."]

"Europe; a Wolfish Hunger for U.S. Fast Foods." *Business Week*, 21 October 1972, pp. 34-35.

"Fast-Food Companies are Hot Again." *Business Week*, 30 September 1972, 54-55.

Newman, E. "Steak, Media, Please." *Atlantic*, 230 (September 1972), 98-100. [satire]

"Fast-Food Franchisers Squeeze Out the Little Guy." *Business Week*, 31 May 1976, 42+.

Vol.4 No.4 + 1983
Transportation Issue

Published Four
Times A Year
ISSN 0706-0904

McDONALDLAND FUN TIMES

A Magazine Especially For Children

Join the pictures that belong together.

Answers on page 14.

Birdie The Early Bird

Connect the dots to find out what she's doing.

What's in a Word? How many words can you find in this word?

RASPBERRY _____

_____

_____

PARTRIDGE _____

_____

Answers on page 14.